Praise for the Bodyguard series:

Brilliant Book Award 2014 – Winner

Hampshire Book Award 2014 – Winner

'Bone-crunching action adventure'
Financial Times

'Breathtaking action . . . as real as it gets'
Colfer, author of the bestselling Artemis Fowl series

'Bradford has combined Jack Bauer, James Bond
d Alex Rider to bring us the action-packed thriller'
Goodreads

'V ly authentic . . . the action and pace are spot on. Anyone
ng in the protection industry at a top level will recognize
that the author knows what he's writing about'
Simon, ex-SO14 Royalty Close Protection

'A oing page-turner that children won't be able to put down'
Red House

'W estle you to the ground and leave you breathless. 5 Stars'
Flipside magazine

'A gripping, heart-pounding novel'
Bookaholic

Chris Bradford is a true believer in 'practising what you preach'. For his award-winning Young Samurai series, he trained in samurai swordmanship, karate, ninjutsu and earned his black belt in Zen Kyu Shin Taijutsu. For his latest Bodyguard series, Chris embarked on an intensive close-protection course to become a qualified professional bodyguard.

His bestselling books are published in over twenty languages and have garnered more than thirty children's book awards and nominations.

Before becoming a full-time author, he was a professional musician (who once performed for HRH Queen Elizabeth II), songwriter and music teacher.

Chris lives in England with his wife and two sons.

Discover more about Chris at *www.chrisbradford.co.uk*

Books by Chris Bradford

The Bodyguard series (in reading order)
HOSTAGE
RANSOM
AMBUSH
TARGET
ASSASSIN

The Young Samurai series (in reading order)
THE WAY OF THE WARRIOR
THE WAY OF THE SWORD
THE WAY OF THE DRAGON
THE RING OF EARTH
THE RING OF WATER
THE RING OF FIRE
THE RING OF WIND
THE RING OF SKY

Available as ebook
THE WAY OF FIRE

B**O**DYGUARD
ASSASSIN

CHRIS
BRADFORD

PUFFIN

Warning: Do not attempt any of the techniques described within the book without the supervision of a qualified martial arts instructor. These can be highly dangerous moves and result in fatal injuries. The author and publisher take no responsibility for any injuries resulting from attempting these techniques.

PUFFIN BOOKS

UK I USA I Canada I Ireland I Australia
India I New Zealand I South Africa

Puffin Books is part of the Penguin Random House group of companies
whose addresses can be found at global.penguinrandomhouse.com.

www.penguin.co.uk
www.puffin.co.uk
www.ladybird.co.uk

First published 2017
001

Text copyright © Chris Bradford, 2017

The moral right of the author has been asserted

Set in 10.5/15.5 pt Sabon LT Std
Typeset by Jouve (UK), Milton Keynes
Printed in Great Britain by Clays Ltd, St Ives plc

A CIP catalogue record for this book is available from the British Library

ISBN: 978-0-141-35950-2

For the Roys,
Good friends to the end!

'The best bodyguard is the one nobody notices.'

With the rise of teen stars, the intense media focus on celebrity families and a new wave of millionaires and billionaires, adults are no longer the only target for hostage-taking, blackmail and assassination – kids are too.

That's why they need specialized protection . . .

BUDDYGUARD

BUDDYGUARD is a secret close-protection organization that differs from all other security outfits by training and supplying only young bodyguards.

Known as 'buddyguards', these highly skilled teenagers are more effective than the typical adult bodyguard, who can easily draw unwanted attention. Operating invisibly as a child's constant companion, a buddyguard provides the greatest possible protection for any high-profile or vulnerable young person.

In a life-threatening situation, a buddyguard is the **final** ring of defence.

The deep snow deadened the men's footsteps as they crept up to the farmhouse. Only the faintest light came from the sickle moon in the winter sky and the five men stole like wraiths through the bone-chilling darkness.

Inside the farmhouse all was warmth and light. A fire burned not only in the grate but in the bellies of the four farmers who sat round the old wooden dining table, knocking back homemade vodka.

'It's an outrage!' snarled a bearded man, who had the bulk and temper of a grizzly bear. 'The Bratva have gone too far with their demands this time.'

'But what can we do, Anton?' asked a rheumy-eyed farmer, his callused hands clasped round his glass as if scared someone might take it. 'If we don't pay their protection tax, they'll destroy our homes, harm our families . . . even kill us.'

'We fight back, Egor.' Anton downed his drink and poured himself another shot before refilling his friends' glasses too.

Slumped like a sack of grain, a ruddy-cheeked man took a drag on his cigarette and stared morosely at his drink.

'How do we fight back when the mayor of Salsk, the man supposed to protect us, is in the Bratva's pocket?'

'Grigori is right,' said Egor. 'We need a new mayor before we attempt to take on the Bratva.'

Anton stabbed at the table with his forefinger. 'What we *need* is a new leader for this country. One that isn't corrupt and backed by the Bratva. But what chance is there of that? None! So we must take matters into our own hands.' He turned to Grigori. 'Strength in numbers, comrade. If all the farmers and local businessmen band together, we can resist. Overthrow this corrupt regime.'

'But surely a bad peace is better than a good war?' Egor argued. 'We've everything to lose.'

'We've everything to gain! Our freedom! Our families' safety! Our lives!' Anton shot back. He slammed his fist so hard on the table that the vodka bottle and glasses rattled. 'This isn't the Middle Ages. This is modern Russia. But it's like we're living in a feudal state, slaves to the Bratva. They steal from our tables, beat our sons, take our daughters. *Enough is enough!*'

'I'm with Anton,' said Luka, the youngest farmer, who had a thrusting jaw of corn-coloured stubble. 'It's time we made a stand.'

Grigori let out a sigh and straightened himself in his chair. With a grimace, he knocked back his drink. 'What choice do we have? The Bratva will take everything anyway.' He looked at Egor, who gave a resigned shrug in agreement. 'So, Anton, what's your plan?'

Anton replied with a grim smile. 'It'll take courage and guts ... and a lot more vodka!' He waved the almost empty bottle in the air. 'Nadia, be a good girl and get Papa another bottle from the cellar.'

His five-year-old daughter glanced up from playing with her baby brother by the fire and responded with an eager nod. She hurried into the kitchen, where her mother was cutting up potatoes and adding them to a thick brown stew bubbling on the stove. As she passed by, Nadia caught its delicious meaty aroma and her mouth began to water.

Her mother smiled. 'Not long now, my little kitten,' she said, with a tender stroke of Nadia's snow-blonde locks.

Swallowing back her hunger, Nadia unbolted the door to the cellar and peered into the black depths. Away from the warmth of the fire, she felt a chill run down her spine. The cellar always frightened her with its dark corners, white wisps of spiderweb and dank grave-like smell, and she couldn't help imagining something terrible lying in wait for her.

Fighting her fear, Nadia fumbled for the light switch. Only a bare flickering bulb lit the gloom. But it was enough to give her courage and she descended the wooden steps. Then, halfway down, the door swung shut behind her, cutting off the kitchen's reassuring light. Trapped in the damp cold cellar, Nadia shuddered. Even though she knew it was just imagination, the crates of potatoes and carrots seemed to crawl with bugs and beetles. The glass jars on the shelves no longer held jam but congealed blood. And the rows of vodka bottles magnified sinister shapes in the gloom.

As the shadows grew, so did her fear.

Nadia hurriedly grabbed a bottle of vodka and turned to go back up the stairs when she heard a crash followed by angry shouts. In the kitchen her mother screamed, then made a strange gurgling sound. With a racing heart, Nadia dashed up the steps ... but stopped at the threshold. Through the narrow gap between the cellar door and its frame, she spied her mother lying on the floor in a spreading pool of blood. Beyond her dead mother, Nadia glimpsed the dining room, where men with knives and clubs were brutally attacking her father's friends. And she saw her father held at gunpoint, forced to watch the slaughter.

Nadia could hear her baby brother crying.

'Shut that child up!' snapped a gruff voice.

A deafening gunshot rang out. Then silence. The man who had given the order smiled. 'That's better.'

Nadia could no longer breathe. In that instant her whole world had gone numb. She could only stare wide-eyed, silent tears running down her cheeks, as the man jabbed the barrel of his gun into the back of her father's head.

'This is what comes of plotting against the Bratva,' he said, as her father fell to his knees weeping.

Tall, with close-shorn black hair and a crooked nose, the man had a crude tattoo of a dagger with three drops of blood just above the neckline. Even at her young age, Nadia recognized these men as members of the local Bratva gang. But there was one who stood apart from the others. His eyes, cold and grey as a winter sky, observed the scene with disturbing indifference. Pale-skinned and lean, he had the menacing air of a government FSB Secret Service officer. But he didn't look Russian to Nadia –

A second gunshot rang out, shattering Nadia's world forever. Her father jerked forward and slumped to the floor.

'That's how we deal with problems in Russia, my friend,' the tattooed man informed the grey-eyed foreigner with pride. 'You can let the mayor know the weeds were rooted out before they got a chance to grow.'

The foreigner glanced round the room. 'Too much evidence ties this back to you . . . and the mayor,' he replied in surprisingly good Russian.

'You're right. We should tidy up.' The tattooed man collected the glasses on the table, then poured the remains of the vodka over the floor and took out a lighter.

'Always important to have a good fire in winter,' he said, laughing, before setting the room ablaze.

Nadia gasped in horror as flames spread through the room. She dropped the bottle from her hands and it clattered to the floor. It didn't break but the noise betrayed her hiding place. The tattooed man and foreigner spun her way. In five quick strides the gang leader reached the cellar. He wrenched open the door to find a vodka bottle wobbling on the top step.

The tattooed man squinted into the cellar's darkness. He tried the light switch but the bulb fizzled out.

'Whoever's down there, come out!' he ordered.

There was no reply. No one appeared.

'Fine,' he grunted. 'You've decided your own fate.'

He picked up the bottle, emptied its contents on to the wooden steps and set the vodka alight. Bolting the cellar door shut, he and his gang left the farmhouse to burn to the ground. As they strode away across the snow-covered fields – the farmhouse now a raging inferno against the cold black sky – a little girl's scream pierced the night.

Ten years later . . .

'You're a dead man, Connor!'

His arm trembling, Connor Reeves gritted his teeth against the pain. His fingers felt like they were being crushed in a vice, his shoulder wrenched from its socket.

'Give up!' Jason grunted, leaning his whole bodyweight into the attack.

Never, thought Connor, as the two of them glared at each other across the table.

'Hey, what's going on?' asked Amir, entering Buddyguard HQ's briefing room.

'Arm-wrestling match,' Charley replied. She crowded round the table with Ling, Marc and Richie, the other three teenage recruits that made up Alpha team.

'Who's winning?'

'Jason, of course.' Ling smirked, with an admiring glance at her boyfriend's bulging bicep.

'It's not over yet,' Charley shot back, wheeling herself closer. 'Come on, Connor! You can beat him!'

But Connor's arm was already halfway to the table, every muscle straining against Jason's drive to pin it down. At over five foot ten and built like a heavyweight boxer, his Aussie rival was significantly stronger than him. Still, Connor had no intention of giving in without a fight. All his hours of gym work and punchbag training hadn't been wasted. He might not be as strong as Jason, but he had stamina. If he could just hold on long enough, Jason would tire as the lactic acid built up in his muscles. He'd weaken first, then Connor could go for the kill.

'Careful, Connor, you're in a break-arm position,' Amir warned as he joined the others. 'Your shoulder must be in line with your arm. Turn your body back towards Jason, straighten your arm and look at your hand –'

'Hey, no coaching!' said Ling, narrowing her jet-black eyes at Amir.

'It's not coaching,' Amir replied with a flash of a smile. 'It's helpful heckling.'

However, before Connor could follow his friend's advice, Jason made a renewed effort to force his hand to the desk. Biting down hard on his lower lip, Connor resisted with all his might. As he fought Jason, he felt his forearm twisting and the pain increased.

'Connor, keep your upper arm close to your body,' Amir hissed into his ear. 'That way, you can combine your arm and body strength. Try to curl your wrist inwards and draw his hand towards you. It's called a "top roll" technique – it'll make it harder for Jason to use his muscles against you.'

'How do you know all this?' asked Richie, eyeing Amir's slight frame. 'You're not exactly Rocky Balboa!'

'Internet,' Amir explained. 'Once saw this video of a professional arm wrestler in the same position as Connor. His arm snapped like a twig. I almost vomited; it was so gross.'

'I'd like to see that!' said Ling with a wicked grin.

'Hopefully not right now,' said Charley, her hands gripping her wheelchair more tightly as she followed Connor's battle with increasing dismay.

Connor blanked out the image of his arm snapping like a twig and repositioned himself so that his body was closer, his arm aligned and his wrist curled inwards. The pain eased and he was able to stop Jason's advance.

'You're nothing but a wuss, Connor!' taunted Jason.

Connor ignored the insult, saving his strength for the battle. They both knew there was more at stake than a simple arm wrestle. Their pride and personal standing with one another rested on the outcome of this match. Jason had clearly expected an easy win. But Connor saw in his rival's eyes both surprise and annoyance that he hadn't yet triumphed – and with every passing second that victory seemed less certain.

'Finish him, Jason!' urged Ling.

Jason grunted as he made another attempt to pin Connor's arm. Connor lost more ground to his opponent before managing to hold his position. But he didn't know how much longer he could last. His arm was shaking so violently he looked like he was having a seizure.

'You're only . . . prolonging . . . the inevitable,' gasped Jason, his face beginning to redden with the effort. The veins in his arm were bulging as if about to burst.

Connor took strength from Jason's evident struggle to defeat him.

'Don't give up, Connor! *Allez! Allez! Allez!*' urged Marc, breaking into his native French in his excitement.

Richie cheered for the other side. 'You've got him, Jason!'

Now everyone joined in with shouts of encouragement, transforming the briefing room into a noisy fighting pit. Connor's knuckles, white under the strain, were now but a centimetre from the tabletop. Sensing victory, Jason threw all his energy into the final push.

But remarkably Connor began to fight his way back from the jaws of defeat. Millimetre by millimetre he was regaining the advantage –

'Heads up! Colonel's here,' interrupted Charley.

The others quickly dispersed to their seats as Colonel Black strode into the room. Connor and Jason broke away from their arm-wrestling match and stood to attention.

The colonel, an ex-SAS soldier with a silver-grey crew cut and the solid square jawline of an action movie star, eyed them both. 'Glad to see you two are bonding at last.'

He gestured for the team to sit, taking his place at the head of the room to begin the morning's mission briefing. As Jason sat down beside Connor, he declared under his breath, 'I won.'

'No, you didn't,' hissed Connor.

Jason glared sideways at him. 'I had your knuckles on the table.'

'They never touched. Besides, the match was interrupted.'

Jason sneered, 'No way were you going to win –'

'Can't you two just call it a draw?' whispered Charley, as Colonel Black powered up the overhead HD screen and turned to face them.

'Never!' said Connor and Jason in unison. They locked eyes and found themselves grinning.

'Rematch?' challenged Jason.

'Any time,' Connor replied. But in truth he hoped it wouldn't be any time soon. He'd never admit it to Jason, but his arm ached like hell.

CHAPTER 2

'Corruption! Crime! Murder! This is the Russia I have grown up in, but not the Russia I want to live in,' declared the man on the podium, his narrow eyes burning with furious zeal. 'The current government is a party of thieves and criminals. They're sucking the lifeblood out of our homeland. Gorging themselves on what is rightfully yours.'

A chorus of jeers and boos rose from the crowd that surrounded the podium he stood upon. Tall, slim and dressed in a smart dark-blue suit and rimless glasses, the man looked more like a stockbroker than a revolutionary, but he was whipping the masses into a frenzy.

He thumped his chest, his voice booming. 'I vow to destroy the mafia-backed state that's been built in Mother Russia. I vow to destroy the system of government where eighty per cent of the national wealth is owned by half a per cent of the population. I vow to fight for the people!'

Cheers now erupted around him.

'But I can't win this fight on my own,' he continued. 'I need YOU, the good people of Russia. You need to make a stand. Take action. The bloated pigs won't leave the trough by themselves. Vote for change. Vote for *Our Russia*.'

The man now raised his arms in a two-fisted salute and his supporters went wild with applause and shouts of 'RUSSIA! RUSSIA! RUSSIA!'

'Viktor Malkov, Russian billionaire and new-wave politician,' explained Colonel Black, ending the video clip and raising the lights in the briefing room. 'He's the leader of the only credible opposition party to the current Russian government. The *Our Russia* movement was founded in response to a series of national scandals, in particular the brutal massacre of a farmer's family and his friends by a mafia gang ten years ago. But the party has only really taken off in the last few years with Viktor as its leader. His anti-corruption stance has proved highly popular with the people. However, it's bringing him into direct conflict with not only the government but the Bratva too.'

'Bratva?' queried Jason.

'The Russian mafia,' the colonel replied. 'Bratva means brotherhood. It's a collective term for the various organized criminal gangs spread throughout Russia. Each gang is headed by a mafia boss known as a Pakhan. Formed of ex-convicts, corrupt officials and business leaders, they virtually run the country. This means Viktor Malkov – with his promise to end corruption – has become their number-one enemy. Which is where we come in.'

The colonel brought up a picture of a young dark-haired lad on the screen. With a narrow nose, thin lips and sharp cheekbones, he was the spitting image of his father, but far more sullen-looking.

'Operation Snowstorm,' announced Colonel Black. 'The Principal you'll be protecting is fifteen-year-old Feliks Malkov. As Viktor's only son, Feliks is the one chink in his father's armour. It is our task to protect the boy from any potential kidnapping or assassination attempts.'

Marc raised a questioning eyebrow. 'Potential? From what you've described, the threat is real, if not guaranteed.'

Acknowledging this with the smallest of nods, Colonel Black folded his muscled arms across his broad chest. He may have been pushing fifty, but as founder and commander of the Buddyguard organization he maintained peak physical condition. 'Our client is well aware of the high threat level against him and his son. That's why he employs his own full-time security team. But Viktor wants to ensure he has the edge over his enemies. So we're the final ring of defence. An invisible shield for his son.'

'What about his mother?' asked Charley.

'Deceased,' replied the colonel. He glanced at his notes. 'Drowned last year in a tragic accident in the mansion's swimming pool. Suspected suicide, according to the coroner.'

'No wonder the Principal looks so miserable,' said Amir, nodding at Feliks's photo on the screen.

Colonel Black tapped his notes with a finger. 'Her death does appear to have hit the son especially hard. He was referred to a psychologist for six months of therapy.'

Connor reassessed the Principal. The boy's sullen expression was understandable. Whoever was assigned to protect him would have to be sensitive to the issue. 'So who's the buddyguard for this operation?' he asked.

The colonel turned his flint-grey eyes upon him. 'You are . . . and Jason.'

Both Connor and Jason did a double-take. This wasn't what either of them had expected. First, Connor had put in a request for a break from any more missions following his brutal assignment in Africa. Second, the colonel knew the two of them weren't exactly best buddies.

'Ah, a match made in heaven!' joked Richie.

'Fat chance,' Jason muttered, his brow furrowing.

'Well, you two have already been holding hands this morning. So after this assignment, who knows, maybe you'll want to get married!' said Ling, shooting them both a wink.

The rest of the team laughed. But Jason and Connor didn't. This was the worst pairing Connor could have imagined. The two of them were always at loggerheads. They agreed on nothing and fought over everything. The first time they'd met, Jason had tried to knock his block off. Granted, it had been part of a recruitment test. But Connor had floored Jason, humiliating him in front of the others. And they had been rivals ever since, always needing to prove who was top dog – whether in fitness trials, combat training, practical jokes or mission deployments.

'Who's in charge on this op then?' said Jason, as if to prove Connor's point.

'Charley will be team leader, as always,' the colonel replied with a respectful nod towards her. 'You two will be working undercover as Feliks's cousins. But Connor will have overall authority on the ground. You'll be 2 i/c.'

'*Second* in command!' Jason's jaw dropped. 'Hang on, I've been a bodyguard far longer than Connor. I should have command on the ground.'

The colonel eyed him sternly. 'I've made my decision. Is this going to be a problem for you?'

Jason held his gaze for a moment, then responded with a curt, 'No, sir!'

'Good. You'll need to have each other's backs on this assignment,' the colonel explained, his tone more serious than Connor had ever heard prior to a mission. 'I won't lie to you: Russia is the most dangerous place on earth to be a bodyguard.'

Nikolay Antonov, a banker with a ratty face and rounded spectacles, walked briskly down the road, shadowed by a tank of a man. Nikolay felt safer having hired the former Chechen soldier to protect him, especially through the almost deserted streets of the Moscow International Business Centre, the financial district having been hit hard by Russia's economic troubles.

As he passed a building site for yet another half-completed skyscraper, two shaven-headed men in black winter jackets stepped into his path. His bodyguard Maxim immediately bristled, thick brow furrowing and hammer fists clenching.

'Nikolay Antonov,' one of the men addressed him. Visible on the back of the man's right hand was a tattoo of a skull, the Bratva symbol for a convicted murderer. And, judging by the long white scar on his brick-like jaw and the thick calluses on his knuckles, Nikolay guessed he was a *krysha*, one of the mafia's violent enforcers.

The banker swallowed hard. 'Yes?' he said, as behind him his bodyguard reached for his gun.

'The Pakhan wishes to speak with you.'

Nikolay held up a hand instructing his bodyguard to back down. '*Me?* But why would the Pakhan want to speak with me?' he asked, his eyes darting around like a panicked mouse cornered by a hungry cat. 'I've always dealt with his bookmaker.'

'You can ask him yourself,' replied the *krysha*, as a coal-black Mercedes with tinted windows rolled up to the kerb. The rear passenger door swung open to reveal a stern-faced man with deep-set eyes and thin lips reclining in the back seat. His hand lay on the central leather armrest; a gold ring, on which the head of a bear was embossed, gleamed in the interior's low light.

The banker's eyes widened in shock. '*Roman Gurov? You're* the Pakhan?'

'You seem surprised,' said the man.

'Of course I am. But you're –'

'Who's the bull?' Roman cut in, pointing his gold-ringed finger at the hulk standing at Nikolay's shoulder.

'Um . . . Maxim, my bodyguard,' replied the banker, standing a little straighter.

Without warning, the two *kryshas* seized the bodyguard, one wrapping his muscled arm round the Chechen's throat, while the other drew a serrated knife and plunged it into his heart. The bodyguard slumped lifeless to the ground.

'Not much of a bodyguard,' Roman remarked. 'Now get in.'

Nikolay stared in shock as his slain protector was dragged through the slush of snow, leaving a trail of blood before his body was tossed like garbage into a builders' skip.

'Don't make me ask you twice,' said the mafia boss. 'Unless you want my men to help you in.'

Hurriedly getting into the rear of the car, Nikolay took the empty seat beside the infamous and much-feared Roman Gurov.

'W-w-what can I do for you?' asked the banker, struggling to keep his composure as the Mercedes pulled away.

'You manage our investments. And I'm very satisfied with the profits they yield, especially in these difficult times,' explained Roman, twisting the gold ring on his finger. 'But it has come to my attention that some of the cream is being skimmed off the top of every transaction.'

'*Really?*' said Nikolay, his exclamation sounding forced even to his own ears.

Roman stared at him. 'As our banker, I thought *you* of all my employees would have noticed this.'

Nikolay wetted his lips. Realizing the mafia boss wasn't to be fooled in the slightest, he changed his tune. 'I *had* actually . . . but I can assure you . . . it's just an accounting error.'

'Twenty million dollars is a rather large accounting error, don't you think?'

Nikolay looked down at his hands and tried to stop them trembling. 'Well . . . yes . . . of course . . . I will correct it immediately.'

'Good,' said Roman, smiling and extending a hand. 'I'm glad this little misunderstanding can be resolved so easily.'

Nikolay stared for a moment at the proffered hand, the gold bear ring glinting at the promise of redemption for his mistake. With a hesitant smile, he reached out to shake it . . . then suddenly found his own hand seized in a vice-like grip. The mafia boss twisted it hard as if unscrewing the banker's wrist from his arm. Nikolay let out a scream. Showing no mercy, Roman applied more pressure to the joint until there was a sickening crack like a branch snapping in two. Nikolay's face drained of all blood and he uttered an agonized moan.

Leaning close to the banker's ear, Roman hissed, 'You *ever* try to steal from the Bratva again, it'll be more than your wrist I'll break. Understood?'

Nikolay gave a feeble nod.

Roman ordered his driver to stop and the rear door automatically opened.

'Careful you don't slip on any ice,' he said, applying his shoe to Nikolay's backside as the banker clambered out of the car. 'You don't want to break anything else, do you?' Then, as the car door closed, he added, 'And I'd advise you to hire a new bodyguard.'

Leaving the injured banker lying face down in the snow, the Mercedes drove away. Inside, the Pakhan turned to his assistant in the front passenger seat. 'Now on to the real business at hand . . . Viktor Malkov.'

'That's a *real* knife!' exclaimed Amir, his eyes on stalks as the blade passed in front of his face.

'Of course it is,' said Steve, their combat instructor, a man so solidly built that he looked to be chiselled from black granite. 'It's time you trained with real weapons. Otherwise you're just swimming on dry land.'

'B-b-but we could get hurt,' Amir stuttered, turning to the rest of the team who stood equally stunned in the sports hall. Having completed the morning's mission briefing and attended Bugsy's vehicle security seminar, they were now on to their daily self-defence class.

Steve nodded. 'That's the point. The first rule about knife defence is there is no defence. You *will* get cut or injured, however skilful or careful you are. That's why this lesson isn't called knife defence. It's called knife *survival*.'

Connor was all too aware of the reality. On his first assignment, protecting the US President's daughter, a mugger had stabbed him with a switchblade. The only thing that had saved him was his T-shirt – a Buddyguard-issued top made from a high-tech stab-proof fabric.

Connor realized that next time he faced a knife he might not be so lucky. Yet, studying the six-inch blade before him, he wondered if their instructor wasn't going a bit too far in his attempt for authenticity. It was perilous enough on missions without being hospitalized during training.

'Trying to catch a knife in motion is like sticking your hand into a blender,' their instructor went on, twirling the weapon in his hand. 'That's why the second rule of knife defence is: run – if you can. Distance is your friend when faced with a weapon like this. Bear in mind that an attacker, pumped on adrenalin, can sprint several paces in under one and a half seconds.'

Without warning, Steve lunged forward and held the razor-sharp blade to Marc's throat.

'*Merde!*' cried Marc, his eyes wide in shock.

'No need to swear, but my point has been made,' said Steve, withdrawing the knife. 'One and a half seconds doesn't give you much time to react.'

'Oh, I think he reacted all right,' said Ling, glancing down at Marc's shorts and smirking. 'Might need a change of pants there.'

Connor and the others laughed as Marc automatically checked himself.

'Ha, ha,' said Marc, his face reddening once he realized he'd fallen for her tease.

'This is no joking matter,' growled Steve, pointing the knife at them. 'Your lives may depend on the technique I'm about to teach you. On the internet you'll see martial arts instructors demonstrating various knife self-defence skills.

Some simple, some fancy, some plain stupid. Most don't work in a real attack situation. The only effective way to deal with a knife-wielding assailant is to Seize, Strike and Subdue.'

He beckoned Jason forward and handed him the knife. 'Come at me.'

'With a stab or a slash?' asked Jason, weighing the knife in his palm. Due to his size and boxing experience, Jason was often chosen to partner up with their mountain of an instructor – and he knew Steve would want him to attack hard and fast.

'It's your choice,' Steve replied, raising his hands into a defensive guard. 'I wouldn't know what was coming in reality.'

Jason nodded, then rushed at their instructor with an overhand strike, aiming for the chest. Steve side-stepped to the right, forearm-blocked the attack, palm-struck Jason in the face, grabbed his wrist, kneed him in the stomach, then drove him to the ground before putting him into an armlock. Barely knowing what had hit him, Jason was forced to relinquish his grip on the knife as Steve applied pressure to the lock. The whole series of moves was over in less than four seconds.

Seeing Jason's face contorted in pain, Connor was glad he hadn't been the one asked to demonstrate.

Jason gasped in relief as Steve released him. 'Right, let me show you the move again, this time at half-speed.'

Loosening up his arm, Jason repeated the overhand strike. Slow and smooth, Steve stepped into the attack with his forearm raised.

'The key thing is to gain full control of the attacker's knife-bearing arm – Seize,' he explained. 'This may require a block first, but if you don't grab hold of the attacker's arm, then they can pull back and go for a second attack.'

Steve gripped Jason's wrist, then in slow-motion hit Jason's neck with the edge of his hand.

'At the same time, you need to Strike. The head or neck is your best option. Then with the attacker stunned and the weapon controlled, you can Subdue. This can be multiple knee-strikes to the head, stomach or lower vital areas, followed by dropping them to the ground.'

He simulated kneeing Jason in the groin. Jason made a high-pitched squeal, crossing his eyes comically and collapsing to his knees. The whole class sniggered. Applying the armlock with enough force to make Jason cry out for real, Steve growled, 'Take this seriously!'

'Only attempt to defang the snake once you have full control,' he instructed. 'Otherwise you might lose your fingers.' Showing them how easily the blade could cut his digits off if he wasn't careful, he continued, 'Then break the arm or do whatever is necessary to eliminate the threat. Don't worry, Jason, I'll let you off this time.'

Jason gratefully stood back in line with the others as Steve released him from the crippling grip.

'Your priority is to ensure your own and your Principal's safety,' Steve explained, handing out more knives. 'The Seize, Strike and Subdue technique isn't pretty, but it's effective. Now pair up and practise.'

Alpha team split off to run through the drill, but everyone was far more cautious now they were training with a live blade.

'Let's hope none of us ever does this for real!' said Richie, inspecting the razor-edged knife he held. 'Especially you, Charley.'

'What do you mean?' said Charley sharply.

'Well . . . you can't . . . exactly . . .' Richie fumbled for the right words.

'Attack me,' Charley dared him. A steely glint entered her sky-blue eyes and Connor knew that Richie was in for it. So did Richie. But there could be no backing down. Nothing riled Charley more than people's low expectations of her abilities, especially for one-on-one combat.

'Are you . . . sure?' Richie said, glancing between the knife and Charley, clearly wondering which was the more dangerous.

Charley gave a single nod. 'Don't hold back . . . just cos I'm in this chair.'

Connor gave Richie a pitying smile as the Irish boy raised the knife and reluctantly launched himself at her. He brought the knife arcing down towards Charley's upper shoulder. Charley spun so fast with her chair that it looked like a fairground ride. Evading the initial attack, she wrenched one of the metal arms from her chair. It sprung out with engineered ease. Now she wielded a lethal *tonfa*-style baton. Before Richie could swing his arm round for a second attack, Charley smashed him across the wrist. He cried out and dropped the knife. The next moment he doubled over as the metal bar caught him full force in the gut. Then Charley hooked the baton behind his left ankle and whipped him off his feet. Richie landed in a crumpled heap on the floor.

'That's how I'd deal with a knife attack,' explained Charley, calmly slotting the metal arm back into her chair as the rest of Alpha team stared at her, open-mouthed and stunned into silence.

'*Another* assignment? But after the last time you promised no more.'

Connor winced as he heard the sense of betrayal in his gran's voice and saw the distinct tightening of her lips as she tried to control her anger.

'I know ... and I'd made a request for a break,' he pleaded into the tablet's webcam. 'But the colonel insisted. Besides, I won't be the only buddyguard on this mission. Jason's joining me.'

'So now there are *two* child targets for the terrorists!' said his gran scornfully. 'How can they miss?'

'It means there's *double* the protection,' Connor argued.

'For the person being protected, yes, but not you. You're in the line of fire. Risking everything. And for what?'

'You know what,' said Connor, trying not to get angry. 'For you and Mum. What I do pays for her care. I have to –'

'You don't *have* to do anything. We will find a way to cope. We always have,' said his gran firmly. 'You shouldn't have to risk your life for ours. If your mum only knew the truth –'

'She *can't* know. Please don't tell her,' Connor interrupted. 'Gran, we've been through this. Part of my agreement with Colonel Black is to keep Buddyguard and my role within it confidential. The organization's effectiveness relies on the fact that few people know it exists. That's how I can be an invisible shield. The best bodyguard is the one nobody notices, remember?'

'But you told *me* about Buddyguard.'

'Of course I did. There's no way I could pull the wool over your eyes. But Mum has to think I'm at a private boarding school on a sports scholarship programme. If she found out the truth she'd put a stop to it and I wouldn't be able to work as a buddyguard any more.'

While Connor didn't like to deceive his mum, she was suffering from the advanced stages of multiple sclerosis and his protection work paid for a full-time carer and all the private medical treatment she needed. Without it, his mum and gran might be sent to separate care homes and he'd be placed with a foster family. So, despite what his gran said about coping, there wasn't really any choice. He had to do this.

'Listen, it's only one more mission –'

'You're just like your father!' his gran snapped. 'Always one more mission!'

For all their arguing, Connor found himself smiling. As much as he hated upsetting his gran, he was pleased to be like his late father. With only fading memories to comfort him, any connection to his father was a blessing that kept his spirit alive. It was one of the reasons Connor had agreed to become a bodyguard in the first place – and the reason Colonel Black had singled him out for recruitment. His father had been an elite soldier in the SAS Special Projects Team, responsible for counter-terrorism and VIP close protection. And Connor was determined to live up to his achievements.

His gran's wrinkled chin now filled the screen. Connor sighed in frustration. He'd recently bought his mum and gran top-of-the-range tablets so they could keep in touch easily – especially now they were less mobile – but his gran often forgot where the webcam was.

'Gran, move the tablet so I can see you.'

He heard a muttering, then his gran's lined face came back into focus. Connor noticed her eyes were watery behind her glasses.

'Where are you being sent this time?' she asked, seemingly resigned to the decision.

'I'd rather not say.'

His gran sniffed. 'And I'd rather not know, to be honest. I'd only worry more.'

'Gran, I'll be careful.'

He saw her bony fingers reach out and touch the screen, caressing his face. 'You were careful last time . . .' Her voice cracked. 'And you almost didn't come back.'

'But I did,' he said. He shifted uncomfortably in the chair as he felt the scars on his back where the leopard had clawed him. They were healed completely now, but the skin still felt tight and the pale white lines were a reminder of just how close he'd come to death.

'How's Mum?' he asked in an attempt to change the topic.

'She's good,' his gran replied, her gaze wandering from the screen. 'No worse . . .'

'Can I speak with her?'

His gran gave a gentle smile. 'She's resting at the moment, but I'll let her know you called. And don't worry, I'll tell her you're doing well at school. Give all my best to that lovely Charley of yours. And take care, my boy, you're very precious to us.'

She ended the call, the last image hanging a moment: her pale hand dabbing at a tear running down the lines of her cheek. Connor set aside the tablet and stared out of his bedroom window, across the windswept hills of the Brecon Beacons. It was a beautiful remote place, perfect for a secret protection agency, but Connor felt far away from his mum and gran. Too far. He swallowed hard, fighting back his own tears. He knew his gran was shielding him from the reality of his mum's condition. But he also knew he could do more for her working as a bodyguard than he could at home as an underage carer with only her widow's pension to support them.

'I agree with your gran. It's time you got out.'

Connor spun round and discovered Charley hovering in his bedroom doorway. He had no idea how long she'd been there, but he was glad to see her. He smiled. 'But if I quit Buddyguard, I wouldn't see you any more.'

She eased beside him at the window and took his hand. 'That's sweet-talking, Romeo, but you've given enough blood for this organization. Three strikes and you should get out . . . before anything *permanent* happens to you.'

Charley glanced down at her chair, then back at Connor, making sure he fully understood her meaning.

'I hear what you're saying, but I need to do this for my mum and gran,' he explained. 'I know my dad faced greater dangers than this and he never quit.'

'No, he didn't,' Charley replied flatly. 'And look what happened to him.'

'Hey! Just because I'm following in my father's footsteps doesn't mean I'll follow him into the grave!' snapped Connor, pulling his hand away.

They sat in frosty silence, both staring at the distant covering of snow on the mountain peaks.

Charley reached for his hand again. 'I'm sorry I said that.'

Connor felt bad about his outburst. They'd only been going steady for the past few months and this was their first-ever row.

'It's just I've lost so much in my life already, I don't want to lose you too,' Charley admitted with a tender squeeze of his hand. 'You're the best thing to happen to me in a long, long time.'

Connor wrapped an arm round her shoulders and pulled her close. 'And you for me.' He moved aside a lock of her long blonde hair. 'You won't lose me. Ever,' he promised, leaning in to kiss her.

But now Charley was the one to pull back. 'Connor, I've got a bad feeling about this assignment . . .'

'It's no different from any other –'

'That's what worries me! You've been lucky so far, but what if you get *really* hurt like I did, or worse.'

Connor saw the deep well of fear in her eyes. 'That was a tragic and unique situation,' he said softly. 'But, seriously, Colonel Black wouldn't send us on a suicide mission.'

Charley held his gaze. 'Are you sure about that?'

Connor stared down the barrel of a loaded gun. He tried to concentrate on the danger in front of him, but his mind kept replaying the words that Charley had heard Colonel Black say: *The size of the contract is worth the risk of a buddyguard or two.*

'Hands behind your head!' ordered the woman who held the pistol in his face, her olive eyes following Connor's every move.

Connor slowly raised his hands. He couldn't believe the colonel would put profit before lives. The Colonel Black he knew was a straight-talking, highly honourable man, and one he trusted. After all, the colonel and his father had been close friends – both serving together in the SAS, the colonel even owing his life to his father. Connor couldn't imagine Colonel Black playing Russian roulette with his life.

The woman's finger curled round the trigger. Forced to act, Connor went for the gun.

Seize. Strike. Subdue.

He just managed to wrap his fingers round her wrist when the weapon went off. Connor flinched and felt the bullet's jarring impact. His face and jacket were splattered red and his vision went dark ... then Connor heard a distinctive guttural laugh.

'Too slow, amigo!' said Jason.

Connor peeled off his safety goggles. The paintball had exploded all over the lenses and covered him in red blotches.

'We'll have to call you pizza face from now on!' Jason teased, not letting up.

Connor narrowed his eyes at him. 'It must be like looking in a mirror then.'

The rest of Alpha team sniggered and Jason fumed.

'Bit difficult,' he snarled, 'seeing you've cracked all the ones in the school!'

'Only to stop you scaring yourself –'

'Enough!' Jody cut in, waving the gun between them. 'Pack it in or I'll shoot you both where it hurts.'

Jody was their close-protection instructor, a young woman with shoulder-length brown hair who had a passing resemblance to Lara Croft. She was the real deal. As a former SO14 Royal Protection Officer, Jody was as tough as their combat instructor Steve, as knowledgeable as their surveillance tutor Bugsy and almost as experienced as Colonel Black. She wasn't a woman to be messed with.

'As you just saw, the odds of disarming a gunman before they pull the trigger are lethally low,' explained Jody as Connor, silenced by her rebuke, wiped away the worst of the paint with the back of his sleeve. 'But it's not impossible to survive a handgun threat. People do it all the time. Your survival depends on three factors. One, the attacker's intention. Two, the distance. Three, the training of both you and the attacker.'

Flicking on the safety catch, Jody set aside the paintball gun on the bonnet of her Range Rover and picked up her insulated coffee mug. Despite the winter chill, she'd taken Alpha team outside to one of the fields for this lesson: Defence Against a Gun. 'Less mess to clear up,' she'd explained.

Pausing to take a sip of coffee, Jody continued, 'If the attacker's intention is to kill, then you or your Principal might be hit before you even know you're under attack. However, if their aim is to kidnap the Principal, the weapon will be used as a compliance tool. Unfortunately for you, that means the bodyguard is likely to be shot. Why?' She looked to Alpha team for an answer.

Ling held up her hand. 'We're a threat to the kidnapper's plans.'

Jody nodded. 'Correct. Why else?'

Marc pursed his lips thoughtfully. 'By shooting us, the kidnapper shows he's serious and the Principal will be more willing to do what he or she says.'

'Exactly,' said Jody. 'That's why you should never admit to being a bodyguard.'

'There goes your chat-up line!' said Richie, giving Marc a nudge with his elbow.

'The second factor in your survival is *distance*,' Jody went on, throwing Richie a warning look to be quiet. 'How far you are from the gunman determines everything.

Handguns are highly inaccurate weapons. If the distance is more than fifteen metres, *run*. Even a top marksman would struggle to hit a moving target at that distance with a handgun. So, shield your Principal with your body, crouch low and run in an unpredictable zigzag manner to make yourselves harder to hit.'

'What if we're closer than fifteen metres?' asked Amir.

'Then do *exactly* as the gunman says.'

'But aren't we supposed to take the bullet for our Principals so they can escape?' said Ling.

'That's the last resort,' Jody replied, her tone as grave as her expression. 'A dead bodyguard is no good to anyone. So I wouldn't advise it unless you're bulletproof.'

'I'm all right then,' Charley remarked with a pat of her wheelchair. Connor knew that her chair had been specially designed for close-protection work and hostile environments. Aside from the armrests that turned into *tonfa* batons, the seat cushion, back and sides were constructed of Kevlar plates and liquid body-armour panels. The carbon-fibre off-road wheels had run-flat tyres. Under the seat was a first-aid trauma kit and three flash-bang smoke grenades. There was even a high-powered rechargeable electric motor in case a fast getaway was needed. Basically Charley sat upon the wheelchair equivalent of a weaponized Ferrari.

Jody smiled at Charley, then turned to the others. 'Well, if you don't have a bulletproof wheelchair at your disposal, you should hide behind a wall, a car or anything else that might stop a bullet. Of course, you're all supplied with ballistic T-shirts and clothes for your assignments. But remember these are only effective against handguns. For anything more powerful like an assault rifle, you'll need mission-grade jackets. Even then you can suffer blunt trauma from the bullet's impact and, of course, your head's still exposed and vulnerable.'

Jason frowned. 'So are you saying we have to surrender at anything less than fifteen metres?'

Jody gave a non-committal shrug. 'Unless the attacker hasn't yet drawn their weapon or you're close enough to grab it, you've no choice but to surrender.'

'But I saw Jason Statham easily disarm a gunman at that distance.'

Jody tried hard to suppress a grin. 'You need to watch fewer movies! Forget the fiction of the hero shooting a villain in the hand at a hundred metres or disarming him before a shot is fired. The reality is that if someone has a gun to your head and you try something, then you're likely to get it blown off – as Connor demonstrated.'

Connor gave a little bow. 'My pleasure,' he said, trying to make light of it, though he knew that on a mission he'd have been scraping his brains off the floor.

'But your chances of survival *can* be improved with training – the third factor,' said Jody, distributing a set of paintball guns among the team. 'Connor's mistake was to grab my wrist rather than the gun. Unlike a knife, a gun needs only to be pointed in the right direction to be deadly. So it's crucial to gain control of the weapon first.'

Jody beckoned Ling forward and instructed her to raise her gun.

'Applying the Seize-Strike-Subdue technique, move your body out of the way at the same time as grabbing the weapon,' she explained, fluidly stepping to the side and clasping the barrel. 'Focus your attention on the muzzle and where it's pointing. You don't want yourself or the Principal shot during the struggle. Your aim is to rip the weapon from the gunman's hand, causing as much pain as possible. Ideally breaking their fingers in the process.'

Jody wrenched the gun from Ling's grasp, stopping short of snapping Ling's trigger finger.

'You see how I rotated the barrel towards the attacker? Their grip is weak compared to the leverage you have. Then once you've got the gun, club them with it *hard* to subdue them, take control of the situation and make your escape.'

Now Jody pointed the gun at Ling. 'Let's practise that. And it goes without saying that once you get hold you must never let go. Your life literally depends on it.'

'I feel like I've been pelted with marbles!' moaned Amir, inspecting the collection of red welts that covered his face, neck and chest. At close range the paintballs might not have killed them, but they left their mark and hurt like hell.

'Let's hope you don't have to disarm anyone on your next mission,' smirked Richie, 'otherwise you'll end up looking like Swiss cheese!'

'Charley, I think you dislocated my finger,' complained Marc, wincing as he tried to wiggle it.

'Yeah, Charley's good at that sort of thing,' said Jason, arching an eyebrow in her direction. By now they'd all heard how Charley had put Jason's little finger out of joint during one of their combat instructor's infamous Gauntlet tests. Although Jason had forgiven her, he never let her forget it.

Charley gave Marc an apologetic smile. 'Sorry, Marc, I got a little over-enthusiastic . . .'

Jody beeped the horn and waved as she drove past in her Range Rover. She'd not wanted the vehicle's leather interior to become smeared with paint so, despite the drizzling sleet, they were now trudging across the field behind her. The squared battlements and narrow windows of the old Victorian school building loomed in the distance. Sheltered in its own valley and hidden from the road, it was the ideal location for the covert training of young bodyguard recruits. From the outside, Buddyguard HQ appeared an old-fashioned private school but, inside, the building was fitted with the latest surveillance equipment, high-tech gadgets and state-of-the-art computers.

Hoping to question Charley on her own about Colonel Black, Connor slowed his pace and walked alongside her. Although the off-road tyres and motor-assist of her wheelchair made light work of the ruts and dips, she was still a little behind the rest of the group. Amir hung back too, but Connor decided to ask Charley anyway. 'Are you sure that's what the colonel said?'

Charley glanced up at him. 'Yes. I overheard the instructors arguing with the colonel in his office about the level of risk this mission entails. They're not happy with the lack of operational information. But Colonel Black's determined to push ahead. And, I quote, "That's what we train them for. The size of the contract is worth the risk of a buddyguard or two."'

Amir's eyes widened in shock at hearing this for the first time.

Connor shook his head. 'I just can't believe the colonel would say that. You *must* be taking it out of context.'

'Well, that's what I heard,' said Charley stiffly.

Amir glanced anxiously at them. 'Knife survival yesterday, medical trauma training this morning, and now gun defence. I certainly get the sense the colonel is preparing us for the worst!'

'He's always prepared us for the worst,' replied Connor. 'That's what makes him so good as commander of Buddyguard. He takes nothing for granted.'

'Apart from us perhaps?' said Charley pointedly.

'Bugsy does seem more tense than usual about this mission,' Amir commented. 'This morning he asked me to *triple*-check the route itinerary for Operation Snowstorm.'

Connor shrugged. 'Bugsy lives by the army's seven Ps: Proper Planning and Preparation Prevents Piss-Poor Performance!' He laughed but Amir and Charley didn't.

'Both Steve and Jody are acting out of character too,' Amir went on. 'Usually they're cool with a bit of banter in their lessons, but it's like their sense of humour has been surgically removed. I agree with Charley. I think this high-level mission to Russia has them spooked.'

'Why would they be spooked?' asked Connor. 'They're both experienced operatives.'

'You're protecting the son of a politician who's in direct opposition to the government *and* the mafia,' said Charley. 'It's not exactly the safest side to be on.'

'But no side is safe in our job,' argued Connor. 'Besides, we've protected other high-profile clients, including Alicia, and she was the US President's daughter! Why should this be any different?'

'It's Russia,' explained Charley. 'Normal rules don't apply.'

'Russia can't be any worse than Burundi,' said Connor. 'Can it?'

Charley and Amir just stared at him.

Ahead of them, Ling suddenly cried out in pain and grabbed her right buttock.

'Bullseye!' Jason laughed. He wielded a paintball gun in his hand.

Ling glared at Jason. 'You're so childish!' she yelled before storming off.

'Hey, it was just a joke,' Jason called out.

Ignoring him, Ling marched fiercely across the field and into the school's main building, slamming the outer door behind her.

'You were supposed to return that,' said Connor, pointing to the gun.

Jason aimed the weapon at him. 'Careful what you say. You're my next target.'

'Aren't you going after her?' asked Charley.

Jason frowned. 'Why?'

Charley sighed in exasperation. 'To apologize.'

'Nah,' he mumbled, kicking at a clod of wet grass. 'I'll do it later once she's cooled down.'

They tramped the rest of the way in silence, Jason brooding over Ling, and Connor thinking about what Amir and Charley had said. Was this mission more dangerous than the others? Would the colonel really risk their lives just for a fat contract payment? Connor didn't think so. The whole point in them learning knife survival, medical trauma and gun defence was to *reduce* the risk.

Charley must have misheard or misunderstood the colonel's meaning.

As they crossed the old playground, the bald head of their surveillance instructor emerged from the building. 'Connor! Jason! Get an overnight Go-bag packed,' ordered Bugsy. 'Your flight's in three hours.'

Connor's pulse quickened. 'But I thought our assignment wasn't for another week.'

'You aren't going to Russia,' said Bugsy.

'Then where are we going?' asked Jason.

'You'll find out when you get there.'

CHAPTER 8

Disembarking the plane at Geneva Airport, Connor and Jason were met by a stocky man in a bright red ski jacket, beanie and snow boots. Despite the unfamiliar outfit, Connor would have recognized Joseph Gunner's weather-beaten face and goatee beard anywhere.

'Gunner!' he cried in surprise. 'What are you doing here in Switzerland?'

The South African park ranger greeted Connor with a hug and a slap on the back. 'I'm your instructor for the next five days,' he explained, his voice as gravelly as his looks. The ranger had been Connor's guide during his last assignment to Burundi, after which Colonel Black had hired him as a specialist tutor. 'Come along. This way to the car park.'

Looking disgruntled at their obvious camaraderie, Jason muttered, 'So what are you teaching us ... skiing?'

Gunner laughed. 'I couldn't ski if you tied me to a tree and threw me down a mountain! My orders are to instruct you in firearms.'

'*Firearms?* I thought the colonel hired you for survival training?' said Connor as they exited the airport and were hit by a blast of ice-cold alpine air.

'This *is* survival training. For Russia,' Gunner replied grimly. 'You won't be facing leopards with claws on this assignment, Connor, but you might have to deal with some Russian "bears" armed with guns. So the colonel thought you'd better have firearms training.'

'Cool!' said Jason, his eyes lighting up. 'Does that mean we'll have our own gun on this mission?'

Gunner shook his head as he tossed their Go-bags into the boot of the hire car. 'No. Besides being illegal, even in Russia, you'd set yourself up as a target and risk revealing your true role. But there's little point learning to disarm an attacker if you don't know how to fire their darn weapon!'

They clambered into the car and set off. The motorway skirted the industrial edge of a large city before heading towards the snow-capped mountains in the distance. They'd only been travelling for half an hour when Gunner pulled up at a motel by a fast-food restaurant. 'That's our digs,' he announced, then pointed to a grey concrete bunker set into the mountainside. 'And that's the firing range.'

After checking in, Gunner wasted no time in taking them over to the range for their first lesson. Inside, the reception was surprisingly warm and cosy, with a coffee bar and sofas in one corner. The only difference from a normal sports club was that racks of weapons were displayed along the walls. Connor and Jason stared in astonishment. It was like a sweet shop for gun fanatics: stacks of pistols, revolvers, auto-loaders, shotguns, assault rifles, sub-machine guns and even tactical sniper rifles.

'Can I try that one?' asked Jason, pointing to a massive Bushmaster assault rifle.

Gunner grinned. 'I like your style, Jason, but these will be your weapons to start with,' he said, as the range's owner placed three compact handguns on the counter top.

Jason's shoulders slumped; he was unable to hide his disappointment.

'Don't be fooled by their appearance. These are Glock 17s,' explained Gunner, signing for the weapons along with several boxes of ammunition. 'An excellent sidearm favoured by security forces worldwide. It's lightweight, easy to use and reliable – just what you need in a high-pressure situation.'

Jason picked one up and weighed it in his hand. 'Yeah, it is light.'

Dropping into a cowboy stance, he pointed the gun at Connor's chest. 'Stick 'em up, punk!'

Gunner snatched the weapon from him. 'It's *not* a toy!' he snapped.

His angry disappointment evident even to Jason, Gunner escorted them to the firing range, a long narrow concrete room with electric runners overhead for positioning the paper targets.

'OK, safety first!' he said, laying the guns on the floor, barrels facing the wall. 'The four unbreakable rules are: one, treat every weapon as a loaded weapon with no exceptions. Two, do not point a weapon at anything you do not intend to destroy. Three, your finger stays off the trigger until the target is in the sights. And four, be sure of your target and surroundings at all times. Understood?'

He eyed Jason fiercely. Both Jason and Connor nodded. Gunner took them through the basics of gun handling before instructing them in the Weaver stance – two hands on the grip, both arms raised and slightly bent, and feet in a boxing stance with the body bladed.

'This is ideal for target practice and learning how to shoot,' explained Gunner. 'But in the real world you won't have time to perform the Weaver. So, once you've mastered this stance and can hit the targets, we'll advance to one-handed shooting and firing on the move. But let's learn to walk before we run, eh?'

Wearing safety goggles and ear defenders, Connor and Jason practised loading and unloading the magazine, quick-drawing the Glock from their hip holster and finishing with the *tap, rack and roll* to clear the chamber of any rounds if the gun failed to fire.

'You seem to be getting the hang of it,' said Gunner with a satisfied nod. 'Let's start shooting.'

When Gunner set up two paper targets with body outlines only three metres away, Jason rolled his eyes. 'That's a bit close. I could spit on those from here.'

'Most handgun engagements are less than two to three metres apart,' explained Gunner. 'And this is the ideal distance to nail your accuracy before shooting at longer ranges.' He indicated they should move to the firing line. 'Now, in your own time, take aim and engage.'

Jason immediately drew his gun, lined up the target between the sights and squeezed the trigger. The *bang* reverberated off the concrete walls and a small hole appeared in the middle of the target.

Gunner cocked an eyebrow. 'Good shooting. You're a natural.'

Jason grinned and reholstered his Glock. Now Connor withdrew his weapon, aimed and fired. He felt the gun's jarring recoil in his wrist but, to his amazement, missed the target entirely. He gritted his teeth and tried again. Still the target remained unmarked.

'You're too tense,' said Gunner. 'Relax your arms, slow your breathing and shoot just after the exhale.'

Connor followed his instructions and this time the bullet clipped the edge of the paper target. But it was still embarrassingly way off compared to Jason's shot. Meanwhile Jason scored another direct hit in his target's torso.

'Maybe my gun's faulty?' Connor said when he failed again to hit anything. 'The sights must be off.'

Gunner shook his head. 'The gun's fine. You're just pulling the trigger too hard. That jerks the weapon down. Shoot with your mind rather than your finger.'

Jason turned to watch, his expression smug. 'We can bring the target closer if that'd help!'

This made Connor even more determined. He couldn't go back to Alpha team with Jason bragging what a crackshot he was compared to him. He'd never live it down.

Before unholstering the gun again, Connor slowed his breathing and calmed himself. Then, slowly and smoothly as if performing a martial arts kata, he pulled out his Glock and took careful aim at the centre of the target. On the exhale, he imagined gently squeezing the trigger. The gun in his hand seemed to almost fire by itself . . .

The bullet went straight into the heart of the target.

Connor felt a frisson of excitement course through him. Beaming at his achievement, he turned to Jason. 'Beat that, hotshot!'

Jason replied by firing a round into the target's head.

Gunner whistled in admiration. 'I can see the competitive spirit brings out the best in both of you. Let's move the targets back a bit,' he said, increasing the gap to seven metres.

'An attacker would cover this distance in less than one and a half seconds,' he continued. 'Now the average handgun round delivers four hundred foot-pounds of force – roughly the equivalent of a strong punch. So there's no guarantee the attacker will go down with your first shot. They may also be wearing body armour or be high on drugs. And it's been known for a bullet to bounce off bone! That's why you need to practise the Mozambique drill – a rapid-fire pattern of two to the body, one to the head.'

Setting up his own target, Gunner demonstrated the technique. In less than a second, he drew his gun, executed a double tap to the target's torso and, after the briefest pause, followed up with the head shot. It all happened so fast Connor wasn't certain he'd even seen Gunner move.

'That's guaranteed to neutralize any attacker,' he said, stepping aside. 'Now it's your turn.'

At seven metres, the target was noticeably harder to hit – especially when attempting the triple-shot Mozambique drill. But Connor's marksmanship rapidly improved with Gunner's expert tuition. After another hour of shooting, the target's distance was increased to ten metres. Jason's draw, aim and fire were now so skilled that he consistently placed a double tap to the target's centre mass and a final shot to the head. Connor was less fluid and his groupings of shots were wider spread, but all his shots now hit the mark.

'Load up a full mag. Let's have a little competition to finish the day,' suggested Gunner, sending two fresh targets down the range to fifteen metres. 'Best out of seventeen rounds.'

Jason glanced at Connor. 'I'll only need half those to beat you.'

'And I'd only need one bullet to hit your big head!' Connor replied, ramming home a new mag.

They took up position on the firing line. On Gunner's command, they engaged with the targets. The range roared with the sound of gunfire, then thirty seconds later fell silent as the two of them reholstered their weapons.

Gunner retrieved the targets and counted the bullet holes. 'Not bad, Connor,' he said. 'Out of a possible seventeen shots, you scored eight to the body and three to the head.'

Connor couldn't help grinning as he glanced at Jason. He thought he'd done pretty well, considering he'd only begun firearms training that morning.

But then Gunner checked Jason's target. 'What can I say? Eleven to the body and five to the head. You're a true Billy the Kid!'

'Eat bullet, Connor!' laughed Jason, drawing his weapon and pretending to blow off Connor's head.

Gunner snatched the Glock 17 out of Jason's hand. 'Don't you listen? NEVER point your gun at someone on the range!'

'But it isn't loaded,' Jason protested. 'I've emptied the magazine.'

Gunner glared at him. 'First unbreakable rule – treat every weapon as a loaded weapon. No exceptions!' He pulled back the slide to reveal the seventeenth bullet *still* in the chamber.

Connor rounded on Jason in shock and horror. 'You could have killed me!'

And for once Jason had nothing to say.

CHAPTER 9

A sharp knock on the wood-panelled door caused Roman Gurov to glance up from the game of chess. '*Da?*' he grunted.

The door opened and a red-headed woman in a dark tailored suit entered. 'Sorry to disturb you, Mr Gurov.'

'What is it, Nika?' said Roman, beckoning his assistant into the elegantly furnished drawing room.

Crossing a red Persian rug in three quick strides, Nika approached the antique chess table upon which a finely crafted set of ebony and ivory chesspieces were in play. She gave a respectful nod to Roman's opponent, then addressed her boss. 'You asked for an update. The banker has adjusted his accounting error and returned the money.'

'Good,' said Roman. 'Now dispose of the banker. *Permanently.*'

'As you wish.'

'What about the Malkov situation?'

'There are plans for another anti-corruption rally,' replied Nika. 'This time much larger. And in Moscow. Malkov's becoming a serious problem.'

Roman reclined in the high-backed leather chair and steepled his long hard fingers beneath his dimpled chin. 'Then *fix* the problem.'

Nika gave a small cough, clearing her throat. 'It's not as simple as that. We can't get near him.'

'Why ever not?'

'Malkov has serious protection in place.'

The Pakhan waved away the excuse. 'That's not stopped us before.'

'True, but our intelligence indicates someone powerful is backing him.'

Roman raised a bushy eyebrow. 'CIA?'

Nika gave an almost-imperceptible shrug of her shoulders. 'That's our usual line. But this doesn't feel like the Americans.'

'Then who?'

'That's what we're trying to find out, but our sources have come up blank so far.'

Roman's deep-set eyes narrowed as his patience wore thin. 'Then they're not looking hard enough,' he growled.

Nika's whole body tensed, bracing herself for a blow. But none came. Not this time, at least. Although Nika was by no means a weak woman, skilled as she was in the Russian art of Systema and able to benchpress her own bodyweight, her boss held a third dan black belt in Kyokushin karate, one of the most brutal styles of Japanese martial arts, and he was notorious for demonstrating his skills on incompetent employees.

'The game isn't won in a few moves,' remarked the Pakhan's opponent, sliding his rook forward two spaces. 'If the king is too well protected, weaken his position.'

Roman's granite face slowly cracked into a sly grin. 'Yes,' he agreed, studying the chessboard closely. He responded to his opponent's move by claiming the rook with his bishop. 'Capture the pieces you can and one by one his campaign will fail. Nika, take someone close to Malkov out of play.'

'Consider it done,' said Nika with a curt nod. Understanding the kill order implicit in her boss's words, she added, 'I'll put our best asset on to this.'

Roman's dark eyes followed his assistant as she strode away. While he appreciated her toned figure and flaming red hair, she was one woman he wouldn't mess with. Like her muscled physique, Nika was as hard as nails and just as sharp. Above all, he valued her brutal efficiency, ruthless nature and absolute loyalty – characteristics that were essential for someone in her position.

Once she'd left the room, Roman returned his attention to the game in hand, his earlier grin quickly fading as his opponent made an unanticipated attack.

'Knight to Queen four,' his opponent announced. 'Check.'

'A new torch? What good is a torch?' said Jason as he examined the contents of the Go-bag Amir had just given him. 'Haven't you read Richie's threat report? What we need are *weapons* for this mission.'

'It *is* a weapon,' Amir replied, switching on the torch and blinding Jason with a bright green laser strobe.

Jason shielded his face. 'Get that out of my eyes!'

Connor laughed. 'Effective, isn't it?' Testing his own torch, he added, 'The Dazzler worked well for me against a Somali pirate.'

Blinking away spots of light, Jason turned to Connor who stood next to him in the logistic supply room. They'd flown back to Buddyguard HQ the previous night after five days of intensive firearms training. Upon their return, Operation Snowstorm had been given the all-go for the next day, so Bugsy had instructed them to gear up.

'We're dealing with gangsters, not pirates,' said Jason. 'A flashlight won't cut it against the Russian mafia.'

'This one will,' said Amir confidently. With a single sharp flick of his wrist, the torch extended to three times its original length.

'Well, *that's* new,' remarked Connor.

Amir slammed the baton down on the countertop with a sharp *crack*. Both Connor and Jason flinched.

'This is an XT tactical torch with hidden extendable baton,' Amir explained, 'constructed from a high-carbon steel alloy. I guarantee it won't break – however hard you hit your target.'

He pointed to the torch's hexagonal prong at the opposite end. 'This reinforced strike-ring will break glass panels if you need a quick escape. And in a fight the ring can do serious damage. You can easily knock out an attacker by hitting them hard on the temple or forehead. You wanted a weapon, Jason? This is the best!'

Amir jabbed the tip down on to the desk, collapsing the baton back into its casing. Once again, it looked like an ordinary torch. Amir shot them a smug look. 'And,' he added, 'it's concealed.' Connor grinned at his friend. Amir could always be trusted to come up with the goods – and he'd put Jason in his place.

Jason took the XT from Amir and re-examined it. 'Well, now we're talking,' he said, extending the baton himself and wielding it like a samurai sword.

'Oi! Watch it!' cried Connor, ducking as the rod skimmed his chin.

'Just testing your reactions,' said Jason with a smirk. He flipped the torch in his hand and tested the strike-ring on the countertop. It gouged a deep hole in the wood. Jason whistled in admiration. 'You're right, Amir – this can do some serious damage.'

'Bugsy won't be happy you've left that dent in his desk,' said Connor.

Jason shrugged. 'I'll just tell him you did it. Amir, you'll back me up, won't you?'

Amir rolled his eyes and held up his hands. 'I'm not getting involved.'

Retracting the baton, Jason tossed the torch into his Go-bag. 'So what else have we got?'

Amir handed them a pair of sleek mobiles along with tiny wireless earpieces. 'I've updated the operating systems on your smartphones. The translation app now works in Russian.'

'Fine, but boring,' said Jason, tossing them in with the rest of his gear.

'How about these then?' said Amir. He placed two small plastic cases, each the size and shape of a thickened ten-pence piece, on the table.

Connor picked one up and unscrewed the lid to reveal its contents. 'A contact lens?'

'Augmented reality system, actually,' explained Amir. 'The lens has a tiny camera and heads-up-display implanted in it for taking photos and film footage, with just the blink of an eye. And –' he looked proud of his device – 'a facial recognition program is installed. Once a suspect is uploaded to its memory, the lens will flash red three times any time it identifies the subject in its field of vision. There's also what I like to call an "eye-translate" feature. Just focus your gaze on a Russian sign, menu or whatever and the lens will scan and display the words in English. Try it.'

Amir held up a printed card with the words: Удачи на русском языке!

Popping the lens into his eye, Connor blinked as he got used to it, then looked at the card. On the lens's display the words now read: *Good luck in Russia!*

'Wow, that's neat!' said Connor, genuinely impressed. 'Shame Jason can't read, though.'

'Oh, don't worry,' Amir replied with an earnest look on his face. 'His lens translates the words into easy-to-understand pictures!'

Jason responded to them both with a thin smile. 'Ha, ha,' he said, as Bugsy entered the supply room carrying a large cardboard box.

'You've also got a new set of stab-proof and bulletproof clothing,' announced their surveillance tutor, depositing a pile of T-shirts, tops and trousers on to the counter. 'Third-generation design, these garments have been interwoven with a graphene fibre so they're lighter, thinner and ten times more effective. They'll now withstand a close-quarter attack from all types of handgun. But you'll still need these jackets for anything more powerful, like an assault rifle.'

Bugsy produced a couple of winter ski-style black coats, complete with hoods. 'The integral liquid body-armour panels will reduce the risk of blunt trauma too,' he explained.

Connor tried on one of the new T-shirts for size. 'I'll need this if Jason tries to shoot me again.'

'Hey, that was just a bit of friendly fire,' Jason said with a shrug. 'Besides, you should be more worried about your own aim. Bugsy, you should see Connor shoot. He's like a blind man playing darts. I'm surprised he ever hit the target!'

Connor sighed. 'Give it a rest.' Right through breakfast, Jason hadn't let up about his own shooting prowess to Ling and the others. It was true Jason had excelled in the firearms training, progressing quickly from static shots to firing on the move, then to one-handed shooting. And, compared with that, maybe Connor was still a novice. But he wasn't the poor shot Jason made out. He could hit the target seven times out of ten – and that was what mattered.

'Well, the report I had from Gunner said you both passed,' replied Bugsy, his jaw working a piece of chewing gum. 'Now, have you got everything you need?'

Connor nodded and slung his Go-bag over his shoulder. 'Yeah, thanks. This should do it.'

'We could do with more weapons,' suggested Jason. 'Like a gun?'

Bugsy shook his domed head. 'That's asking for trouble. Remember: don't rely on your gear, rely on your wits to avoid danger in the first place.'

Our wits will have to be razor-sharp then! thought Connor, remembering Charley's warning. But he felt confident they could deal with most threats using the gear they'd just been given..

'That's good advice, Bugsy, to use your wits,' said Jason, heading for the door. 'That's why I'll leave Connor to explain what he did to your desk.'

'Jason's a loose cannon,' said Connor as he tossed his washbag into the suitcase for that night's flight to Moscow. 'He's a danger to me and the Principal.'

'Just because you two don't get on doesn't mean he's not up to it,' replied Charley.

Connor looked at Charley, her slender cheekbones half-lit by the low winter sun shining through his bedroom window. He'd hoped she'd be on his side. 'Our relationship's got nothing to do with it. I question his judgement. Jason almost shot me in Switzerland!'

'From what I hear, that was a momentary lapse of concentration.'

'That's all it takes,' said Connor. 'Jason's gung-ho, doesn't listen and doesn't follow safety protocol. With that attitude, he shouldn't be assigned to this operation.'

Charley frowned. 'I know Jason can be brash and big-headed sometimes, but he's dependable and a decent bodyguard. Just look at his track record.'

'Yeah! Like when he got second-degree sunburn on a Caribbean assignment!' Connor replied, throwing a spare fleece into the suitcase. 'I question if Jason's really been *tested*. It's not like he's had to fight off Somali pirates or rebel gunmen.'

Charley pursed her lips. 'Perhaps the fact that nothing's happened on his assignments is down to his close-protection skills.'

'Or to luck,' Connor shot back. He stopped packing and turned to her. 'Why are you defending him anyway?'

'Because he stood by me when I needed a rock to cling to,' Charley replied, her hands unconsciously clasping the arms of her wheelchair. 'Look, I'll admit we weren't the best of friends to begin with, but once Jason accepts and respects you he's fiercely loyal. I'd trust him with my life.'

'Well, that's OK for you,' said Connor. 'But we don't exactly see eye to eye on things. And he's not taken well to me being in charge on the ground. This operation is a disaster waiting to happen.'

Charley edged herself away from the window and took Connor's hand. 'Listen, I understand your concerns about Jason. He can be full of himself and a bit of a joker. But he's also dedicated, experienced and more than able to handle himself *and* protect the Principal. The problem is you're both alpha males.'

Connor made a face. 'What do you mean?'

'You're like two tigers in a cage,' Charley explained. 'But instead of fighting one another you should be combining your strengths. And, from what I heard the colonel say, you'll need to watch each other's backs. This mission is more dangerous than most. So *please*, work it out with Jason, not just for me but for your own safety.'

Connor slumped down on the bed. He realized Charley was most likely right; perhaps his pride was getting in the way. He hadn't liked it when Jason outgunned him in Switzerland and disliked it even more that everyone knew. Ever since joining Buddyguard, he'd always been in competition with Jason and maybe that was the real reason he didn't want to partner with him on Operation Snowstorm. It seemed more of a contest than an assignment – and one neither of them could afford to lose, if only for the sake of their Principal.

But he had to give Jason some credit. He'd stood by Charley after the accident left her in a wheelchair. Whatever their differences, he respected Jason enough for that alone to work at his side. But he didn't know if the reverse was true.

'OK, I'll give him the benefit of the doubt,' he said, 'but only because you vouch for him.'

'Trust me,' said Charley, squeezing his hand. 'Jason won't let you down. And, once you show him what you're capable of, he'll come to respect you. What worries me more in all this is that Colonel Black had you two learning firearms in the first place.'

Connor frowned. 'Surely it's good we're being taught how to defend ourselves?'

'Then why didn't the rest of Alpha team receive firearms training?'

Connor shrugged. 'I don't know. Time? Expense? What's with all this questioning about the Buddyguard organization and the colonel? You're his star recruit –'

'*Was*,' corrected Charley. 'You have that honour now.' She glanced with rare contempt at her chair. 'I can't exactly go on missions any more.'

Connor knelt beside her. 'Maybe not, but you're the heart of Alpha team. Without you, the operations would fall apart. I couldn't do what I do without knowing you're there to back me up.'

A tentative smile replaced the scowl on Charley's face. 'Just take care, Connor. I'm worried –'

Connor put a finger to her lips. 'It's only cos we're together now. You never used to worry like this.'

Charley looked deep into his green-blue eyes. 'I've always worried about you, Connor.'

Unable to resist, Connor leant forward and kissed her. Charley responded and for a moment all their concerns and fears melted away. Then, from down the corridor, they heard raised voices.

'For heaven's sake, that isn't what I meant!' cried Ling.

'*Isn't it?*' Jason shouted back. 'Then why do you keep going on about him? Do you fancy him or something?'

'*What?*' exclaimed Ling. 'Get a grip! I only asked you to be nice. Why do you have to be such a pig-headed oaf about this?'

'Me? Pig-headed? You're one to talk, *Lippy Ling*!'

There was a sharp slap, then Ling yelled, 'Shove off to Russia and freeze, for all I care!'

Connor and Charley watched Ling storm past the bedroom door and down the stairs. Jason briefly appeared, his cheek red, before retreating back into his own bedroom. Charley glanced at Connor and whispered, 'I wonder what that was all about?'

ASSASSIN
CHAPTER 12

The businessman's black leather shoes scraped on the edge of the Moshe Aviv Tower as he tried to keep his footing. His pudgy arms flailed and his heart beat so fast he thought his pacemaker was short-circuiting.

'No use trying to fly, Mr Agasi,' said the lean-faced man, gripping his tie like the lead of a misbehaving dog. Despite his apparently slender build, the man stood firm as a rock on the rooftop helipad of the tallest building in Israel, one foot planted against the metal runner for anchorage. The sun was fierce in the desert-blue sky and the air hot and still, despite the immense height they were at.

'*Please, I beg you, Mr Grey!*' rasped Mr Agasi, his piggy eyes fixed upon the frail lifeline that was his silk Armani tie.

Mr Grey glanced at the city of Ramat Gan far below, the cars as small as bugs and the pedestrians as insignificant as ants. 'Some people believe if you fall from a great height you'll be dead before you hit the ground,' he said, ignoring the man's pleas. 'I'm afraid the reality isn't so pain-free.'

Mr Agasi tried to reply, but his tie had pulled taut like a noose round his neck. He clawed desperately at Mr Grey's arm.

'If I let go, Mr Agasi, you'll fall exactly two hundred and thirty-five metres to the pavement below,' Mr Grey went on, his wintry eyes showing no pity for his victim. 'In the seven seconds that will take, you'll accelerate to over one hundred miles per hour. Not quite terminal velocity. But it won't be the fall that'll kill you. It's the dead stop when you hit the ground.'

Mr Grey released his grip for a fraction of a second. Mr Agasi's eyes widened in horror before he jerked to a halt as Mr Grey reclasped the very end of the tie.

'A sudden deceleration from such a speed to zero will cause everything in your body to effectively weigh seven and a half thousand times more than normal,' Mr Grey explained in a monotone, suggesting he was delivering a university lecture rather than a death threat. 'Your brain will momentarily peak at ten tonnes. In that instant, your body's cells will burst open and your blood vessels will be torn apart. Your bones will shatter. And your aorta will rip loose from your heart. For a few beats, your heart will continue to pump blood into the cavity surrounding your lungs, but no longer to your brain. After the initial impact, your weight will of course return to normal. But that makes little difference since your blood is now seeping through your irreparably damaged brain. What doctors refer to as massive internal haemorrhaging.'

Mr Agasi spluttered in panic, one foot slipping off the edge of the tower. The abyss opened up below him and he experienced a sickening distortion of vision – the buildings warping and the ground rippling like a wave beneath him. Somehow he regained purchase with his foot. All the while, the assassin observed his futile efforts to survive with the sadistic pleasure of a child torturing a spider.

'Now there was a case of a parachutist who survived a freefall when her chute failed to open,' said Mr Grey, with an attempt at a comforting smile that had all the warmth of a shark's grin. 'However, as I understand, the ground was very soft. I'm not sure the concrete pavement will be as forgiving.'

Mr Agasi held up his trembling hands. 'OK, OK,' he gasped. 'I'll give you the names. Elias Borgoraz, Nir Levy, Beni . . .'

'Now we're getting somewhere, Mr Aga–' Mr Grey's mobile vibrated in his pocket. 'Hold on.'

With the man still dangling over the precipice, Mr Grey tapped his wireless earpiece to answer the call. After a short burst of static on the encrypted line, a voice said, 'Where are you?'

'Israel,' replied Mr Grey.

'You're needed in Russia.'

Mr Grey frowned slightly. 'I'm in the middle of a negotiation.'

'That can wait,' said the caller. 'We need you to take care of Viktor Malkov.'

'How soon?'

'Immediately. Drop everything.'

'Whatever you say,' said Mr Grey, releasing his grip on the tie and heading for the stairwell.

Confusion and terror briefly registered on Mr Agasi's face before he plummeted out of sight.

When Mr Grey emerged from the Moshe Aviv Tower a few minutes later and hailed a taxi, a small crowd had gathered round a deformed and broken body on the pavement.

'Did you get any sleep on the flight?' asked Connor, rubbing his eyes and yawning.

'Not much,' grunted Jason as they stood in line in the immigration hall of Sheremetyevo International Airport. The passport queue for foreign arrivals seemed to stretch on forever, snaking back and forth across the grey tiled floor like an over-extended concertina. Every so often the queue would shuffle a few steps forward, then come to a shuddering halt again.

Connor glanced at his watch: 5:30 a.m. They'd landed an hour late and still had to collect their bags. 'We're supposed to be meeting Malkov's contact in half an hour.'

'Nothing we can do about that,' mumbled Jason.

Connor sighed in frustration, irritated at Jason's tetchy mood. He texted Charley to let her know they'd landed safely, but were held up at passport control. Despite it being three thirty in the morning there, Charley responded almost immediately:

Will let client know. Stay safe C x

Connor smiled. That was why Charley was team leader, and why he admired her so much. Quick to respond, quick to solve any issue – big or small. He slipped the phone back into his pocket, then turned to Jason. 'So, did you sort things out with Ling before you left?'

Jason scowled at him. 'None of your business.'

'Sorry, only asking.'

'Well, don't. Me and Ling are over.'

'*What!* Why? You two have been going out for ages –'

'I said, it's none of your business!'

Connor shut up and they stood in silence. Connor couldn't believe that Ling and Jason had split up. No wonder Jason was so grouchy. They'd been an item since before Connor had joined Buddyguard. He just hoped Ling was all right. She was one tough cookie, but he knew she adored Jason. It was such bad timing. Now Jason was on a mission, the two of them would get little chance to make up. Connor glanced at the thunderous scowl on Jason's face and hoped the break-up wouldn't affect his judgement as a bodyguard.

After another fifteen minutes the queue had barely shifted. Then an immigration officer pushed his way through the lines of people. Dressed in a dark grey-blue uniform with three gold stripes on the shoulder, and with a red-rimmed cap pulled down tight over his brow, the officer had a severe military bearing. His hawk-like eyes swept the hall of sleep-starved arrivals, scanning each face against a piece of paper in his hand. His gaze fell on Connor and Jason and he made directly for them.

Connor nudged Jason as the officer approached. Double-checking their faces against the paper, the officer demanded in a thick accent, 'Connor Reeves? Jason King?'

They both nodded.

'*Pojdem so mnoj,*' said the officer, turning on his heels. In their earpieces the translation app barked, 'Come with me.'

Connor exchanged an uncertain glance with Jason. However, after a curt order of 'Now!' from the officer, they picked up their Go-bags and followed. The queue parted, almost fearfully, as the three of them cut through the lines to the opposite side of the immigration hall.

'Where are we going?' Jason asked the officer.

The man strode on without replying.

'Is there a problem?' asked Connor.

But still the officer remained tight-lipped as he halted beside a door, stabbed a code into the keypad, then escorted them along an empty corridor and into a private windowless room. As Connor stepped inside, a sinking feeling gripped the pit of his stomach. Overhead the strip lights burned harsh and bright. The beige paint on the walls was peeling. And there was an ominous dark stain in the centre of the threadbare carpet. The only furniture was a row of moulded-plastic brown chairs bolted to the floor, opposite a counter-and-glass partition that divided the room in half. An unpleasant smell of stale sweat, urine and cigarette smoke tainted the air. This wasn't any 'Welcome to Russia' reception area, Connor realized. It was a detention room.

'Passports,' demanded the officer, thrusting out a hand.

'What's this about?' asked Jason.

'*Passports!*' repeated the officer, his tone sharp and unforgiving.

Reluctantly they handed them over. The officer gave their credentials and entry visas a cursory glance before striding out of the room. The door automatically locked behind him.

'He's got our passports,' Jason snarled.

'I know,' Connor replied, his eyes darting round the room.

'Do you think they –?'

'I'm sure it's just routine,' Connor interrupted before his partner blurted out any details of their operation and raised suspicion in the Russians' minds. With a subtle nod he directed Jason's gaze towards a CCTV camera in the corner of the room. Then he urged Jason to sit next to him on one of the plastic chairs, seemingly moulded for maximum discomfort.

'Ah! I see what you mean,' said Jason, taking his seat. 'Probably routine.'

But there was nothing routine about their detention. His brain in overdrive, Connor ran through the possibilities. The Russians obviously knew their names and faces. They could've been pulled aside simply because they were unaccompanied kids. Possibly the airline had alerted the authorities. But they had to assume the worst ... that Malkov's enemies were on to them already!

Connor pulled out his mobile to text Charley, but he no longer had a signal. 'Is your phone working?' he whispered.

Jason checked and shook his head. 'Must be blocked in here.'

Connor's blood ran cold. They were cut off from help, in a foreign country notorious for disregarding human rights. They could be held here for hours, maybe days. With no communication to the outside world, they could simply disappear. The room, already airless, began to feel suffocating. Connor dry-swallowed. He noted there was no water fountain or toilet. He stared at the ominous dark red stain on the carpet at their feet, wondering what had happened to the last occupant of this room.

Jason typed a text on his mobile, then tilted the screen towards Connor.

We need to get our story straight.

Connor was about to text a reply when the door burst open and two brutes of men strode in. Despite the smart suits they wore, their jackets couldn't hide the hardened muscle beneath, nor the tattoos rimming their wrists and stout necks. One was tall and broad-chested, with a menacing air that tainted the room like bad aftershave. The other was short, squat and bald, with rings like knuckledusters on his fingers. Connor and Jason both leapt to their feet, instinctively on guard. If these two men had come to interrogate them, Connor realized they had little chance of resisting.

Then the immigration officer entered the room. Unsmiling, he handed back their passports, their visas stamped and authorized.

'Let's go,' said the taller of the brutes in heavily accented English. With a severe buzzcut of black hair, a heavyset jaw and a nose that must have been broken at least twice, he wasn't a man to argue with.

Still wary, Connor asked, 'Where? Who are you?'

Clearly aware of the surveillance, the man's eyes flicked towards the CCTV camera, then back to Connor. 'We're your bodyguards. My name's Lazar. Your uncle is looking forward to meeting you.'

Connor allowed himself to breathe again. Lazar's last line was the code phrase that had been agreed for the rendezvous with their contact at the airport. The uncle in question could only be Viktor Malkov.

Jason whispered out of the corner of his mouth to Connor, 'Bodyguards for bodyguards! We're in deep trouble here.'

Not wanting to stay in the detention room any longer than they had to, Connor and Jason seized their Go-bags and headed for the door. As they left the room, Connor noticed Lazar slip the immigration officer a fistful of roubles.

Connor knew from the operation briefing notes that Viktor Malkov's residence was set in a ninety-acre wooded estate in the super-rich suburb of Rublyovka, Moscow's equivalent of Beverly Hills. With nine bedrooms, two swimming pools and every room lavishly decorated in mahogany, marble and gold, the mansion was more like a palace than a home. But the billionaire politician had spent his money on more than just decorating the property. As the silver Mercedes wound up the driveway to the gravel forecourt, Connor peered through the darkness and noted armed guards on the main gate, electrified fencing on the perimeter wall, surveillance cameras and floodlights every hundred metres, and the torchbeams of security men patrolling the pine-forested grounds. To Connor's trained eye, the mansion was as much a fortress as a palace.

The Mercedes rolled to a stop beside the forecourt's central fountain – a Baroque-style marble masterpiece featuring an enormous white statue of Neptune spouting water. Lazar and the other bodyguard, Timur – his name the only word he'd grunted during the entire two-hour drive from the airport – opened the passenger doors. Connor and Jason clambered out.

'*Jeez*, it's freezing!' exclaimed Jason, his breath clouding in the deep winter chill.

Sunrise was another hour away, so it was still dark and the air bitingly cold. Zipping up his jacket, Connor was glad he'd packed that extra fleece. A porter collected their luggage from the boot as the two of them were escorted up a flight of stone steps into the mansion's entrance hall. Inside they were met with a welcome wave of warmth and light.

As their eyes adjusted to the brightness, Jason let out a low whistle. They both gazed in awe at the huge gleaming chandelier dangling over their heads.

The grand entrance hall took Connor's breath away too. This room alone had to be larger than his mother's terraced house in east London. Encircling the chandelier, a viewing gallery on the upper level looked down on to a white marble floor inlaid with pure gold. Alabaster walls boasted expensive works of art from the Renaissance period, while ornate antique furniture completed the hall's majestic design. Connor had never seen such a display of opulence and wealth in his life.

A set of double doors swung open to reveal Viktor Malkov in a designer blue polo shirt, chinos and his trademark rimless glasses. The dark-haired politician smiled. 'Welcome to my humble home,' he said. 'How was your flight?'

'Good, thanks,' Connor replied, shaking the man's hand.

'You lie! Aeroflot are the *worst* airline.'

Connor flinched, wondering if he'd somehow offended the man.

Then Viktor laughed. 'You should have flown British Airways!'

He shook Jason's hand. 'Sorry for the delay at passport control. The FSB's border security service recently ordered the closure of fast-track services at airports. Security reasons, they say. More government restrictions is what I say. So now it takes a little more *effort* to ease people through the line.' He rubbed his fingers together to indicate the extra money required. 'But you're here now and I'm sure you're hungry. Have you had breakfast?'

Jason nodded. 'We had some on the plane.'

'Another lie!' exclaimed Viktor, wagging his finger. 'Speak truth. Aeroflot meals are like cardboard. Come, let's have a proper breakfast.'

Flanked by the two bodyguards, Connor and Jason followed Viktor down a corridor to a magnificent conservatory overlooking an enormous garden covered with deep snow. A long table was laid with fresh fruits, yogurts, pancakes, cheeses and pastries – so much food it looked like a buffet at a five-star hotel.

'Sit,' Malkov ordered, as a housemaid poured out coffee for her boss. 'You want some? Or juice?'

'Orange juice would be fine,' replied Connor, taking a seat.

'For me too,' said Jason.

Lazar and Timur stationed themselves by the door, where they stood like granite statues as the maid filled the boys' glasses with freshly squeezed juice.

Viktor sipped from his coffee and took a bite of a pastry. 'I'm very glad you're both here. While I've complete confidence in Lazar and his men –' Viktor nodded respectfully at his personal bodyguard – 'it can never hurt to have too much protection. Especially in Russia. My enemies would dearly love to take me down – any way they can – which makes my son a target too.'

'Don't worry, we'll keep Feliks safe,' said Jason, helping himself to a chocolate croissant.

'Have you eaten *syrniki* before?' asked Viktor.

Jason and Connor shook their heads.

'Then you must! You're in Russia.' He clicked his fingers at the maid, who served them each three thick fried pancakes along with a small pot of sour cream and another of jam.

'Traditional cottage-cheese dumplings,' Viktor explained, as he spread a layer of cream and bit into a steaming *syrniki*. 'Always loved these as a child – and still do.'

Connor tried one with jam. To his surprise, he discovered the outside was crisp and the centre warm and creamy.

'You like?' asked Viktor.

Connor grinned and took another bite.

'Good. They're very nutritious and high in protein. Fill you up for the winter mornings. And the mornings in Moscow are enough to freeze the –'

A knock at the conservatory door alerted them to a new arrival. Lazar let in a bearded man wearing a charcoal-grey suit. The top of his head was as bald as a boiled egg, as if his hair had parted and slid down to form his sideburns and neatly trimmed beard, peppered white at the tips. He had a slightly pudgy nose and small plump lips, but his eyes were sharp and watchful.

'Ah, Dmitry, you're early,' said Viktor, beckoning the man to join them at the breakfast table. 'Please meet my nephews, Connor and Jason.'

A slight frown wrinkled the man's bald brow. 'Nephews?'

'Second cousins, once removed, really. On my mother's side,' Viktor explained with a disarming smile. 'Dmitry Smirnov is my personal adviser,' he told Connor and Jason. 'He's responsible for orchestrating the campaign for *Our Russia.*'

'It's a joint effort,' said Dmitry humbly.

Connor was intrigued to note that Viktor hadn't revealed their role as bodyguards to his right-hand man. Viktor's trust circle was evidently very small and he was taking no chances with the covert security measures for his son.

'We need to talk,' said Dmitry as the maid filled his coffee cup. 'In private.'

'Of course,' said Viktor. He waved a finger to get Timur's attention. The squat bodyguard lumbered over. 'Timur, take the boys up to see Feliks. I'm sure he'll be excited to meet his cousins at long last.'

Feliks Malkov spooned another pile of cornflakes into his mouth and continued to stare at the colossal TV dominating the end wall of the mansion's recreation room. A horror movie about the living dead was on and the screen was so large that the zombies appeared almost life-size, the blood splatters gruesomely real.

'That's some TV,' remarked Connor, trying not to wince as a young woman had her guts devoured. He was amazed their Principal still had an appetite watching this sort of stuff.

'Mmm,' Feliks agreed half-heartedly as he reclined further in his La-Z-Boy armchair, his spindly legs stretched out in front of him, eyes transfixed on the screen.

'What would one of these TVs cost?' asked Jason, nodding at the screen.

Feliks shrugged as if to say, *What does it matter?* and shovelled in another spoonful of cornflakes.

Exchanging a glance with Connor, Jason raised his eyebrows. Timur had left them with Feliks ten minutes ago, but they'd barely got anything out of the boy beyond a disinterested response to their questions. Their Principal certainly matched the photo in the operation folder: sullen, moody and pale-faced, as if he rarely saw the sun. With his flop of dark hair, narrow nose and thin lips, Feliks could easily be mistaken for a vampire. Connor got the sense the boy didn't socialize much either – despite the rec room being kitted out with every game and entertainment imaginable. A one-lane bowling alley ran the length of the far wall. In the centre was a football table, air hockey and a full-size pool table. Arcade games machines were dotted around, including a vintage Space Invaders, pinball machine and state-of-the-art VR units. It was a billionaire's toy shop – with no one but the billionaire's son to enjoy them.

The film ended with a suitably grisly bloodbath and the credits began to roll. Feliks glanced up at Connor and Jason for the first time since they'd entered the rec room. 'So, you're my new bodyguards, eh?'

'Yes,' Connor replied, making a renewed effort to smile. 'We'll be ensuring your safety during your father's campaign.'

Feliks looked them both up and down. 'Well, *you* look as if you can handle yourself,' he said, nodding at Jason, whose broad chest puffed out at the compliment. Then Feliks turned to Connor, noting his spiky brown hair and slim, athletic build. His eyes narrowed. 'Not sure about *you*, though.'

Jason smirked and Connor tried not to appear offended. 'I was the UK junior kickboxing champion,' he replied defensively.

'*Was?*' Feliks questioned, frowning with disappointment. 'Who beat you?'

Connor bit back on his tongue. He was fast coming to dislike his new Principal. He reminded himself the boy had lost his mother – but that didn't excuse his rudeness. 'No one beat me. I've been working as a bodyguard ever since.'

Feliks dumped his bowl of cornflakes on a table and ambled over to a large American-style fridge in the room's refreshment zone. He took out a chocolate milk but didn't offer them one.

'So, my father thinks you two can protect me from the Bratva. The most feared and ruthless mafia organization in the world!' He snorted a laugh, then shook his head in dismay. 'My father's finally losing it.'

'We're an invisible ring of defence,' explained Connor. 'Lazar and his team are obviously bodyguards. They draw too much attention and turn you into a high-profile target. But Jason and I can blend in. Follow you where they can't. Go to school. Parties. Whatever. So wherever you are, you have a hidden shield protecting you.'

Feliks drained his chocolate milk and wiped the froth from his top lip with the back of his hand. 'Well, I hope you last longer than my previous bodyguard,' he said, tossing the empty carton into the bin.

'What happened to him?' asked Jason, as Connor wondered why this information hadn't been in their operation folder.

'He got fired . . . *literally*.' Feliks sniggered and made a gun with his hand, pretending to shoot both Connor and Jason.

But Connor and Jason didn't laugh.

CHAPTER 16

Early next morning, Connor's alert level shot up to Code Orange. They were on the slow commute to Feliks's school and he was studying the traffic through the rear windscreen, when a black Toyota Corolla appeared five cars behind. He'd spotted the same vehicle earlier as they'd turned out of the road leading to Malkov's estate. If it hadn't been for the street lamp on the corner, Connor would never have noticed it. With its jet-black paintwork and headlights switched off, the car was a shadow in the pre-dawn darkness.

Only now in the reflected red glow of brake lights could Connor make out the number plate. But he was certain this was the same Toyota that had tailed their SUV through the Rublyovka suburbs and on to the Moscow Ring Road.

'We're being followed,' he told Timur, who sat in the front passenger seat.

'*Da,*' replied the bodyguard, his bowling ball of a head not even looking round.

Connor frowned. 'Aren't you worried?'

'*Nyet.*'

'Shouldn't we –'

'The FSB always follow,' he cut in.

Connor was surprised at the bodyguard's lack of concern. The FSB was the main security agency of the Russian Federation. Responsible for counter-intelligence, counter-terrorism and surveillance, the organization was the strong arm of the government and sometimes used to intimidate political opponents – and even, it was rumoured, to assassinate them. As the natural successor to the infamous KGB, their presence wasn't to be taken lightly. So Connor realized it shouldn't be a complete shock that FSB agents were following them. As the primary opposition to the current government, Viktor Malkov would be the subject of intense investigation and his movements closely monitored. And that would include his son too.

As they pulled off the ring road at the next exit, so did the Toyota.

Connor couldn't help glancing over his shoulder every so often. He found the shadowy figures in the vehicle sinister and unsettling.

'You'll get used to it,' said Feliks, without looking up from the shoot-'em-up he was playing on his phone. He was in the seat next to Connor, but until then hadn't made any attempt at conversation. Connor wondered whether Feliks's aloofness was due to social awkwardness or simply rudeness. Whatever the reason, the Principal seemed totally disinterested in both him and Jason.

Connor glanced at Jason. He was on their Principal's other side, dozing against the window. He felt compelled to wake him. Jason should be alert in Code Yellow in case of any threat. But Connor couldn't blame him either. It was about 5 a.m. UK time and, despite having had a day to adjust, he was struggling to keep his own eyes open. On top of that, the journey was taking forever, the traffic snarled up along the entire route.

The Toyota pulled up on the opposite side of the road as they eventually reached the International Europa School, a leading independent school for the children of Moscow's elite. Connor turned to rouse Jason. But, sensing their arrival, he'd already snapped awake and looked refreshed and alert. Now Connor envied his partner's power nap. Stifling a yawn, he stepped out of the vehicle. At once his tiredness was blasted away by the ice-cold wind.

'Does the sun ever rise round here?' Jason asked, pulling up his hood and surveying the darkened sports field.

'Around nine,' Feliks replied. Shouldering his school bag, he headed for the gates.

Timur accompanied them to the main school entrance, then handed over protection duties to Connor and Jason with a monosyllabic grunt. The three of them crossed the inner playground, the previous night's snow a mish-mash of footprints as more and more students arrived. As they walked, Connor instinctively fell in on Feliks's right-hand side. The prime position for the personal bodyguard.

But so did Jason – and they clashed shoulders. For a moment they jostled for dominance.

'Take point,' Connor ordered in a whisper, nodding to the forward position that a second bodyguard would normally assume.

'*You* take point,' said Jason.

Connor glared at Jason, but his rival wouldn't give ground. 'We'll take it in turns,' he hissed.

'OK,' said Jason with an appeasing smile. 'You go first.'

Connor clenched his jaw in annoyance, but didn't want to make a scene in front of their Principal. He moved slightly ahead and to the left of Feliks. This ensured that between them they had a full arc of view and their Principal was protected from the front, behind and to either side.

Reaching the main building, Connor opened the doors, quickly scanned for threats – not that he expected any – then stepped inside. The school was busy with students arriving, teachers heading to classrooms and friends catching up after the weekend. As they made their way down the central corridor, Connor noted few people actually acknowledged Feliks, though some stared at him. Connor wondered if this was because of his and Jason's presence, two new kids on the block . . . or was it something else?

They stopped beside a row of lockers to hang up their coats and dump their gym bags. Connor and Jason kept their Go-bags to hand, masquerading them as normal school bags. As Feliks dialled in the code to his padlock, a slim girl with a high rollneck sweater and long ice-blonde hair approached. She wore a black oblong backpack and clasped a timetable in one hand.

'Excuse me,' she asked. 'Do you know where Grade Ten maths is?'

Feliks just stared at her, goldfish-like.

She smiled at him. 'Well, do you?'

'D-d-down the hall on the left,' Feliks mumbled, a slight flush to his cheeks as he fumbled with the padlock and opened his locker door, almost hiding behind it.

'Thanks,' she said with another burst of a smile. Her pale blue eyes briefly fell upon Connor, then Jason, before she strode away down the corridor.

'Who's she?' asked Jason keenly, his gaze trailing the blonde beauty.

Feliks buried his head in his locker. 'No idea. Must be a new girl in my class.'

Jason smiled. 'I'm liking it here already.'

Connor jabbed him in the side with his elbow. 'Focus on the job,' he hissed.

'I am!' protested Jason. 'I'm identifying potential threats.'

'And *is* she a threat?' asked Connor, his tone sarcastic.

'No . . . but I might be to her,' he replied with a rakish grin.

Connor rolled his eyes, wondering how Jason could forget Ling so quickly. 'Let's get to class.'

Closing their lockers, they headed down the corridor only to discover the way blocked by two hulking lads. Like a couple of young bulls, they stood shoulder to shoulder, arms folded, nostrils flared and their brows furrowed.

'Excuse us,' said Connor, still on point and subtly shielding his Principal.

The two Russian lads looked straight through him, glanced at Jason, then eyeballed Feliks.

'Who are these two losers? Your *bodyguards*?' sneered the slightly better-looking of the two. Blond-haired with a broad nose, square jaw and dimpled chin, the boy had an air of menace that went way beyond his intimidating bulk.

Although he did his best to hold the boy's glare, Feliks visibly shrank from his presence. '*Kuzeny*,' he answered in Russian, a slight quaver to his voice.

'Long-lost cousins by the looks of it,' snorted the other boy, his rounded face pockmarked with acne. 'Your papa having to buy in friends for you now?'

The two lads laughed at their own joke as Feliks's cheeks flushed.

'What's your problem?' said Jason.

'Him,' the first boy replied, narrowing his eyes at Feliks. 'And unless you two want to become part of that problem, beat it!'

Connor held up a hand, ostensibly in peace, but primed for a one-inch push if the situation became violent. 'There's no need for –'

'*You* beat it!' Jason interrupted, stepping between Feliks and his aggressors.

Both the boys' eyes widened in disbelief, evidently stunned that someone had the nerve to talk back at them. Recovering fast, the boy with acne squared up to him. 'Or else what?'

Despite Jason's bulk, the Russian boy still had two inches on him and fists like rock-hammers. Connor laid a hand on Jason's arm, signalling him to back down. But Jason shook it off.

'Or else you'll be swallowing teeth,' Jason threatened.

The lad grinned to reveal a mouth reinforced with metal braces. 'Go on – take a swing at me. If you dare.'

It was clear Jason would have to hit the boy very hard to dislodge *any* teeth. And if he did his knuckles would be shredded to pieces by the wire. Yet Connor could see Jason clenching his fists, the temptation to wipe the grin off the lad's face too much for him.

Connor had no idea what Feliks's history was with these two bullies, but this *wasn't* the best solution. And definitely not the best way to start their first day on the mission. As he moved to diffuse the situation, the bell rang for the start of lessons. In that brief moment of distraction, Connor grabbed Feliks and herded him along with the rush of other students past the two lads. Jason followed close behind, keeping guard from the rear.

'We're not finished!' warned the boy with acne, jabbing a finger at Jason.

Jason stared back, undaunted. 'No, we've not even started.'

'Who were those two?' asked Connor, as the three of them took their seats towards the back of the maths classroom.

'Stas and Vadik,' spat Feliks, his voice and courage returning now they were gone.

'What's their beef with you?' asked Jason.

'Stas's father is the Director of the FSB,' Feliks explained bitterly, 'so Stas acts like the school's own head of secret police, with Vadik as his henchman. Since my father is in opposition to the government, they consider me fair game for *interrogation*.'

'Well, they seem like a pair of knuckleheads to me,' said Jason as their maths teacher walked in, sat down and began the register.

'*Luka Azarov . . . Stefan Artenyev . . . Klara Balashova . . . Jean Claude . . .*'

Connor leant over and whispered to Jason, 'Yes, and *you* almost got us into a fight with them.'

Jason looked blankly at him. 'So?'

'That *isn't* the way to deal with this problem.'

'Of course it is,' he argued under his breath. 'We need to make a show of strength. Otherwise they'll think they can walk all over us.'

Connor shook his head. 'Our job is to deflect threats, not create them.'

Jason frowned. 'Surely it's better to neutralize any threat *before* it becomes a problem.'

'No! It's better if they underestimate us.'

'I disagree.'

'Well, if you haven't forgotten already, I'm in charge and –' Connor suddenly became aware that the classroom had gone quiet and everyone was staring at them.

'Sorry, gentlemen, am I interrupting you?' the maths teacher enquired, glaring at them over the top of his half-rim glasses.

Connor and Jason shook their heads. 'No, sir,' they replied.

'Then pay attention!' The teacher tutted, then returned to the register. '*Jason King . . .*' he repeated as if talking to a five-year-old.

'Yes,' Jason replied somewhat sheepishly.

'. . . *Anastasia Komolova . . .*'

'Here!' The blonde girl who'd earlier asked for directions put up her hand.

Connor, Jason and Feliks all looked over to where she sat by the window, her hair glistening like frost in the morning sunshine. While there was no denying she was beautiful, there was also something hard about her; perhaps it was the way her mouth was set in a tight solemn line, or the way her eyes constantly scanned the classroom, the door to the hallway and the playground outside the window. To Connor, she seemed in a constant state of Code Orange, 'focused awareness' – a level up from the Code Yellow 'relaxed awareness' that they'd been taught to maintain as bodyguards. He guessed Anastasia was highly strung. Then again she was the new girl and probably hadn't settled in yet.

Once the register was complete, the teacher switched on the interactive whiteboard and instructed, 'Turn to page thirty-six of your textbooks.'

Connor did so and was confronted by a bewildering array of algebra and complex equations. Fortunately for him and Jason, since the Europa School was a mixed international school, English was the primary teaching language. But it was still a mental shock to go from 'real world' Buddyguard training and return to traditional education. During the course of the lesson, Connor's mind was stretched and strained by the challenging mathematics. At Buddyguard they continued to have lessons on the core subjects, but everything was geared towards its application in close protection. In contrast, the equations set in front of Connor were far more abstract and demanding. The end of the period couldn't come quickly enough for him. Nor for Jason.

'I forgot how boring real school is!' Jason complained later, as they finally escaped their third-period geography lesson for the lunch break.

They crossed the frozen playground, passing clusters of pupils chatting excitedly, or playing football, or else heading towards the canteen. But Feliks made his own solitary path over to the food hall.

In the canteen, they encountered Stas and Vadik again. The two bullies were pushing to the front of the queue, the other students stepping aside in fearful respect. It was evident Stas had inherited the formidable reputation of his FSB father.

Connor and Jason flanked Feliks as they chose their lunch from the hot-food counter, collected their cutlery, then headed for a free table. As they passed Stas's table, someone in their group heckled, 'Dead man walking!'

The jibe at Feliks triggered a burst of sniggers. Feliks did his best to shrug off the taunt, but Jason spun towards the source of the heckle.

'Dead man *talking*, more like,' he said, his stare daring the culprit to speak again.

The heckler, a boy with dark cropped hair and a breeze-block head and body, rose from his seat. And kept rising. Connor wondered what the hell Russian kids were fed on – this one looked like he devoured at least a dozen *syrniki* every morning for breakfast.

But Jason to his credit didn't show any sign of fear . . . or backing down.

A teacher on supervision duty glanced over at the scene. Connor turned to Jason, warning him to let the remark go. With reluctance, Jason backed down and walked away.

'Thanks,' said Feliks to Jason as they seated themselves. 'It's good to have some muscle on my side for once.'

'Stas and his friends seem to have it in for you,' Jason remarked, not taking his eyes off the bullies' table.

'All sheep are afraid of the lion,' said Feliks. 'My father's exposing Russia for what it is and they don't like it. Because many of their parents work for the government or have businesses connected with it, they're worried their parents will be exposed too.'

'Well, at least we know who to look out for now,' said Connor, memorizing all the faces of Stas's gang.

As they tucked into their lunch, they heard Stas call, 'Hey, new girl! Come and sit with us.'

Anastasia, tray in hand, gave him a cool look and kept walking. She passed a table of her girl classmates – a spare seat available – before stopping beside Connor, Jason and Feliks. She glanced at the free chair next to Feliks.

'May I sit with you?' she asked. The smile she gave Feliks was dazzling. It melted the initial icy impression Connor had of her.

'Sure.' Feliks swallowed, looking half-delighted, half-shocked by the request.

Jason sat up straighter, ran a hand through his shaggy hair and grinned as she settled down opposite him. 'Hi, my name's Jason.'

Anastasia's pert nose crinkled slightly in a question. 'Are you ... English?' she asked, her accent soft, the *r* rolling off her tongue.

'Crikey, no!' exclaimed Jason, looking truly appalled. 'Connor is, I'm afraid. But I'm one hundred per cent Australian.' He leant forward, his elbows resting on the table. 'I take it you're Russian?'

'And proud of it,' she replied, shrugging off the hard oblong backpack and setting it down at her feet.

Still trying to assess their new friend, Connor asked, 'Any reason you sat with us and not the girls?'

'I saw you guys stand up to *them*,' Anastasia replied, glancing over her shoulder in the direction of Stas and Vadik. 'No one else here seems to. And I hate bullies.'

'Well, I don't like bullies either,' said Jason.

Anastasia looked at Jason, gave a single approving nod, then forked some salad into her mouth. 'So how do you three know each other?' she asked, directing her question at Feliks.

'We're . . . cousins,' Feliks mumbled through a mouthful of food.

Anastasia's ice-blue eyes narrowed slightly as she compared their features.

'Second cousins,' Connor explained quickly. 'Visiting for a while on a student-exchange programme. How about you?'

'My parents have gone away. New job. *Again*,' she explained with a weary sigh. 'So I've just started boarding at this school.'

Connor eyed the unusual-shaped backpack on the floor. 'What's in the case?' he asked.

'A violin,' she replied. 'I'm on a music scholarship.'

'Cool,' said Jason, impressed. 'I play a bit of guitar.'

Reassured that the girl presented no threat to their Principal, Connor continued eating his meat and potato stew. Feliks single-mindedly focused on his lunch as Jason

96

and Anastasia talked, but Connor noticed he kept sneaking furtive glances at her. He was obviously cripplingly shy when it came to girls.

Towards the end of lunch, Stas and Vadik strode up to their table. Connor and Jason tensed, readying themselves for another confrontation. But Stas ignored them and smiled in the way a snake might. 'Anastasia, isn't it?'

She nodded.

'I realize you're new here, but you don't want to be hanging out with the son of a political traitor.' He sneered at Feliks.

But Anastasia's gaze didn't falter. 'Thank you, Stas, but I think I can choose my own friends.'

'Then join us for the party,' Stas persisted, pointing to a large red and black poster on the canteen wall. *PANTHER SOCIAL CLUB. Youth Night This Friday. U18s. Dress to impress.* 'I've VIP access. Come as my guest.'

'I'd love to,' Anastasia replied with a smile, 'but Feliks has already asked me.'

Feliks's mouth dropped open. He looked as stunned as Stas – and Jason – by the news.

'So, what's your room like?' asked Charley, her face a welcome glow on his smartphone's screen. Connor was four days into the mission and – aside from the official report-ins – this was their first opportunity to talk in private.

'It's mad. See for yourself,' said Connor, switching to the rear-view camera so he could show her the antique mahogany furniture inlaid with mother-of-pearl, the velvet burgundy curtains that draped like royal robes across the huge bay window and the solid gold lampstands that stood ceremonial guard either side of his king-size bed. 'Even my bathroom has a chandelier!'

'Wow, it's like a presidential suite!' gasped Charley. 'Your host is certainly treating you like a king. How are you getting along with the Principal?'

'He's rude and unfriendly,' Connor admitted, switching the camera back. 'To be honest, I think Feliks might have a problem. He seems disconnected from the real world, always on his phone playing games or else totally uncommunicative ... I suppose it's understandable, considering ...'

Charley gave him a questioning look.

'Well, apart from the obvious hardship of his mother's suicide, Feliks is being bullied at school. Stas and Vadik, the main culprits, are victimizing him because of his father.'

'Well, his father is ruffling quite a few feathers in Russia,' conceded Charley. 'He's announced plans for another anti-corruption rally in Moscow at the end of the month. So expect things to get heated over the coming weeks.' Charley's expression darkened. 'I've also discovered what happened to Feliks's previous bodyguard.'

Connor sat up on the bed. Despite rereading the operation folder, he'd found no reference to it and had asked Charley to investigate.

'According to a Russian newspaper report I found online, the bodyguard was shot during an attempted carjacking. Feliks was in the back of the vehicle at the time. The bodyguard managed to drive away but later died of his wounds. The police reported it as a random attack, but Viktor suspected it was premeditated – an attempt to kidnap his son.'

'So he employed Buddyguard's services,' said Connor.

'Yes.' Charley nodded. 'No wonder the instructors were tense over this assignment. But if the colonel didn't include this in our briefing, what else is he keeping from us? I don't like it. This mission is too risky, however fat the contract! I'm going to have a word with him.'

'Good idea,' said Connor, who didn't like being kept in the dark either. They needed the full facts to protect Feliks effectively – and keep themselves safe at the same time. 'Don't worry, though – we'll be on guard. Apart from the school bullies, there's no sign of any other threat.'

'Not yet anyway,' said Charley. 'How are things working out between you and Jason?'

Connor shifted awkwardly against the velvet pillows at his back. 'OK, I guess.'

Charley gave him a look that said, *I know you're lying.*

'Not brilliant,' he finally admitted. 'Jason and I clash constantly.'

'In what way?'

'In every way!' said Connor, only half joking.

'Come on, surely it isn't that bad. Remember, you two need to watch each other's backs on this mission.'

Connor sighed. 'I know, but he won't listen to me. Or follow orders. He considers taking point to be beneath him and dozes on the journey to school when he should be alert. On top of that, he's easily distracted.'

'By what?'

Connor was thinking of Jason's roving eye and his attempts to chat up Anastasia. He was clearly on the rebound. But it didn't feel right telling on his partner. And he didn't want to make Ling any more upset than she probably was already. Besides, surprisingly, Anastasia seemed more interested in Feliks than Jason.

'Doesn't matter,' said Connor. 'What does, though, is that we disagree on how to handle Stas and Vadik. Jason wants to go all out. Give a show of strength. But I think that's asking for trouble. It'll probably end in a fist fight or worse. The problem is Feliks encourages this approach.'

'So how do *you* think it should be handled?' asked Charley.

'Avoidance of the threat.'

Charley chewed thoughtfully at her lower lip. 'You can't hide Feliks every day you're at school.'

'But we can ignore Stas and his crew. Or simply laugh off the insults. We need diplomacy, not aggression. Otherwise we might get suspended or expelled from the school, then we couldn't protect Feliks at all.'

Charley nodded. 'I agree you don't want an all-out brawl. But Jason's method has merit.'

Connor blinked in surprise. 'Really?'

'Russians respect strength,' Charley went on. 'Jason's calculating that Stas and Vadik will back off if you two prove you can stand up for Feliks. So perhaps you need to mix both your approaches?'

'Jason isn't one for compromise,' replied Connor, 'but I'll give it some thought.'

After signing off on the video call, Connor stared out of the bay window at the flurries of snow. Charley could be right. Stas and Vadik weren't the sort of bullies to be ignored. But there would have to be a balance between his negotiating style and Jason's physical deterrence, otherwise there'd be a full-out war with the two FSB boys.

The ballerina fluttered across the stage, whirling to the ebb and flow of the orchestral strings. Spellbound, the audience watched as her lithe arms swayed in a constant dance, her body bending to the notes and her feet gliding with such grace that she barely seemed to touch the ground.

From his private gilded box in the upper tiers of the Bolshoi Theatre, Roman Gurov had the best view of the star's performance. But his attention often wandered. Beside him sat a beautiful young woman, half his age, with auburn hair that shimmered like bronze, and dark bewitching eyes that promised sleepless nights. Draped in a long white satin gown, his date proved a far more appealing affair than the ballet.

His assistant Nika wished for a similar distraction herself since she hated ballet. Mid-performance, her phone vibrated in her clutch bag and she was glad of a reason to leave the auditorium. Quietly excusing herself, she stepped through the red velour privacy curtain and out into the carpeted hallway. Apart from two bodyguards stationed by the private box's entrance, the hallway was deserted.

Moving a discreet distance from the two men, the strains of the ballet fading to a muted soundtrack, Nika glanced at the number on her phone's screen, then answered the call.

'You're in Moscow?' asked Nika, speaking softly. The line was secure, but she didn't want to risk being overheard.

'Yes,' replied the gruff voice on the other end of the line.

'You have the package we left.'

'Yes.'

'When will you fulfil the contract?'

'Friday night.'

'You understand the job must look real. Convincing,' insisted Nika. 'We want no suspicion raised.'

'I understand.'

'*But* make the message clear.'

'Crystal clear, you have my word.'

To Nika's surprise, the assassin ended the call first – possibly to ensure his mobile signal wasn't traced and his position triangulated. Nika slipped the phone back into her bag and took a moment to reapply some lipstick. She always felt a touch uneasy arranging a hit. Not out of any pity for the victim, but because there was an unavoidable element of risk. A danger of blowback and unwelcome connections being made back to her and her boss. But the assassin had a strong track record and she had no reason to doubt the attack on the target close to Malkov would be both surgical and untraceable.

Returning to the private box, Nika slid into the seat behind her boss. Roman now had his hand on his date's knee, his gold ring gleaming in the low light. On stage the ballerina was twirling like a feather in a storm, the music rising to a crescendo. At its peak, Nika leant forward and whispered in her boss's ear, 'The asset is in play.'

'Good,' said Roman. 'What's the deadline?'

Nika smiled. 'This time tomorrow Malkov will be in mourning.'

'We should have got here earlier,' said Jason as they joined the long queue outside the Panther Social Club on Friday night. Located in a stylish eco-building on the west side of Gorky Park, the new youth club boasted an outdoor skate pool, mini-velodrome and parkour assault course. Sponsored by Panther Sports, it was *the* hip place for the young and trendy of Moscow to gather, even in winter.

A muffled *boom-boom* of bass thrummed from within the venue.

'This is early!' said Anastasia, who was wrapped in a thick fur coat against the bitter cold. 'Most Russian parties don't kick off until gone midnight.'

'Well, this party had better be worth it,' Feliks muttered, stamping his feet to keep warm. Night having fallen, the temperature had dropped to a bone-chilling minus ten degrees. Luckily, Connor and Jason's mission-issued jackets were proving freeze-proof as well as bulletproof.

'Looks like it'll be good,' Connor said, peering through a misted window into the club. He knew his Principal had never planned, or even wanted, to go to the party until

Anastasia had sprung the idea on him. But the venue had promise. Inside there was both table football and table tennis, a bowling alley, pool tables, and on a central stage a band was setting up for the night. 'The club's kitted out like your rec room, Feliks!'

'So we needn't have bothered coming out then?' he shot back sarcastically.

'Hey, don't be such a sourpuss,' said Anastasia, taking his arm. 'This'll be fun.'

'Yeah, loads of fun,' Feliks murmured as Stas and Vadik strutted past, up to the front of the queue and walked straight in.

'Guess they did have VIP passes after all!' said Jason with a snort. He squinted through the window. 'It's only half full in there. What's holding up the queue?'

Jason shot Connor a look to say, *We shouldn't be exposing our Principal like this!*

Connor was in full agreement with Jason for once. They were in a public park on a Friday night where *anyone* had the right to wander through. Dog-owners, shoppers, tramps, courting couples, muggers, kidnappers, assassins . . . It was a high-risk location. But Feliks's father had approved, in fact encouraged, the trip, since he was so delighted that his son had actually been asked out for a social event.

Connor scanned the immediate area, looking for any suspects among the late-night gathering of students. There was no one obviously out of place, but he could only see so far. While a halo of light spilled from the venue's entrance, and the skate pool and parkour course glowed with neon strips, beyond the club's terrace area the park was swamped in darkness. It was the perfect cover to spy on a target, launch an attack or conceal a sniper.

As his eyes swept the nearby bushes, Connor spotted the red glow of a cigarette. It flared brightly as its owner inhaled, giving his position away.

That FSB agent has to be on his third cigarette by now, thought Connor. He'd been aware of their tail ever since Timur had dropped them off at the edge of the park, when the familiar Toyota Corolla had pulled up at the kerbside and disgorged a shadowy figure. The agent's presence was both unsettling yet strangely reassuring in that someone 'official' was watching them. Still, Connor had no reason to trust the FSB and kept the agent in his peripheral vision at all times.

'So, Feliks, you never did tell me who your father is,' said Anastasia.

Feliks stiffened, eyeing her with distrust. 'Viktor Malkov,' he replied, fixing her with a glare that dared her to comment.

Anastasia's eyes widened. '*Our Russia!* My parents are great supporters of his cause. They too want to stamp out corruption in our country.'

Connor noticed Feliks visibly relax at her words. 'That's good to hear,' he said. 'So what do your parents do?'

'Oil exploration.' She gave a weary shrug. 'That's why they're away so much.'

'And where are they now?' asked Connor.

'In the Arctic somewhere. It's all very hush-hush, since new oilfields are so scarce.'

'My father owns an oil company,' said Feliks casually. 'That's where he made a lot of his money, along with banking and computing.'

As they continued to chat in the queue, Feliks's mood lightened and, to Connor's surprise, by the time they reached the club's entrance he seemed almost eager for the party. It was the first time Connor had seen their Principal enjoying someone else's company. But, if Connor was honest with himself, it would take a blind and deaf man not to enjoy being with Anastasia – a fact not lost on Jason, who couldn't keep his eyes off her.

So it fell to Connor to maintain a vigilant watch on their surroundings. The FSB agent was on his fifth cigarette and, apart from a couple of kids graffitiing the skate pool, Connor hadn't spotted any obvious threats. However, he was glad they'd soon be entering the warmth and relative safety of the venue. Since it was a social night organized by the school, the door was manned by a couple of students. One of them Connor recognized from Stas's gang – Boris – the breeze-block boy who'd heckled Feliks in the canteen. If he was on the door, no wonder Stas and Vadik had walked straight in.

Jason handed over their tickets. Boris narrowed his eyes at Jason but waved him through. He welcomed Anastasia with a lopsided leering grin while acknowledging Connor with a half-hearted nod.

'Not you,' said Boris, barring Feliks with a hand.

'But I've got a ticket,' he protested.

'You're still not coming in.'

Jason and Anastasia stopped by the cloakroom, wondering what was holding them up.

'Why can't he?' Connor asked.

Boris crossed his arms in front of his breeze-block chest. 'Because I say so.'

'This is a school event,' Connor argued. 'Every student has the right to be here.'

Hearing the commotion, Stas and Vadik appeared at the entrance. With wide grins on their faces, they leant against the wall to watch.

'Give me one good reason Feliks can't come in,' Connor demanded.

'Face control,' said Boris with a smirk.

Connor frowned in confusion. 'What?'

'Face control,' he repeated, and stabbed a finger at Feliks. 'I don't like the look of his face.'

The other students in the queue sniggered. A flush of humiliation coloured Feliks's cheeks.

'Well, I don't like the look of yours either,' said Jason, striding back and squaring up to Boris. 'Now let Feliks in before I face-control you . . . with my fist!'

Boris let out a dismissive snort at the threat – and the other bouncer stepped up as reinforcement.

'*Back down, Jason!*' Connor hissed into his ear. '*We're Feliks's bodyguards, not his enforcers.*'

Connor had tried negotiation and failed, but he knew that brute force wouldn't get them anywhere either.

'As I said, you three can come in,' Boris repeated with overt politeness, pointing at Anastasia, Jason and Connor. 'But he can't. Now stop blocking the entrance.'

Connor glanced over at Stas, who was delighting in Feliks's public humiliation. Connor realized this was a set-up by him – to split Feliks from his only friends and belittle him in front of everyone else.

Feliks knew it too and glared at his classmate. 'You'll regret this, Boris,' he said coldly.

Boris laughed. 'Not as much as you'll regret being the son of a traitor.'

Feliks clenched his fists and stormed off. Connor and Jason immediately followed, Anastasia in tow.

As they hurried after him, Connor noticed a red ember fall to the ground and blink out. The FSB agent was on the move too. But, at the same time, Connor caught sight of another cigarette being extinguished in the darkness.

'The party didn't look that good anyway,' said Anastasia kindly, trying and failing to placate Feliks.

Alert as a wild cat, Connor's eyes darted from tree to bush, path to park, silhouette to shadow. He hunted the darkness for any sign of their two stalkers – the FSB agent and the mystery threat. But the night concealed all movement.

'Why don't we go somewhere else?' suggested Anastasia. 'The outdoor ice rink at VDNKh will be open.'

Feliks shook his head. 'Another time. I've lost the party mood.'

Anastasia pouted her lips in disappointment.

'Sorry . . . if I've ruined your night,' he mumbled.

She put on a smile for him. 'You didn't . . . That idiot did!' she replied, her smile switching to a scowl at Boris on the door.

'Don't worry, he'll come to regret it.' Feliks jammed his hands deep into his pockets against the bitter cold. 'I'll get Timur to drop you back.'

Connor instructed Jason to call the bodyguard on his phone and have the car waiting for them. They'd obviously not planned to leave so early and Connor didn't want to hang around in the dark and cold any longer than they had to . . . especially if they were being followed.

Their boots crunched in the thick snow as the four of them trudged along the unlit path. Digging into his jacket pocket, Connor pulled out his XT tactical torch and switched it on. The beam cut through the darkness like a knife.

Anastasia looked at him with an amused half-smile. 'You're prepared,' she said.

'Scouts' motto,' he replied, directing the beam along the path.

Ahead Connor spied an old homeless man shivering on a bench, a bottle in a brown paper bag clasped in his ungloved hands. Feliks and Anastasia barely gave the wretch a glance, but Connor kept his attention fixed on him, watching for the slightest warning he might attack or be anything other than he seemed.

As they drew closer, Connor had his finger primed on the Dazzler button, ready to stun the homeless man with its light – and, if necessary, use the hidden baton. But the man kept his head bowed, a hand raised to his eyes as he protested irritably against the bright glare of Connor's torch.

'Timur's on his way. Three minutes out,' Jason informed Connor.

The sound of muffled footsteps from behind made Connor stop and turn. But there was no one there, the bench empty, a trail of footprints disappearing into the bushes . . .

Was the man now following them too, or had he simply gone to relieve himself?

'What's got you so jumpy?' asked Jason, keeping his voice low, aware they couldn't alert Anastasia to their true role.

In a whisper, Connor explained what he'd seen back at the club – and his fears about the apparent homeless man.

Jason immediately withdrew his own torch, gripping it as a weapon rather than for light alone. 'I spotted the agent, but not the other one,' he said. 'You sure it wasn't just a student sneaking a cigarette?'

'We can't take that risk,' said Connor under his breath. 'Now you take point while I cover Feliks.'

Increasing their pace, Connor came up behind his Principal and subtly urged him along the path.

'Can you slow down!' protested Anastasia, her high-heeled leather boots driving pinholes in the snow.

'Sorry, getting cold,' explained Jason, who for once did as instructed and took point. He led the way through the pitch-black park, his torch sweeping like a lighthouse ahead of them. Snow fell in waves, reflecting the light and making visibility poor.

'You Aussies need to toughen up!' teased Anastasia.

'And you Russians need better weather!' Jason replied grimly, his focus on the path ahead.

Every few paces Connor swung the torchbeam behind them. Once or twice he caught the flash of a ghostly figure in the bushes. *The homeless man? The FSB agent? Some other threat?* Whoever was tailing them was keeping a discreet distance. But if there was more than one, then others could have run ahead. Perhaps the plan was to cut them off at the entrance . . .

Connor hurried Feliks towards the main gate, the immense stone pillars looming against the Moscow skyline and offering the promise of safety.

'Hey, what's the rush?' complained Feliks, panting slightly with the rapid pace.

'Car's waiting,' Connor replied, hoping that it was.

As they approached the pillars, Anastasia lost her footing in the snow. She slipped and Connor caught her by the arm.

'Thanks,' she said, stopping to lean on him and test her ankle. 'I thought we decided not to go ice-skating!' she joked.

'Your ankle all right?' he asked, his eyes scanning the snow-filled darkness behind. He didn't want to delay any more than he had to.

'Yes,' she said. 'But –'

Connor spotted movement. He took her by the hand and, ignoring her protests to slow down, dragged her out of the park with Feliks. Exiting the gate and passing a dilapidated merry-go-round, he spied the stocky figure of Timur dutifully waiting at the kerbside. He breathed a sigh of relief.

'Problem?' asked the bodyguard, opening the rear door for Feliks as they approached.

Feliks answered with a scowl, then muttered quietly to him. Connor caught the bodyguard's attention, signalling the situation was potentially far more hostile than a refusal of entry.

'Let's go,' said Timur, ushering Feliks into the back seat.

As a breathless Anastasia clambered in after him – followed by Jason – Connor made a final sweep with his torch. But Gorky Park refused to give up its secrets.

CHAPTER 22

Connor and Jason were having a leisurely breakfast the following morning with Feliks and his father when Dmitry dashed into the conservatory, a newspaper clasped in his hand. The adviser's pale and anguished face told the whole story before he'd even laid the paper on the table in front of Viktor. Connor caught the headline at the top, his contact lens translating the Russian: *Malkov Lawyer Shot Dead in Street*.

As the billionaire read the article, his expression passed through varying stages of shock, grief and finally anger.

'A *mugging*?' Viktor exclaimed, tossing the paper back on the table. A picture of the dead lawyer took up most of the front page. His body lay in a pile of bloodied snow, a bullet through the right eye, according to the photo caption. 'How the hell have the police come to that conclusion?'

Dmitry shrugged. 'They say Sergey's wallet and phone were stolen, and his briefcase broken into.'

'I don't believe it.' Viktor sighed, taking off his glasses and pinching the bridge of his nose. 'Sergey only called me last night to say he'd secured the city permits for the rally.

He was supposed to come over this morning and hand-deliver them. His death is too much of a coincidence.'

'You think it was murder?' asked Dmitry.

'Worse, it was an assassination!' Viktor slammed his fist so hard on the table that their plates rattled.

Connor and Jason remained silent. The potential threat level to the billionaire and his son had just rocketed. But Feliks buttered a piece of toast and continued to eat his breakfast as if this sort of thing happened every day.

Viktor replaced his glasses and stared at his adviser. 'This was definitely a premeditated attack. A message job.'

Connor exchanged a puzzled look with Jason. *A message job?*

'What makes you say that?' asked Dmitry, a note of horror entering his voice.

Viktor stabbed his finger at the picture of the lawyer. 'Among the Bratva, a shot through the eye is a message to say, *We're watching you*. This so-called mugging was a hit by the Bratva to warn me off. They knew Sergey was carrying those permits. This is a blatant attempt to sabotage my rally.'

The billionaire politician downed his black coffee, thrust back his chair, then stood with his fists planted on the table. 'But I *won't* be threatened into silence,' he declared furiously. 'Dmitry, I want copies of City Hall's permit papers by the end of the week. We're going ahead with this rally . . . if only to honour my good friend Sergey.'

'But what if the next message is more *personal*?' asked Dmitry, tugging at his beard and looking decidedly uneasy.

Viktor strode over and laid an arm round his adviser's

shoulders. 'This is exactly the sort of intimidation and corruption we're fighting against, my friend.'

'But we don't know *who* we're fighting against,' argued Dmitry. 'No one has the faintest idea as to the identity of the Pakhan. It could be the President, for all we know.'

'The Bratva is the Bratva, whoever is heading it. And it's their links with the government that are the heart of the corruption. Besides –' a sly smile slid across Viktor's lips – 'the Bratva don't know who they're fighting against either. Listen, if we don't make a stand, no one will, and this country will be lost for another generation. So let's give those in power a message of our own.'

Forcing his own smile, Dmitry nodded. 'I'll get those permits,' he promised, and headed out of the door.

Viktor beckoned his personal bodyguard over. 'Lazar, this is just the start of my enemy's campaign to undermine and destroy me. You and your men –' he glanced over at Connor and Jason to ensure they were listening to his directive too – 'need to be on full alert. Take no chances. Treat everyone and everything as a potential threat.'

By now Feliks had stopped eating and was watching his father intently.

'So it's begun?' he asked flatly.

Viktor looked over at his son, his jaw set. 'Yes, it has.'

Feliks gave a resigned nod of his head and returned to his breakfast.

'Don't worry, my son – these two boys will protect you with their lives.' Viktor's steely gaze turned on Connor and Jason. 'Won't you?'

'This is more like it,' said Jason as he knelt beside Connor and Feliks on the tatami mat in the school gymnasium. 'A *proper* lesson.'

Dressed in the white cotton jacket, *obi* and trousers of a *judoka*, Connor was equally at home. With a junior black belt in jujitsu, he was familiar with many judo techniques and was itching to get back on the mat and practise his martial art skills. Feliks looked less happy at the prospect of the school's obligatory judo lesson. But the President of Russia was an eighth dan black belt and actively encouraged the sport as part of the national curriculum.

Stas and Vadik knelt at the far end of the row, black belts tied tightly round their stocky waists. They shot a glance down the line at Connor and Jason, sneering at their novice white belts. Connor smiled inwardly. Little did they know.

As the class waited for their teacher, a girl with rounded cheeks and hair in a tight black bun whispered, 'Ana, you joining us for ice-skating this weekend?'

Anastasia glanced up the line and nodded. 'Sounds good, Elena. Can Feliks and his cousins come too?'

Elena shrugged, seemingly indifferent to Feliks, then her eyes lit on Connor and she grinned. 'Sure, why not?'

'See you Sunday then,' said Anastasia, before turning to Feliks. 'Good with you?'

Tongue-tied by the unexpected invite, Feliks managed a small nod. Jason grinned, obviously keen to spend more time with Anastasia. But Connor wasn't so eager to go ice-skating, not after the mystery stalker in Gorky Park and the brutal murder of Viktor's lawyer on the same night.

Connor still couldn't believe the Bratva were so ruthless that they'd kill someone just to deliver a message. If that was the case, then the threat level to Feliks was critical and a couple of school bullies were the least of their problems. No wonder Colonel Black had warned them Russia was the most dangerous place to be a bodyguard. Operation Snowstorm wasn't a matter of *if* an attack might occur, but *when*.

And it seemed that Feliks was fully aware of the danger he was in – perhaps another reason for his dark moods, besides his mother's suicide. Now Connor felt the same unnerving shadow over himself. It was clear that Viktor Malkov had hired Connor and Jason not as bodyguards but as human shields. And, although they'd both nodded when he asked them to sacrifice themselves for his son, Connor hoped it wouldn't come to that. But it felt like any outdoor trips were the equivalent of putting his head above the parapet during a siege.

'What happened to Boris?' asked Anastasia in an astonished whisper.

Connor looked up as Boris limped in on crutches and plonked himself on a bench. The side of his face was badly bruised and his leg was in a plaster cast.

Elena replied down the line, 'I heard he slipped on some ice after the party.'

'Nasty fall by the looks of it,' said Feliks, a faint smirk on his lips.

Connor noted the distinct pleasure in Feliks's tone . . . perhaps too much pleasure. But his Principal's lack of pity was understandable after Friday night's face-off when Boris had barred his entry to the party. The injured Boris glanced their way, then quickly averted his gaze, his former arrogance replaced by what looked to Connor like a flicker of . . . *fear*?

'*Rei, Sensei!*' bellowed Stas as their judo teacher, a large barrel-chested man with limbs like steel girders and a bush of wire wool for a beard, entered the gymnasium and took up position on the mat.

The students bowed as one and the lesson began. After a warm-up, their sensei led them in a session of *ukemi*. Break-falling across the mat, Connor was in his element, flinging himself over and rolling neatly out of each fall. This was followed by demonstrations of key throwing and grappling techniques. Although a little rusty, Connor quickly came to grips with them again – enjoying the simple effectiveness of the outer leg reap *osoto-gari*; relishing the speed and power of the hip throw *o-goshi*; mastering the easy dominance of the scarf hold *kesa-gatame*; and logging for future use the joint-breaking potential of the arm bar *juji-gatame*.

Although Jason had never trained in judo or jujitsu, he had boxing and Mixed Martial Arts experience, which meant he excelled in grappling. And, judging by his progress, he was also a quick learner.

Then it was time for *randori*, free-sparring. This was the students' opportunity to put all they'd learnt during the lesson into practice. First Connor partnered with Feliks, an orange belt. But Feliks lacked confidence. He could do the basic techniques well enough, but they seemed to jerk out of him rather than flow.

'You're too stiff,' said Connor, going easy on him.

'But I don't like to fall,' he replied, tensing as Connor moved in for a leg reap.

'Relax your body. Go with it. That's the purpose of the *ukemi* training.'

Connor got the sense that Feliks's usual training partners practised hard and fast, with no consideration for their opponent's ability level. So, when he swept Feliks's leg from under him, he gently threw him to the mat. Once Feliks realized he wasn't going to be brutally dropped, he loosened up and his *randori* improved.

After a couple of rounds, Connor found himself paired with Anastasia. Like him, she wore a white belt. Not wanting to damage her confidence either, he played down his skills. They gripped each other's collar and sleeve and began the mock combat.

Anastasia was impressively light on her feet, moving like a dancer. Connor went for a couple of foot sweeps, but she evaded them with remarkable ease. Shifting round the mat, Connor made himself open for an attack. Anastasia saw it and moved with startling speed. She spun into him, drove her hip against his and lifted him high off the ground. Then, with a complete lack of mercy, she pounded him into the mat.

A perfect *o-goshi*.

Connor wheezed, the wind knocked out of him. '*Impressive!*' he gasped. 'I thought . . . you were on a music scholarship.'

Anastasia dazzled him with that smile of hers. 'Russian girls are full of surprises.'

Taking her proffered hand, Connor got to his feet. This time he wouldn't be so forgiving with her. He faked an inner leg reap, then went for *harai-goshi*, a sweeping hip throw. But Anastasia countered with *ura-nage*, grabbing hold of his hips and throwing him directly over her shoulder. Having sacrificed herself, she struck the mat at the same time, flipped her body over and pinned Connor to the mat with *kesa-gatame*. She held Connor close in the clinch, her ice-blue eyes locking with his.

'You like being pinned down by me?' she teased. Under her intoxicating gaze, Connor could see why Jason was so enamoured. It was easy to fall under her spell.

Connor struggled in her grip and tried to dislodge her. But she was deceptively strong for her size. His estimation of Anastasia went up yet again. But Connor wasn't to be beaten. Bridging his body, he rolled her over and trapped her in his own scarf hold.

'You like being pinned down by me?' he joked.

Anastasia laughed before tapping out to signal her submission. Connor released his grip, but in the struggle her jacket and T-shirt had been pulled aside and he caught a glimpse of waxy white skin at the base of her neck. Usually hidden by her long hair and clothing, the ripple of scarring appeared to spread down her back. Anastasia saw him staring and quickly tugged her T-shirt back into place.

'Don't worry – I've got scars too,' he said, trying to make light of it. He pulled his *gi* to one side to reveal the four long pale score marks on his left shoulder. 'A safari that went badly wrong,' he explained.

Her eyes downcast and suddenly sad, Anastasia offered him a sympathetic smile and seemed about to tell him her story when the sensei called, '*Yamae!*' bringing the *randori* to an end. Without another word, she hurried back into line.

Seeing her sensitivity to her scarring, Connor decided he wouldn't bring it up again. Besides, if they were to compare scars, he'd have a whole lot more explaining to do. Not many teenage boys had a set of leopard claw marks, a knife wound and a bullet hole in the thigh before the age of sixteen.

'We'll finish with a round of *shiai*,' announced the sensei, his voice booming like an artillery gun. 'First up, Stas, and –' his steely gaze ran down the line of kneeling students – 'Feliks.'

Feliks groaned and reluctantly got to his feet. 'He always does this,' he muttered, directing a scowl at the judo teacher.

Connor patted him on the back, wishing him luck. Unlike *randori* in which the principle was to learn, *shiai* was a full-on competition with the sole aim to win. And against a beast like Stas it was a contest Feliks would undoubtedly lose.

'Keep your centre of gravity low and use his own body weight against him,' Jason whispered as Feliks trudged past. But Jason could have been talking Greek for all their Principal understood of his advice.

Feliks and Stas faced one another in the centre of the mat like a David and Goliath re-match. On their sensei's command they both bowed. Then he barked '*Haijime!*' and the fight began.

Not even giving Feliks a chance to blink, Stas lunged forward, gripped the front of his jacket and yanked him off balance. Feliks's face registered a look of shock as he was jerked forward. Then Stas planted his right foot into Feliks's stomach and rolled backwards. Connor recognized *tomoe-nage* as soon as Stas committed to the sacrifice throw. Feliks, who hadn't even managed to get hold of his opponent's jacket, was tossed over Stas's head like a crash-test dummy flung from a car. With a bone-shattering impact Feliks slammed into the mat, all the air expelled from his lungs in a great *whoosh*.

Connor winced for him. Now he understood why his Principal wasn't keen on judo training. The rule of this dojo seemed to be one of no mercy – and one encouraged by the sensei. The sacrifice throw was worthy of a straight *ippon*, an outright win. But their teacher let the fight play out.

Following through on his backward roll, Stas mounted the winded Feliks, seized control of his right arm and wrapped both legs across his chest. Pinned to the mat, Feliks was utterly defenceless. Then Stas straightened out the arm, leant back and applied pressure to Feliks's elbow joint.

Connor watched with increasing concern. *Juji-gatame* was the most powerful armlock in judo. It took hardly any force to dislocate, or even break, the elbow.

Feliks gasped in pain and tapped the mat twice with his free hand. But Stas ignored the submission. Apparently, so did the sensei.

Feliks's eyes bulged. His already pale face turned white, his arm on the verge of snapping.

'Hey! He's tapped out!' Connor shouted as he realized Stas had no intention of releasing the lock.

'Sensei, stop the fight!' Jason protested, getting to his feet.

As Feliks's hand slapped the mat like a dying fish, the teacher called '*Yamae*' with what sounded like reluctance. Connor stared in disbelief at him. Did Feliks's persecution extend to the teaching staff? Surely not.

The sensei awarded the fight to Stas. After bowing out, Feliks limped back into line, clutching his hyper-extended elbow.

'Are you all right?' Anastasia asked. Feliks nodded, but wouldn't meet her eye. Connor saw he was trying to hold back the tears.

Their teacher didn't appear to care one way or the other about his student's welfare and moved straight on to the next *shiai* match.

'Vadik and . . . what's your name?' The sensei pointed at Jason. 'You appear to have had some training before.'

'A little,' Jason replied cagily.

Connor frowned. He got the distinct impression this was another pre-arranged match. It couldn't be coincidence that Vadik had been paired with Jason. 'Make mincemeat of him,' he urged his partner.

Jason cracked his knuckles. 'Diced or sliced?'

He took up position opposite Vadik and bowed. Both looked like they wanted to tear each other apart.

'*Hajime!*' called the sensei.

Vadik charged. Jason neatly side-stepped him, making the boy look like a lumbering rhino. Infuriated, Vadik snatched for Jason's *gi* and got hold of his collar. They tussled, both fighting for dominance. Vadik yanked Jason hard to one side, throwing him off balance. Jason countered by diving at Vadik's leading leg for an MMA-style takedown. The attack failed, but only after Vadik illegally kneed Jason in the head.

The sensei acted blind to this and Connor seriously began to question his eyesight, if not his judgement. It seemed the reach of the FSB extended to the teaching staff too.

As Jason reeled from the blow, Vadik tried an *o-goshi* hip throw. But Jason managed to keep his centre of gravity low and prevent the technique being executed. Vadik took a step back and Jason, spotting an opportunity, went for an inner leg sweep. His foot connected, bone hitting bone . . . but Vadik's legs were rooted like tree trunks and he didn't go down.

Then, as Vadik surged forward for an outer reap, Jason surprised him by not resisting. Instead he retreated, allowing Vadik's own momentum to over-balance himself. Combining this with a hard tug on Vadik's sleeve and a sharp rotation of his own body, Jason threw a surprised Vadik over his outstretched leg and pile-drove him into the mat.

Connor whooped in celebration. It was a match-winning *tai-otoshi*.

But the sensei didn't call it, even though it was a clear *ippon* to everyone in the class. The problem was Vadik had managed to keep hold of Jason's *gi* and pull him to the ground too, making the technique look messy. With sheer brute strength, Vadik rolled Jason on to his back, mounted him and trapped his throat in a cross-strangle. Vadik wrenched on the jacket's lapels and pressed down hard, causing Jason to splutter and choke.

Despite being strangled, Jason wouldn't tap out.

Instead he palm-struck Vadik straight in the nose. An illegal move in judo. But no more so than a knee strike. The boy grunted as a spurt of blood splattered his white *gi*. Vadik let go, clasping his nose, then raised a fist to retaliate –

'*YAMAE!*' shouted the sensei. He pulled the two boys apart. 'This is not a cage fight,' he growled.

'Sorry,' said Jason, holding up his hands. 'It was an accident. I panicked.'

The sensei narrowed his eyes. 'An accident?' he said doubtfully. 'If that was an accident, then I'm the President of the United States. You should have tapped out if you were in trouble.'

'Didn't seem to work for the previous match,' shot back Jason, boldly holding the teacher's gaze.

Dumbstruck by Jason's cheek, the sensei's face reddened like a geyser about to explode . . . but the school bell rang, signalling the end of the lesson and cutting off the teacher's tongue-lashing before it had even begun.

'You were lucky,' said Connor as they headed for the changing rooms.

Jason replied with a conquering grin. 'Vadik was lucky.'

Feliks kept pace with Jason, his earlier injury seemingly forgotten. 'I've never seen anyone beat Vadik in a *shiai* match, or any fight for that matter!' he said with genuine awe. Feliks seemed to be walking a little taller. 'Stas and Vadik will think twice now before taking me on.'

However, as they approached the changing rooms, the two bullies were blocking the doorway, Vadik with tissue paper plugging his bleeding nose.

Stas glared at Feliks. 'We know you're to blame for Boris's accident,' he snarled.

Feliks responded with a blank look. 'What?'

'Boris won't talk about it, but we know it was no accident.'

Connor frowned, as perplexed as Feliks apparently was. 'We weren't even at the party, thanks to Boris! So how can you blame Feliks?'

'Ask Feliks,' said Stas.

Jason stepped right into Stas's face. 'Listen, just cos your idiot friend slipped and made a pancake of his face, don't go accusing Feliks. He was with us all the time, so had nothing to do with Boris's little accident. Now step aside unless you want a bloody nose too.'

Stas stood his ground and puffed out his chest, daring Jason to make good on his threat. Then they both noticed the teacher was looking on.

Standing aside, Stas pointed a finger at Feliks. 'Next time I *will* break your arm!'

Roman Gurov leant forward in his chair, rubbed his chin and studied the chessboard intently. His next move was crucial. It could alter the balance of power on the board – either to his opponent's advantage, or to his own.

After several minutes' consideration, he reached for the bishop, then thought better of it. The bold attack would capture a significant piece – a knight – but he'd be sacrificing his own bishop two turns later. The gain didn't add up against the loss. Instead he decided to advance his rook three squares forward, in order to squeeze his opponent's king into the corner.

'Interesting move,' commented his opponent, his tone guarded, revealing neither dismay nor satisfaction at Roman's choice.

A polished silver samovar sat steaming on the coffee table between them, along with a china teapot, two gilded tea glasses, a bowl of honey, slices of lemon and a selection of savoury cakes. His opponent poured a small draught of concentrated tea into a glass, then topped it up with boiling water from the samovar. The single slice of lemon he added for flavouring drifted like a pale half-moon in the black tea.

Savouring a long sip from his glass, he asked, 'How did your *other* move work out?'

Roman eased back in his chair, shifting on the seat as if the soft red leather had hardened and was causing him discomfort. 'The assassin proved as good as his word,' he said.

'And did the Black King get the message?'

'Message delivered, understood and *ignored*,' replied Roman, his tone bitter and hard as if he'd just swallowed a lump of lead. 'He plans to push ahead with the rally.'

His opponent took another draught of strong tea. 'Not good.'

'No, not good,' agreed Roman.

'So, your opening gambit has failed. Perhaps a bolder move is required?'

Roman raised an eyebrow. 'We've executed his lawyer. Last year we drowned his wife – though we made it look like suicide – how much bolder must one be before he'll get the message?'

His opponent set aside his tea glass, reaching forward to rest his index finger on the small head of one of his white pawns.

'The pawn is the weakest and most vulnerable playing piece on the board,' he said, sliding it forward one space. The surprise move put Roman's rook into a

dangerous predicament and he silently cursed himself for
overlooking it.

'Yet a single pawn can decide the outcome of the game,'
said his opponent with a spider's smile. 'In your case,
capture the pawn and the king will yield.'

CHAPTER 26

'This is the start of Moscow's winter festival,' explained Elena cheerfully as they strolled past a spotlit stage overlooking the frozen lake in Izmaylovsky Park. 'It's great fun. We have traditional folk dances, live concerts, a farmer's market, an ice rink and even a funfair.'

She nodded ahead to where a huge Ferris wheel dominated the tree-fringed skyline. Connor's eyes swept round the snow-covered park, feigning interest while keeping a sharp lookout for potential threats. He knew the FSB agent had to be somewhere, the black Toyota Corolla having parked at the same time as their silver Mercedes. As always, Timur had dismissed the threat with his singular grunt. His concrete bulk now followed several paces behind their little group, no passer-by daring to cross his path.

Elena stuck close to Connor as she guided her three friends, along with Jason, Feliks and Anastasia, in the direction of the ice rink. Feliks seemed to be favouring Jason after his performance in the *shiai* match, so Connor reluctantly took point while Jason held primary position on their Principal's right-hand side. Jason made no comment, but a smug grin plastered his face. Yet as long as Feliks was being properly protected, Connor felt they were doing their job.

Despite being one of the largest parks in the city, the whole place buzzed with Muscovites enjoying the winter festivities. There were people everywhere, wrapped in heavy coats, their feet encased in boots and their faces partly obscured by scarves, hats or hoods. This made identifying potential suspects far harder, since many wore similar clothing and any distinguishing features were hidden.

Glancing in the direction of the funfair, Connor noticed a man standing near a candyfloss stall. His face was concealed in the shadow of a fur-lined black hood and Connor wouldn't have spotted him at all had the man not been as motionless as a dead fish in a pond, while everyone else moved round him.

Connor felt an involuntary shudder run down his spine. The man's gaze appeared fixed in their direction –

Elena looped her arm through his. 'We can hop on a troika, if you like,' she said, pointing to a wooden sleigh pulled by three dapple-grey horses. 'Snuggle under a blanket, if you're getting cold.' She gave Connor a coy smile.

'Err . . . perhaps later?' Connor replied. Apart from the fact he had Charley as a girlfriend, he didn't want to be separated from his Principal. Especially not with a potential threat in the vicinity.

'I'll hold you to that,' said Elena as he glanced back towards the candyfloss stall.

But he'd barely turned his head when a harsh *CLACK-CLACK-CLACK* ripped through the air. Recognizing the sound of automatic gunfire, he spun round, shouted 'GUN!' and launched himself at Feliks. Jason reacted too. Both of them threw Feliks to the ground, shielding him with their bulletproof-clothed bodies. Connor braced himself for the bruising rounds about to hit them.

But none did. And the gunfire ceased.

Connor looked round for their attacker, his search starting at the candyfloss stall. But the prime suspect had vanished. Like a ghost.

Scanning the park, he realized no one else had reacted to the gunfire. In fact, Anastasia, Elena and the other girls were staring at the three of them on the ground in shocked amusement. Several paces behind, Timur's rock-hard face had broken into a smirk, his professional contempt for Connor's reaction summed up in a roll of his eyes.

'Connor . . . it's just a shooting gallery,' said Elena gently, as more gunfire rang out.

He and Jason turned towards a fairground stall, spilling over with stuffed toys, where a young man was firing an adapted Kalashnikov assault rifle at a paper target – obliterating it in the process.

Connor closed his eyes in dismay. Only in Russia would there be an AK-47 shooting gallery! His blunder was not just embarrassing but risked exposing his and Jason's true role in guarding Feliks.

'Let me up!' said Feliks impatiently, still pinned to the snow beneath them.

'Sorry,' said Connor, his cheeks flushing with humiliation as the girls began to snigger. He stood and helped Feliks back to his feet.

'You two are a little jumpy,' remarked Anastasia.

'Err ... just not used to gunfire in Britain, that's all,' said Connor, trying his best to shrug it off.

'Well, you're certainly *protective* of your cousin,' she said.

Jason patted Feliks on the back and put on a smile. 'That's what family's all about, isn't it?'

'Come on, let's go skating before Connor decides to dive on one of us!' laughed Sofia, one of Elena's friends, a tall girl with blonde plaits.

'Let's try the shooting gallery first,' suggested Elena, striding off towards the stall. 'I want to win one of those cute Minion toys.'

As they tagged along behind, Jason muttered, 'Well, that was *embarrassing*!'

'Better embarrassed than dead,' Connor replied defensively.

'Maybe for you,' said Jason, glancing in Anastasia's direction. 'Next time confirm the threat before you shout *gun*.'

'Hey, you reacted too!' said Connor.

'Only because you did first.'

Connor glared at him. He couldn't believe that he was getting all the blame. Then again, he *had* made the call. And he was first command on the ground, which meant he had to bite the bullet for his mistake.

The AK47 thundered in Elena's grip, the recoil so great she was almost knocked off her feet.

Despite the noise and power of the weapon, she failed to even graze the target. In fact her aim was so off that the stall vendor was forced to press himself against the gallery wall to avoid being shot himself by the rubber pellets. Even the stuffed Minions lining the shelves looked scared for their lives.

'Hey, Ana, your turn,' said Elena, a wide grin on her face despite not winning anything.

Anastasia gave the assault rifle an uneasy look and shook her head. 'No, it's all right. I don't like guns.'

'How about the boys then? One of you needs to win us a prize.'

Much to Connor's surprise, Feliks stepped up to the challenge. He'd barely uttered a word since their arrival and, apart from Anastasia, the girls had ignored him. But now they flocked round him as he shouldered the rifle and took careful aim at the target. Connor could tell by the way he handled the weapon that he'd had experience with guns before.

Feliks needed to obliterate three red bullseyes to win any prize.

With a controlled burst of the AK47, Feliks hit the target but his shots were a good six inches to the left.

The girls groaned in disappointment.

'Hey, the sights are off!' Feliks complained, glaring at the vendor.

'Maybe it's your eye that's off,' the vendor sneered.

Scowling at him, Feliks returned his attention to the gun. Connor took the opportunity to glance round the funfair, keeping his eyes peeled for the man in the fur-lined black hood. *Perhaps he's the FSB agent? Perhaps he's no one?* But the suspect *had* been watching their group. Whoever it was, he was no longer making himself so obvious. The problem was complicated by the fact that a large number of men in black jackets were wandering around the park. Connor counted at least four nearby. The suspect could be any one of them. But Timur stood like a sentinel near Feliks and none of them made an approach.

A deafening blast of gunfire cut through the fairground noise as Feliks squeezed the AK47's trigger. This time he found his mark, clipping the first bullseye. It then took six long bursts to completely clear the red. After a quick glance at Anastasia to be sure she was watching him, he moved on to the next target. His first shot was much closer to this bullseye but still off-centre. After another five volleys of gunfire he managed to take out the entire second bullseye. As Feliks lined up on the final target, the vendor

139

crossed his arms and began chewing hard on the toothpick jammed between his lips.

'You can do it,' whispered Anastasia. Everyone round him held their breath.

Feliks pulled the trigger. The AK47 gave a dry click. Out of ammo.

'Oh, unlucky,' said the vendor with a vampire's grin.

Fuming, Feliks dumped the rifle on the counter. 'This stall is fixed!'

'Everyone hates a sore loser,' said the vendor.

'Let me have a go,' said Jason, picking up the gun.

After Jason had handed over a five-hundred rouble note, the vendor loaded a new magazine clip into the weapon. Jason studied Feliks's shooting pattern, checked the sights, then aimed the rifle purposefully off-target. His first rubber bullet clipped the edge of the bullseye. Then with surgical precision Jason worked his way across the red, keeping his bursts short and sharp, conserving ammo. Once clear, he moved on to the next target. Connor was amazed at how much of Gunner's firearms training Jason had absorbed. He obliterated the second bullseye with sniper-like skill. As he destroyed the final target, the girls clapped and whooped. The stall vendor bit down so hard on the toothpick in annoyance that it snapped in half.

'I thought you English boys weren't used to guns,' said Elena, sidling up to Jason.

Jason winked at her. 'I'm an Aussie. We're good at everything!'

As if being forced to prise out his own tooth, the vendor reluctantly handed over a large banana-yellow Minion.

'Ta-da!' said Jason, presenting the toy with a flourish to Anastasia. Connor noticed Elena's nose wrinkle in envy, while Feliks glared at Jason. He'd clearly wanted to impress Anastasia himself. But Jason didn't seem to notice, too busy bathing in the glory of his win and Anastasia's smile.

'I'll admit those gun sights *are* dodgy, but I wasn't going to let that stop me!' Jason bragged.

'Connor, aren't you going to win *me* one?' Elena asked, her expression hopeful.

'Sorry. Closed,' said the vendor, pulling down the gallery's shutter with a forceful snap.

'Now that's a real sore loser!' laughed Connor, quietly relieved that he wouldn't have to measure up to Jason's shooting skills.

They headed across to the ice rink, Jason and Anastasia walking at the front with the doe-eyed Minion in her arms. Connor thought about reminding Jason of his duty, then decided to move into primary position next to Feliks. Jason could take point for once!

'Have you done much skating before?' asked Anastasia, tugging on her boots.

'A little,' said Connor. He smiled to himself, recalling the times his father had taken him to Lee Valley Ice Centre in north-east London. Whenever he was on leave from the army, his father had always encouraged him to learn new things: swimming, riding a bike, making a campfire, navigating by the stars, kickboxing ... anything he thought might be a useful life skill. Little could his father have known that ice-skating would help him protect a Russian billionaire's son!

Although Lee Valley had been an international-sized rink, it was nothing compared to the one they were about to skate on now. Stretched out before them like an airport runway, the park's outdoor rink was the length of three football pitches with a capacity for over four thousand skaters. With a wooden pedestrian bridge arching over the top, the huge rink encircled a neon-lit island of a snowy winter scene, complete with miniature houses, Christmas trees, reindeer and sledges piled high with presents.

Connor couldn't even see to the end and just hoped his skating skills would be enough to get him round and back to the start!

'How about you, Jason?' asked Anastasia, rising from the bench and heading for the rink.

Jason responded to Anastasia with a cocksure smile. 'Australia doesn't get much ice. But I'll give anything a go.'

Feliks was booted up and ready to skate but didn't look too thrilled at the prospect. A frown darkened his expression, suggesting he was still angry that Jason had won Anastasia the cuddly toy.

Elena led the way on to the ice, her friends gliding round with practised ease. Timur stationed himself at the rink entrance, his excuse being that he wasn't 'built to skate'. And, judging by the sudden look of trepidation on Jason's face as he hobbled towards the rink, Connor guessed he wished he could opt out too. After a couple of faltering steps on the ice, Jason's feet went from under him and he landed hard on his backside in comical style.

Feliks laughed loudly and cruelly, his mood instantly improved.

Connor couldn't help chuckling too. After the shooting gallery, his partner's ego needed some deflating. Stifling his own laughter, Connor skated over and helped Jason back to standing. It was a welcome change not having to compete with him.

'This is harder than it looks,' said Jason, his legs wobbling like a newborn deer's.

'Just have to get your balance,' said Connor.

'Let me help you,' offered Sofia, gliding over with the graceful movement of a swan.

'What about Feliks?' Jason whispered to Connor as Sofia took his hand. Their Principal was still sniggering at his fall.

'Don't worry,' Connor replied. 'I'll stick close to him. You can be the back-up.'

Leaving Jason clinging to Sofia, the group headed off round the rink. To Connor's relief, skating was like getting back on a bike. While he probably wouldn't attempt any fancy tricks just yet, he was more than comfortable moving forward, turning and stopping. For his Russian friends, skating seemed as natural as walking and Connor had to work hard to keep up. He skated as close to Feliks and Anastasia as he could.

'Nice not to have Stas or Vadik spoiling the party for once,' remarked Anastasia.

'Yeah,' Feliks agreed, suddenly turning shy.

Anastasia looked at him. 'It's good to see you relaxing and laughing too. You don't do that often enough.'

'Well . . . I've a lot on my mind,' he admitted.

'I'm sure you have, considering who your father is. It can't be easy.'

'No, it's not,' said Feliks, the frown returning.

'But you must be proud of your father too, for taking a stand against corruption,' said Anastasia. 'I think it is very brave of him.'

'And foolish!' muttered Feliks, his answer surprising Connor. 'He's going to get us both killed.'

'But he's hired a bodyguard for you,' Anastasia pointed out, glancing back at Timur. 'And I suppose he has bodyguards too?'

Feliks nodded.

'And other security measures?'

'Yeah, we've armed guards on the gates, electrified fencing, cameras in all the ro–'

'Wow, look at them go!' Connor interrupted, trying to stop Feliks blabbing about the mansion's security details in public. *Anyone* could be listening. A conga-line of skaters zipped past like an express train.

'Let's join on to the end next time,' said Anastasia with an enthusiastic grin. 'Sorry, Feliks, you were saying?'

Feliks was about to reply when Elena came up alongside. 'You're a pretty good skater, Connor,' she remarked.

'Thanks, it's been a while,' he said, already starting to feel the ache in his legs.

'Let me show you how to skate backwards.' Elena took his hands and spun so that she was facing him. Their pace slowed and Feliks and Anastasia pulled ahead. 'See how I turn the toes in and make a C cut with each step?'

Connor nodded. While he appreciated the lesson, he needed to stay alongside Feliks. He tried to speed Elena along. As they passed beneath the pedestrian bridge, he happened to glance up and caught sight of a black-hooded face staring at him. It was the briefest glimpse and Connor wasn't even sure it was the same man. Coming out of the other side, he looked back over his shoulder, but there were too many people on the bridge to confirm the identity.

Yet Connor was deeply aware of his surveillance tutor's motto: *Once is happenstance. Twice is circumstance. Three times means enemy action.*

If he spotted the hooded man again, he'd have to assume the worst.

'Are you paying attention?' said Elena.

'Err, yes,' he replied, turning back to her.

'Then you have a go.'

As they were about to swap positions, a large man in a black ski jacket barged them aside and sent them spinning into the barrier. Elena crashed heavily on to the ice, cracking her head.

'Hey, careful!' shouted Connor.

'You vatch it!' the man spat back in a heavy accent. He powered ahead as if on a mission.

Connor helped the dazed Elena back to her feet and leant her against the rail. As she recovered from the blow, Connor looked down the rink. He was now a worrying distance behind Feliks and Anastasia. He'd have to catch up fast. Then he noticed three more muscled men in black ski jackets go flying past with no regard for other skaters. They appeared to be moving in a coordinated pattern: a pincer formation.

All four of them were converging on Feliks.

This time Connor knew he wasn't about to cry wolf. Feliks was definitely being targeted.

Too far behind to warn his Principal, Connor launched himself away from the railing.

'Hey, where are you going?' asked Elena groggily.

'Stay there,' said Connor as he sped off down the rink in pursuit of Feliks and Anastasia. His blades cut deep into the ice, the adrenalin-fuelled muscles in his legs driving him forward, faster and faster.

Ahead, the four men were bearing down on Feliks like an unseen avalanche.

Connor weaved between the other skaters, ignoring their protests as he clipped their arms.

'Jason!' gasped Connor, activating his hidden earpiece and throat mic. 'Where are you?'

'*Still near the main entrance,*' came the reply.

'Code Red. Little Bear under threat,' said Connor, using the official call sign for Feliks.

'*Are you* sure *this time?*'

'One hundred per cent! In pursuit of four suspects now,' he panted, almost careering into a young girl. 'Tell Timur. Possible kidnap or kill.'

Connor heard Jason swear under his breath, then: *'Meet you at Point Lima.'*

From their pre-trip briefing Connor knew that meant the ice-rink entrance. 'Doubt we'll make it that far!' he replied as he watched the four black jackets close in on their prey. 'FELIKS!' he shouted.

Feliks and Anastasia both turned. Connor waved his arms frantically at them to keep moving. 'DON'T STOP! HAILSTORM!'

Several skaters glanced up at the clear sky with confused looks on their faces. But Feliks knew what Connor meant. Connor had forewarned him of certain call signs, *Hailstorm* being the code word for a full-blown attack. Feliks's eyes widened in horror as he saw the four huge men heading towards him.

One of the black jackets spun on the spot and began skating backwards, hunting for the source of the warning. His eyes locked on to Connor. Skidding to a stop, ice chips flying, the black jacket now thundered towards him instead.

'GO!' Connor screamed at Feliks.

Quick to spot the danger too, Anastasia grabbed Feliks's arm and raced off with him, the three other black jackets chasing them down like a pack of wolves.

Connor powered on. He was on a direct collision course with the fourth black jacket, who was shouldering people aside like bowling pins. An ice-rink attendant tried to stop the man but was knocked down with a vicious punch to the face. Other skaters jumped aside, leaving a clear path between the black jacket and Connor. As they charged at one another in a deadly duel of chicken, Connor pulled the XT tactical torch from his pocket. Closer and closer they got. Faster and faster they sped. The man's eyes focused on his target, fists primed. Everything looked set for Connor to be mown down and sliced in half by the skater's blades.

Connor steeled himself. Then, at the very last second, he flicked out the extendable baton, dropped on his side and slid to the left of the black jacket. As he slipped past, evading the man's outstretched arms, the baton smashed across the black jacket's kneecaps. There was a sickening crunch of bone and the man flipped forward and slammed face first into the unyielding ice.

A collective gasp of horror rose from the onlookers, but Connor didn't even look back as he slid to his feet and kept skating. The black jacket was down and out for the count. That was all that mattered.

Further along the rink, Feliks and Anastasia were rounding the corner at top speed and heading back down the long straight to the main entrance. But the remaining attack unit was almost on top of them.

Connor skated hard, trying to catch them up. But it was futile. He could never make it in time.

One of the men grabbed Anastasia, her scream cut off by a large gloved hand. The other two caught Feliks either side by his arms and carried him off.

Leg muscles burning, Connor put on a desperate burst of speed as Feliks disappeared into the crowd.

'Jason!' he gasped into his throat mic. 'Little Bear's been taken! Heading your way.'

'*I don't see him. I repeat, I don't see him.*'

Connor was fast approaching Anastasia. She was struggling wildly in her attacker's grip. But Connor knew he couldn't stop to save her. Feliks was his priority. His *only* priority.

Still, as he closed in on the two of them, Connor readied his baton to strike the man's head. All he needed was a glancing blow. *Twenty metres ... fifteen metres ... ten metres ...*

Just as he raised the baton, Anastasia drove the edge of her skate down the man's shin and on to his foot. The sharp edge of the blade cut open his trouser leg and sliced off a layer of skin. Her attacker howled in agony. Then she elbowed him in the gut and in a miraculous display of skill and balance threw her assailant over her shoulder with a perfect *o-goshi*. The man landed with such devastating impact that the ice cracked beneath him.

By the time Connor reached Anastasia, she was free from her captor's grasp and racing alongside him.

'You OK?' he asked, retracting the baton and concealing the torch in his hand.

'Fine,' she replied, her snow-white cheeks slightly flushed and her ice-blue eyes blazing. 'Who are these guys?'

'No idea. But I have to rescue Feliks.'

'I'll help,' said Anastasia.

'It's too dangerous.'

'I can handle myself,' she replied firmly. 'Besides, I'm a better skater.'

Connor couldn't argue with that. Ahead, he caught a glimpse of the two black-jacketed kidnappers, Feliks still trapped between them, his legs kicking wildly. They were heading for a side exit. Skating in Anastasia's slipstream to maximize his speed, Connor gradually closed the gap. But they were running out of time. Feliks would be off the ice and gone before they reached him.

Then out of nowhere Jason came barrelling up the rink the wrong way. Arms wheeling, body swaying, he careered down the ice and ploughed straight into Feliks and his kidnappers. The whole group tumbled over in a heap of arms and legs, more skaters tripping and landing on top of the pile.

As the two black jackets scrambled to free themselves from the tangle, Connor and Anastasia finally caught up, Anastasia 'accidentally' connecting her knee with one man's jaw, and Connor driving the hexagonal strike-ring of his torch into the forehead of the other man. They both went out like blown light bulbs.

With the four black jackets neutralized and the rink in chaos, Connor grabbed Feliks and Anastasia held Jason as they skated hard for the main exit.

'You did well to keep my son safe,' praised Viktor, patting both Connor and Jason on the shoulders. 'More than I can say for this useless lump of meat!'

He shot Timur a contemptuous look. The bodyguard was propped up in a chair in the mansion's kitchen, an ice pack held to his bald head. One of the black jackets had coshed him from behind and left him unconscious outside the ice-rink entrance. As they were escaping, Connor had spotted his bulky form laid out like a discarded drunk in the snow.

'You should be thanking Anastasia too,' said Connor, their blonde friend having been dropped off on the way back to the mansion. 'She tackled two of Feliks's attackers by herself.'

'Who's Anastasia?' asked Viktor, turning to his son.

Feliks was perched on a stool at the breakfast bar, cradling a hot chocolate. 'Just a friend,' he replied shyly.

Viktor's eyes narrowed. 'The same friend who invited you to the social club?'

Feliks nodded.

An impressed grin spread across Viktor's face. 'I'd like to meet this young lady. She sounds spirited. Let's invite her to lunch.'

'Don't get too excited,' mumbled Feliks. 'She's not my girlfriend or anything.'

'Not yet anyway,' said Viktor with a wolfish wink.

Feliks's face flushed red and he buried himself in his mug of hot chocolate.

'Anyway, gentlemen,' said Viktor, turning back to Connor and Jason. 'Thank you again for your efforts. I –'

Dmitry dashed into the kitchen. 'My apologies, Viktor. I came as soon as I got your message,' he panted. 'Are you all right, Feliks?'

Feliks worked hard to put on a brave smile. 'Just about,' he sighed.

Dmitry looked to Viktor. 'Was this another Bratva *message*?'

'At least another attempt at one,' replied the billionaire. 'The boldness of it has all the marks of the Bratva. But Connor says the men were all dressed in black ski jackets – a sign it could be an FSB agent job. Lazar has spoken with the police. Predictably there are no witnesses and none of the attackers were arrested. So, another cover-up, which indicates government involvement. So my guess is all three.'

Dmitry plonked himself down at the breakfast bar and held his head in his hands. 'This is getting out of control, Viktor. It's becoming more like a war than a campaign.'

'Yes, and a war we will win,' said the billionaire, pointing his finger confidently at his adviser. 'We have the backing. We have the voters' support. We have the will.'

'Viktor, they went for your *son*,' reminded his adviser, staring at the billionaire in disbelief. 'Your enemies are taking no prisoners in trying to stop you. Are you sure you want to continue risking Feliks's life for this cause?'

'It's *his* future that's at stake here. *His* country. And I've already lost too much to give in. We must fight on.' When Dmitry didn't reply, the billionaire frowned at his adviser. 'You aren't losing your backbone, are you?'

Dmitry shook his balding head. 'No, of course not.'

'Good, because change doesn't happen without sacrifice,' stated Viktor. 'Their failed kidnap attempt is our success. Proof they're running scared. We can use it as a rallying cry for our cause. Expose the government's dirty tricks against us.'

Dmitry glanced from Viktor to Feliks and back again. 'You must be careful not to use your son as a political pawn.'

Viktor walked over and laid a hand on his son's shoulder. 'Don't worry, Feliks is well protected,' he said, giving his son a reassuring squeeze. 'Now come, let's discuss this elsewhere,' he continued, ushering Dmitry out of the kitchen.

Once they'd left, Feliks remained staring into his hot chocolate.

'You OK?' asked Connor.

'I just want to be on my own,' he mumbled, not looking up.

Timur stood up and lurched away, the ice pack still clamped to his head. Jason shrugged and headed out of the door too. Connor hesitated, wondering if he should hang around a little longer. Feliks had been through a traumatic kidnap attempt and could be in shock. And Connor was sure it hadn't helped Feliks to hear that his father valued his cause more than his son. Then his phone vibrated in his pocket. Checking the number, he saw that it was Charley. He stepped out of the kitchen and into the hallway to take the call.

'Hi, Connor, thanks for the en-route update,' she said. 'Is Little Bear safe in his cave now?'

'Yes,' Connor replied, glancing back through the doorway at Feliks. The boy still sat with his head bowed over the hot chocolate. 'But I think he's suffering from shock.'

'I'm sure he'll recover. How are you doing?'

'All the better for hearing your voice,' he admitted, and could almost sense Charley smile at the other end of the line. 'You can tell Amir his XT torch makes a fine weapon.'

'You did well to deal with four hostiles. And on ice!'

'It was certainly a challenge. I just wish you'd seen Jason's counter-attack.' Connor laughed. 'He was the most dangerous thing on that rink. A human cannonball! To be honest, I don't even know if Jason was intentionally trying to hit the attackers or not. It seemed more luck than skill!'

'The Principal's safe, and so are you. That's all that matters,' said Charley. 'I spoke with the colonel, by the way. He insists he didn't know about Feliks's former bodyguard. But he admits there are a few holes in the information Mr Malkov provided.'

'A *few holes*?' exclaimed Connor. 'The shooting of a bodyguard seems a pretty big hole to me! You mean there are *more* surprises to come?'

'Hopefully not,' replied Charley. 'Oh, and the colonel denies ever saying *the size of the contract is worth the risk of a buddyguard or two*. He insists that he said it is *never* worth the risk.'

'Do you believe him?'

'I don't know what to believe at the moment.' There was a pause on the line. 'How's Jason?' Although her tone had lightened, Connor sensed she meant something more than this.

'He's OK. Why?'

'Well, Ling wants to talk with him and he's not answering her texts.'

'Oh . . . I think he's just focused on the mission,' Connor replied, wondering why he was covering for his partner, especially when he owed more loyalty to Ling than he did to Jason.

'Give him a prod to call her, will you? Ling's still really upset. You know, after their split. I think she wants to make up.'

'Sure,' said Connor. 'Anything else?'

'Yes, in your update, you mentioned additional support in dealing with the hostiles? What additional support?'

'We had help from a school friend of Feliks's,' he explained. 'A girl called Anastasia.'

'What's her background?'

'She's new at the school. A boarder on a music scholarship. Really nice girl with . . . well, some surprising talents.'

'What do you mean?'

'She's very switched on, has fast reactions in a crisis and *seriously* impressive self-defence skills,' Connor explained, smiling at the memory of her pounding her attacker into the ice.

'I hope you're not falling for this Russian girl!' said Charley, her tone sharp but teasing. 'Remember, I've some seriously impressive self-defence skills too! Perhaps you'd like a reminder?'

Connor laughed. 'No, thanks. I've witnessed them in full force on Richie. Don't worry, Charley, I've only got eyes for you. But I *am* interested in Anastasia for another reason.'

'What's that?'

'I've been thinking . . . she has the potential to make an excellent Buddyguard recruit.'

'Really?' said Charley. 'Well, if that's the case, I'll dig a little deeper into Anastasia's background before you recommend her to Colonel Black.'

'Hey, Jason, hold up!' called Connor, running down the hallway as his partner headed towards the mansion's personal gym. To keep themselves fit for the job they worked out daily, enjoying the state-of-the-art weights room with computerized running machines, indoor pool and sauna and steam room. 'We still need to debrief after today's attack.'

Jason stopped and turned, a towel slung over his shoulder. 'Debrief what? Principal's safe and sound.'

Connor nodded. 'True, but we need to debrief our handling of the situation.'

Jason shrugged. 'There was a situation. We dealt with it. Job done.'

'It wasn't exactly textbook perfect,' said Connor. 'In the park, you didn't always stay on point. That meant the Principal was unprotected. And you couldn't ice-skate. You should have mentioned that, so we could plan our protection better.'

'Hey, my skating was good enough to take out two heavies,' said Jason, stabbing a finger at Connor's chest. 'Besides, *you* overreacted to the funfair shooting gallery.'

Connor held up his hands. 'Fair enough, which is why we need to debrief before I put in our official report to HQ.'

Jason rested a hand on Connor's shoulder and smiled. 'Listen, mate, you go ahead and do the debrief yourself. You're in command on the ground. *I'm* just a lowly 2 i/c.'

He strode off towards the gym again. Connor fumed. Jason was playing him for a fool – both disrespecting his authority and using it to skive off his duties.

'There's also the matter of you and Anastasia,' said Connor pointedly. 'Perhaps I should mention that in the report?'

The implied threat stopped Jason in his tracks. He shot Connor a glare. '*What* matter?'

'Come on, Jason.' Connor sighed, not really wanting an argument with his partner. 'You're hitting on her when you know Feliks likes her too. You can't do that to a Principal. It's a conflict of interest that will cause issues.'

Jason blinked as if something didn't quite compute. 'But Anastasia's *way* out of his league.' He sailed a hand into the air. 'I mean, way out.'

Connor shrugged. 'Anastasia doesn't seem to think so. In fact, she shows more interest in Feliks than in you.'

Jason made a face. 'Oh, give over! You're just jealous.'

'No, I'm not,' snapped Connor. 'I've got Charley back at base. Talking of which, you've got Ling.'

Jason squared up to Connor. 'Listen, mate, me and Ling split up. So I'm free to do what I want. And, just to be clear, *she* ended it. Broke my heart. But I'm not going to mope around.'

'Well, if you're so upset about breaking up, why haven't you called her back?'

'It's none of your business.'

'Yes, it is. I've covered for you so far. But Ling is keen to talk to you. Sounds like she wants to make up. What was that argument about anyway?'

Jason crossed his arms and stared at Connor. After a long silence, he said, 'You!'

Connor frowned. 'Me?'

'Yeah, Ling was going on and on about me needing to be nice to you,' explained Jason, rolling his eyes. 'That I should accept being 2 i/c to you on this mission. That we should be combining our strengths and not competing all the time. That once I got to know you, then I'd come to respect your skills as a bodyguard. Blah . . . blah . . . bl–'

Connor started to laugh.

Jason scowled at him. 'Why are you laughing?'

'Because Charley said the exact same things to *me* about *you*!'

'Then you know why me and Ling argued. And why we –' he pointed to himself and Connor – 'will always clash. We're too alike.'

'We don't *have* to clash,' said Connor, getting exasperated. He clenched his fists, wanting to thump some sense into his partner.

'Mate, it's like our arm-wrestling match,' Jason explained, edging closer. 'I won, but you won't accept it. Likewise, you may have won command of this operation, but that doesn't mean I have to accept it.'

With that, Jason strode off and disappeared into the gym, leaving Connor furious and frustrated in the hallway. Connor punched the wall with his fist, making a knuckle-sized dent in the plasterwork. It hurt his hand, but he felt a whole lot better for it.

Steam rose in great wafts from the hot coals. The sharp scent of eucalyptus infused the air, clearing the lungs of the two great men who sat sweating on the wooden benches in the *banya*. Bell-shaped felt hats kept their heads cool and protected their hair from the intense heat.

Roman Gurov whipped himself with a bundle of birch branches, getting his blood flowing – and venting his frustration.

'It's good to beat the toxins from one's body, eh?' said his comrade, who was just a ghost among the wreaths of hot steam.

Roman laid aside the birch branches, savouring the tingle of his lashed skin in the humid heat of the sauna. He just wished it was as easy and pleasurable to get rid of Viktor Malkov.

A fierce prolonged *hiss* like a nest of vipers cut through the sweltering haze as his comrade ladled another scoop of water on to the glowing coals.

'Tell me, how did your latest move against the Black King work out?' he asked, dropping the ladle into its bucket and leaning back against the spruce-panelled wall to let the heat roll over him.

Roman let out a heavy sigh as the scorching wave of steam hit him. 'The pawn's capture was thwarted by unexpected resistance.'

His comrade gave him a hard stare. '*Unexpected?*'

'Our assets were defeated by a bunch of kids!' explained Roman, his expression seething as red-hot as the coals in the stove.

His comrade raised an eyebrow in disbelief. 'And who are these kids?'

'According to my source, the target's second cousins, although we're having trouble verifying the family connection. Also a girl, a friend from the target's school.'

'Yet she too took out a trained asset?'

Roman nodded. 'The man can barely walk.'

'Impressive,' said his comrade, picking up his own bundle of birch branches. 'Still, the kidnap attempt will have got the Black King's attention.'

'Yes, it did. But it's only hardened his resolve!' Roman muttered irritably. 'He's using the failed attack as a sympathy vote and rallying cry for his cause.'

His comrade began to lash himself, leaving a rash of red scratches across his broad back. 'So, what's your plan now?'

Roman barely paused to consider this. 'Kill the king.'

His comrade stopped whipping himself and shook his head in mild disapproval. 'Don't want to make him a martyr.'

'What do *you* suggest then?'

'Better to kill a man's reputation,' he replied, standing and stretching out his back. 'Destroy his credibility and you destroy the cause.'

Roman weighed up this option as his comrade stepped out of the sauna, crossed the marble-floored antechamber and dived head first into a plunge pool of ice-cold water. Enduring the sauna's heat a few minutes longer, Roman thought, *But what's to stop me killing both the man* and *his reputation?*

'Your bodyguards can't come in,' said the maître d' with an apologetic but unyielding smile.

Viktor frowned. 'Why not?'

'House rules,' replied the slick-haired man, his hooded eyes narrowing in distaste at the dagger tattoo just visible above Lazar's collar line. He gave Timur an equally derisory glance. With his bulging muscles and semi-automatic pistol barely contained by his jacket, Timur looked like a suited bear and was totally out of place among the elegantly dressed guests at Vivosti, Moscow's most fashionable and expensive restaurant.

'They must wait in the lobby,' insisted the maître d'.

Viktor turned to Lazar and Timur with a shrug. 'The price of exclusivity, I suppose.'

His two bodyguards grunted, clearly unhappy with the arrangement. But Connor and Jason walked straight into the restaurant unquestioned with Feliks and his father. As the maître d' escorted their party through the frosted-glass doors and over to their table, Connor saw that Dmitry and his family were already waiting with Anastasia.

Viktor greeted his adviser with a firm handshake, then turned to his other guests. 'So you must be Anastasia,' he said warmly, briefly glancing at Feliks in clear approval of his son's taste. 'I had no idea Feliks's friends were so elegant and refined.'

Anastasia's pale cheeks flushed. 'It's a pleasure meeting you too, Mr Malkov. I've been looking forward to it.'

'Viktor – call me Viktor.' He cocked his head to one side. 'You're from the southern provinces, are you not?'

'No,' said Anastasia, a frown marking her brow. 'Why would you think that?'

Viktor shrugged. 'Your accent sounds southern. I thought you might be from the Rostov region where I began my political career. Anyway, you're welcome and I'm truly thankful for your assistance at the ice rink.'

'Oh, it was nothing,' she replied, lowering her gaze and studying the handbag she clutched.

'Not according to Connor,' said Viktor, raising an eyebrow. 'In fact I'm seriously thinking of hiring you to protect *me*!'

Anastasia met his eye. 'Don't you already have protection?'

'Yes, but not as deadly as you!' Viktor laughed. Then he turned to embrace his adviser's wife, a tall woman with a cascade of golden blonde hair and large drop diamond earrings that hung like glittering chandeliers. 'Ah, Natasha, so good to see you,' he said.

Natasha glanced past his shoulder. 'No date?'

Viktor smiled agreeably. 'Too busy for romance.'

Natasha tutted in mild disapproval, then directed her attention to Connor and Jason. 'And who are these fine gentlemen?' she asked.

'Feliks's cousins,' Viktor replied, stepping aside. 'Connor and Jason.'

'Ah, the boys who saved your son. Well, this is my daughter, Tanya,' said Natasha proudly, introducing a wide-eyed girl with the blonde locks of her mother and the plump lips and pudgy nose of her father.

Tanya smiled shyly and they nodded back. Connor noted no warm greeting passed between her and Feliks, just the weary look of a forced friendship through parents.

Viktor invited them all to sit, offering Anastasia the seat next to his and beside his son. Jason moved swiftly to sit on Feliks's right-hand side. To Tanya's obvious delight, Connor took the chair next to hers. But he'd only chosen the seat since – much to his irritation – Jason had stolen prime position beside the Principal. If his partner continued to undermine his authority like this, he'd be forced to raise the issue with the colonel – but he knew that would only worsen the situation between them. Still, his own chair faced the entrance and he had a clear view of the restaurant, making it ideal from a security standpoint.

A waiter presented them with menus and Viktor immediately ordered water, bread, pickles and a bottle of top-brand vodka for the table.

As the others studied their menus, Connor's eyes swept the room. The restaurant was stylish, with dark woods, granite and glass. A mock waterfall trickled down a neon-lit wall into a tank filled with exotic fish. The eighteen tables were all taken for lunch, waiters slipping like well-oiled machines from guest to guest. Through the frosted glass that separated the lobby from the restaurant, Connor could just make out Lazar and Timur's bulked-up silhouettes. Although they had to wait in the lobby, at least they could guard the entrance. Connor also identified the fire exit and location of the toilets, as well as the route to the kitchen – just in case they needed a quick escape.

'Do you need help with the menu?' Tanya asked, noticing Connor seemed to be staring at it for a long time.

Breaking away from his surveillance of the other guests, Connor shook his head. 'No, I'm fine. Thanks.'

He took a moment to actually study the menu. Just as Amir had boasted, the contact lens he wore in his right eye instantly translated the Russian into English. The words appeared clearly on the lens's heads-up-display: *Икра* ... Caviar; Пельмени ... Beef Dumplings; Борщ ... Beetroot Soup ...

As soon as the waiter had taken their orders, Viktor reached for the vodka.

'Allow me,' offered Anastasia, taking the bottle and prising open the cap. 'At home I always pour for my father.'

'Really?' said Viktor, with a pleased curl to his lips. 'He has brought you up well.'

Anastasia selected a shot glass and poured out a measure of the clear liquid, twisting the bottle at the end to prevent drips. Then she served Dmitry and his wife.

'She could get a job here,' remarked Dmitry.

'Oh, I think Anastasia has a great deal more potential,' replied Viktor, winking at his son.

'You should raise a toast,' suggested Anastasia.

'Agreed. But first let's get business out of the way,' said Viktor. 'Give me some good news, Dmitry.'

Dmitry smiled. 'I have obtained the permits for the rally.'

'Wonderful! This will be a momentous day in our country's history. Have the media been updated?'

Dmitry nodded and the two of them talked a few minutes longer. Then, as Viktor reached for his vodka glass, Connor caught a flicker of movement through the lobby's frosted glass. Multiple shadows shifted in precise, coordinated yet urgent patterns, all converging on the door.

'Jason!' hissed Connor, directing his partner's attention towards the lobby.

Viktor raised his glass in a toast. 'To *Our Russia*!'

'To *Our Russia*!' chimed Dmitry.

Just as they went to down their shots, there came a yell of warning: Lazar's voice. A group of armed men in black combat gear burst into the restaurant. Guests screamed. Waiters dropped their trays. Connor and Jason both leapt from their seats and grabbed Feliks. They pulled him to the floor, shielding him with their bodies. Connor was glad to see that Anastasia had reacted fast too, diving beneath the table and hiding behind the tablecloth. But Tanya still sat frozen in her seat.

'Get down!' Connor hissed at her. But she seemed not to hear. Looking to the fire exit, Connor saw that the gunmen had already covered both entrance and exit. Within seconds their table was surrounded. There was no escape.

'Viktor Malkov,' said an iron-faced man, his gun levelled at Viktor's chest.

It wasn't a question; it was a statement.

Viktor calmly held up his hands. 'What's all this about?'

As the gunman stepped forward, Connor spotted three bright yellow letters emblazoned on his back: ФСБ.

The contact lens's heads-up-display translated the Russian letters into the forbidding acronym: FSB.

'You're being arrested under suspicion of tax evasion, money-laundering and embezzlement,' declared the Secret Service officer, seizing Viktor's wrists and binding them behind his back.

Dmitry rose from his chair in fury. 'Those are ridiculous accusations!' he cried.

Another FSB agent hammered the adviser in the small of the back with the butt of his rifle. Dmitry collapsed, sprawling across the table, knocking over the glasses of vodka and scattering the plates.

'Stay down!' warned the agent. 'Unless you want to be arrested too.'

Groaning feebly, Dmitry lay where he fell, his wife weeping beside his prone body, his daughter still too shocked to move.

The FSB officer shoved Viktor Malkov out through the lobby doors. Connor caught a glimpse of Lazar and Timur held at gunpoint, powerless to stop the FSB task force taking their boss.

'Papa?' cried Feliks, frightened and bewildered at his father's dramatic arrest.

As Viktor was dragged away, the billionaire shouted to Lazar, 'Protect my son at all costs!'

None of the FSB officers noticed the man standing in the doorway opposite as they bundled Viktor Malkov out of the fancy restaurant. Nor did the pack of photographers who eagerly snapped away as the disgraced billionaire was dragged through the slush of dirty snow and thrown into the waiting police van. Nor did any bystanders as they watched the van doors being slammed shut and the FSB task force drive off, sirens blaring.

No one noticed him.

Like a concrete chameleon, his ashen skin blended into the dull grey of the office building's bricks. His absolute stillness attracted zero attention, his body seemingly as much a permanent part of the street scene as the surrounding buildings, street lamps and pavement. A pedestrian could walk past within a few feet of the doorway and remain completely oblivious to his being there.

Mr Grey was all but a ghost. An assassin without presence.

He waited until he was convinced all the FSB agents had departed. Then he took out his phone and silently dialled the memorized number. It was answered on its second ring.

'He was arrested before I could get to him,' he informed his contact.

There was a pause on the line.

'Too much depends on Malkov. Deal with the situation.'

Mr Grey observed a silver Mercedes with blacked-out windows drive up to the restaurant and stop beside the kerb. The restaurant's doors opened and two heavies in suits stepped out, surveyed the street, then beckoned to a dark-haired boy waiting in the lobby.

'What about the son?' asked Mr Grey.

'Ensure he is taken care of too,' ordered his contact. 'This is a prime opportunity. The boy is vulnerable without his father.'

Mr Grey's eyes turned to shards of ice as he watched Feliks being escorted to the Mercedes by a lean boy with spiky brown hair. Mr Grey recognized the assured gait with which the boy walked, the hyper-alert manner in which he scanned his surroundings and the protective body position he maintained with his charge. Mr Grey had encountered the boy before. In Somalia. In Burundi. And now in Russia.

Mr Grey knew Connor Reeves wasn't any ordinary boy.

'Malkov's son might not be as vulnerable as you think,' he informed his contact.

CHAPTER 35

Connor was showering in the changing room after basketball practice when he heard a familiar and unwelcome voice call out, 'Hey, traitor boy! I hear your father's been arrested.'

'You *know* he's been arrested,' Feliks snapped back. '*Your* father at the FSB ordered it!'

'Of course he did,' said Stas. 'He was handed evidence of your father's illegal business dealings. So much for Viktor Malkov's campaign against corruption. He's as corrupt as the Bratva themselves!'

'It's lies! All lies!' cried Feliks. Connor heard the distress in his voice and wondered where Jason was. He should have been guarding their Principal.

'Perhaps we should arrest you and put you on trial too?' said Stas.

'Get your hands off me!'

Connor grabbed his towel, wrapped it round himself and rushed out of the showers. He found Feliks surrounded by Stas, Vadik and two other members of the gang: the mop-haired Alexei and the sumo-shaped Gleb, both of them meatheads. Jason was nowhere to be seen. Connor barged his way through the gang.

'Leave him alone!' he ordered, breaking their grip on his Principal's arm.

With a dismissive snort at Connor's demand, Stas squared up to him. 'It's time I taught you a lesson in *respect*.'

With lightning speed, he caught hold of Connor by the throat and slammed him against the lockers. A galaxy of stars burst before Connor's eyes as his head cracked against the metal frame.

'Here's lesson number one,' said Stas, raising his fist.

'Respect this!' said Jason, coming up behind them from the direction of the toilet block.

Vadik moved to intercept him and Jason flung open a locker door, smashing Vadik in the face. There was a clang and a crunch as the Russian's nose crumpled under the impact. Vadik dropped to his knees and clasped a hand to his face, blood dripping through his fingers.

'You're making a habit of that!' smirked Jason.

With Stas distracted by the downfall of his right-hand man, Connor brought a forearm down on to Stas's elbow joint. His arm crumpled and Connor broke free from his grip. Then, with a sharp snap-kick to the stomach, he sent the bully toppling over a bench.

In the mayhem that followed, Alexei swung a wild punch at Jason as Gleb shoved Feliks to the floor and went to kick him. Snatching a can of deodorant from his open locker, Connor sprayed it in the boy's eyes. Half-blinded,

Gleb screamed and staggered away. Meanwhile Jason had blocked Alexei's punch, then one-inch-pushed the boy in the chest. Struck with brutal force in the solar plexus, Alexei flew backwards and crashed into a stack of lockers, the impact sounding like a head-on collision with a truck. The boy slid down to the floor in a wheezing heap.

Connor yanked Feliks back to his feet. Then he and Jason stood shoulder to shoulder, fists raised, shielding Feliks behind them as an enraged Stas advanced.

'Hey, what's going on in here?' said their basketball coach, storming into the changing room.

Connor and Jason lowered their fists. The winded Alexei slunk off to his locker. Stas neatly turned on his heel and helped Vadik stand up.

'He slipped on a wet tile,' Stas explained.

The coach shot him a dubious frown. Then he nodded at Gleb, who was rubbing his eyes as if they were on fire. 'And what happened to *him*?'

'Soap in his eyes,' said Connor.

The coach's face twisted into a livid scowl at their pathetic lies. 'My office, all of you, now!'

After five minutes of awkward silence where no one admitted to anything, they escaped the coach's office with a severe reprimand and a detention each. Back in the changing rooms, there was an uneasy stand-off between the two groups.

Feliks, cocky with Connor and Jason's combat skills, goaded them. 'Hey, Vadik, I can see your big nose in this.'

He pointed to the rounded dent in the door of Jason's locker. 'That'll teach you to mess with me.'

Glowering, Vadik made a step towards him, but Stas held his friend back.

'You'd better watch out, traitor boy,' warned Stas. 'You won't have your guardian angels with you *all* the time!'

'Hey, where have you been?' Anastasia called, tramping across the snowy playground. School was long since over and the pale wintry sun was dipping below the horizon.

'Detention,' Feliks replied glumly, his breath frosting in the frigid air.

'Oh yeah, I heard about that.' She looked at Jason and raised an eyebrow. 'You face-planted Vadik into a locker?'

Jason held up his gloved hands. 'Guilty as charged.'

'We're all guilty in Russia,' she said, a half-smile on her lips, 'whether we're innocent or not.'

'Unless, of course, your father is the Director of the FSB,' Feliks muttered sourly.

Connor explained, 'Stas got out of *his* detention with one phone call to his father. So did Vadik.'

'There's Russian justice for you,' said Anastasia with a shrug. 'Speaking of which –' she glanced at Feliks – 'how's your father getting on?'

Feliks kicked at a pile of snow. 'He's still being held in jail. Dmitry supposedly has the best lawyers working on his case and hopes to have him released on bail by the weekend. But who knows?'

'Let's hope he is, for your sake,' said Anastasia, gently touching his arm. Connor noticed the gesture of affection. So did Jason.

As they traipsed over to the main gate, Connor asked, 'Why are you still here this late?'

'Music lesson,' Anastasia replied, holding up her violin case.

'You should play for us some time,' suggested Jason. 'I like Mozart and . . . all that sort of stuff.'

Connor almost laughed out loud. He knew Jason hated any sort of classical music.

Anastasia suddenly came over all shy, a flush to her cheeks. 'I'm . . . really not that good.'

Connor was surprised by her modesty. 'But you're on a music scholarship,' he remarked.

'I know, but –'

'My father loves the violin,' said Feliks to no one in particular.

On hearing this, Anastasia's resistance appeared to weaken. 'Well . . . perhaps when he's out of jail, I can play a short piece for you all?'

'Really?' said Feliks, brightening at the idea. 'He'd love that.'

'Sure. It'd be my pleasure.' Anastasia smiled. Then the smile froze on her lips. 'Who's that?'

Connor spun, following the line of her gaze. In the darkening twilight a figure appeared at the gate, triggering the security light. Tall, broad and imposing, with cropped black hair, the hardened ridge of a boxer's nose and a dagger tattoo visible on his neck, Connor could understand why Anastasia was so alarmed by the bodyguard's sudden presence. His appearance was meant to deter attackers far more threatening and dangerous than a schoolgirl.

'That's only Lazar, my father's bodyguard,' said Feliks with a laugh.

'Are you all right? You look like you've seen a ghost,' said Jason.

Anastasia's already snow-white face had paled to the colour of bone. 'I was just startled, that's all,' she explained, quickly recovering. 'You know, after yesterday, I'm a little bit jumpy.' She turned to Feliks. 'So where's your other bodyguard?'

'You mean Timur? He's probably in the car.'

'And does Lazar go with you everywhere now?' asked Anastasia.

'Pretty much,' Feliks replied with a resigned shrug. 'My father's worried for my safety.'

'Considering what happened at the restaurant, I can understand why. To be honest, I'm surprised you don't have bodyguards following you round the school!'

Connor and Jason exchanged a glance and tried not to grin.

Stopping short of the gate, Anastasia checked her violin case. 'Sorry, I've just realized I forgot my bow.' She turned back towards the music block.

'We'll wait for you,' said Jason.

'No need, I'll be fine,' she called back. 'By the way, I'm thinking of going to the Red Square at the weekend. To see the ice sculptures. Would you like to join me?'

'Sure thing,' said Jason, a little too eagerly.

'That depends on Feliks,' said Connor, reminding Jason of his duty. 'And Lazar.'

Feliks frowned and studied the snow on his boot before kicking it off. 'Well . . . I don't know . . . after the ice rink and now my father's arrest . . .'

'Could take your mind off things?' suggested Anastasia. 'Unless your bodyguard won't allow it, of course.'

This seemed to make up Feliks's mind. 'My bodyguard doesn't tell me what to do! He's just supposed to take a bullet for me. So I'll be there.'

'Great!' said Anastasia, and headed off into the darkness. 'See you all Saturday morning at ten.'

CHAPTER 37

'I guess diplomacy is over,' said Charley after Connor had updated her on the locker-room brawl with Stas and Vadik.

'You could say that war has been declared!' Connor agreed with a hollow laugh. Smartphone in hand, he sat cross-legged in one of the high-back leather chairs in the mansion's oak-panelled library. Quiet and seldom used, the library was the ideal location from which to report in without being disturbed or overheard. In the black granite hearth of the library's fireplace, a fresh log crackled and spluttered, occasionally spitting out a glowing ember like a lone shooting star.

'Vadik won't let Jason get away with smashing his nose twice,' Connor continued. 'And Feliks is stirring the pot any chance he gets now that we're around to back him up.'

'Have you spoken with him about that?' asked Charley.

Connor nodded. 'I tried on the drive back from school. Feliks barely listened to me. To be honest, I think he *likes* having the upper hand over Stas and Vadik.'

'Can't blame him really,' said Charley. 'Given they've bullied him so much, it's only natural he wants to get his own back.'

'True. But we're his bodyguards, not bullies for hire.'

Through the leaded windows he could see snow falling in silent waves, covering the garden with a deep blanket of white.

'What does Jason think?' asked Charley.

Connor shrugged indifferently. '*Bring it on!* was his response.'

'You two still not seeing eye-to-eye?'

Connor shook his head. 'Jason followed my lead when there was that potential threat in Gorky Park. But otherwise he's acting like *I'm* 2 i/c or else simply ignoring my orders. He may have backed me up in the locker room, but he wasn't where I'd told him to be – guarding Feliks. Instead he was in the toilet, having a dump!'

Charley tried to suppress a grin. 'Well, when you've got to go, you've got to go!'

'Maybe, but he should've waited for me to finish in the shower first. Anyway, he's always undermining my authority by taking prime position or shirking his duties.'

'Have you brought up the problem with him?'

Connor snorted. 'I tried but didn't get very far. He compared our relationship to an arm-wrestling match! One that we think we've both won.'

Charley smiled. 'Well, I suppose that's progress. At least you're combining your strengths in an arm wrestle!'

'We'd better do, if we're to stand any chance of protecting Feliks at the winter festival this weekend. We can't afford to be shoulder-barging each other in a public place!'

Charley's expression turned grave. 'If it's got that bad, perhaps you should mention the issue to the colonel?'

Connor shook his head and sighed. 'No, that'll only make matters worse. I can just imagine Jason's teasing: *Aw, the big baby, went running to the colonel!* No, I'll handle it myself.'

His gaze drifted towards the window again as a security guard passed by on his patrol through the garden.

'You look worried,' said Charley.

Connor rubbed a hand across his face. 'I just have a feeling Red Square is a disaster waiting to happen.'

'How so?'

'With Viktor still in jail, this trip seems an unnecessary risk. The Bratva have already shown they'll go to any length simply to deliver a message. And the ice rink proves Feliks is a target. The winter festival is a prime opportunity for the mafia, or any of Malkov's enemies, to attempt another attack or kidnap.'

'What's Lazar's opinion?' asked Charley. 'Isn't he the one with final say on security matters?'

'Lazar's confident Feliks will be safe,' replied Connor. 'He says Red Square's one of the most heavily guarded areas in Moscow.'

'Well, that's certainly true,' said Charley. 'The square is a stone's throw from the Kremlin. The area has countless surveillance cameras, plainclothes officers and round-the-clock armed security. If you are going anywhere in Moscow, this is probably the safest location. You'll just have to trust Lazar's judgement on this.'

'I don't know who to trust,' said Connor. 'We both know certain key information isn't being passed on for this assignment.'

Charley gave a reluctant nod. 'On that point, the colonel's working on plugging any gaps in the mission file as soon as our client is released from custody. But, to be honest, getting any reliable information out of Russia is a problem.'

'How do you mean?'

'I've had real difficulties researching Anastasia's background. Russian bureaucracy is a nightmare, and the language barrier isn't any help either. Beyond the information you've given me and what I've read in her school scholarship application, there appears very little to be found on her.'

Connor smiled. 'This all sounds very promising,' he said, realizing Anastasia's lack of an obvious past made her an even more ideal recruit.

'She's not even that active on social media. Another plus,' remarked Charley. 'Anyway, I'm going to try the local registry office next. I'll let you know if I discover anything odd. Otherwise, I think you can recommend your Russian friend to the colonel.'

Red Square was frosted like the icing on a wedding cake. The candy-coloured onion-domes of St Basil's Cathedral glistened in the bright morning sun in stark contrast to the tall towers and imposing red-brick walls of the Kremlin. In the vast cobbled square itself, row upon row of craft stalls were dusted in snow like sugar-coated gingerbread houses. Fairground rides twinkled and spun like fancy decorations. And, sparkling in the golden sunlight, elaborate ice sculptures of breathtaking size rose up from the ground as if a frozen army had been summoned. Overhead the sky was festooned with streamers, flags and fairy lights, turning the square into a magical winter wonderland through which strolled hundreds of people wrapped in thick coats and woolly scarves, all enjoying the season's festivities.

Above the grand edifice of the GUM department store that bordered the square's north-eastern edge, a lone figure crouched on the roof. Concealed from public eyes behind a stone parapet, white gloved hands removed a Vanquish .308 collapsible sniper rifle from its oblong backpack and assembled it with workman-like efficiency: extending the telescopic shoulder butt, deploying the bi-pod supports, screwing the slender barrel on to the stock. Then attaching a suppressor to the barrel, ramming home a full magazine of 7.62 mm calibre bullets, and finally chambering the rifle with a live round.

All in under sixty seconds.

Careful to stay behind the glare of a mounted spotlight, the sniper knelt down in the icy snow and put an eye to the rifle's tactical scope.

The scope's cross hairs swept the square, seeking out their target.

But the multitude of constantly shifting people hampered the search. There were also other factors to consider.

First, the cold. The longer the wait, the more stress on the body. So the harder it would be to control the breathing – and, as a consequence, the smooth pull of the trigger finger.

Second, light. There was a risk of glare in the magnified view of the scope from the dazzle of sun on the ice sculptures, perhaps with temporary loss of vision. There was also a danger that the scope itself would be spotted by a stray reflection of sunlight on its lens.

Third, wind. The flags were fluttering in the breeze, indicating a crosswind speed of at least twelve kilometres per hour: enough to cause the bullet to drift. Depending upon the range of the shot, the rifle would need to be aimed anywhere between two to ten centimetres to the left of the target in order to compensate.

Finally, distance. The kill would have to be made over a range of anywhere between fifty and three hundred metres. There would be little time to take aim and adjust for the shot.

As soon as the target entered the cross hairs, the trigger would have to be squeezed.

The ice dragon loomed over Connor and the others, its taloned wings spread, fanged jaws open wide and tail raised to the sky like a scorpion's, ready to strike. Connor was struck speechless by the colossal ice sculpture. From its sheet-thin wings to the needle-sharp teeth, the dragon was a magical work of art and intricate craftsmanship. Through its ice-block body, fiery rays of sunshine lent the dragon's skin a glistening sheen and the eerie impression that it was alive and moving.

Among the other ice sculptures on display were a royal carriage pulled by two horses, a swan in mid-flight, a scene from a Russian folk tale and a huge bear rearing up on its hind legs. Now, despite his security concerns about visiting Red Square, Connor was glad they'd made the effort. The winter festival was truly worth seeing.

Connor's gaze swept along the rows of wooden stalls, decorated with holly, silver baubles and multicoloured fairy lights. On sale were Christmas ornaments, nesting dolls, wooden spinning tops, painted boxes, handmade shawls and sheep-felt *valenki* boots. The sweetness of warm pancakes and cinnamon bagels filled the air, along with the odd whiff of vodka fumes from passing revellers and the sharp tang of citrus, vanilla and aromatic spices from various teas being brewed in a steaming bronze samovar on a nearby stall.

Jason's phone beeped with a text message and he glanced at the screen. 'Ana's running late,' he told them. 'Delays on the metro.'

'I told her we should have picked her up!' Feliks muttered irritably.

He seemed more annoyed about Anastasia texting Jason instead of him than the fact she'd be late. Connor was surprised at this development too. He hadn't known that Jason and Anastasia had exchanged mobile numbers. Perhaps she *was* switching her affections . . .

'Let's get a pancake while we wait,' Jason suggested, completely unaware of the reason for Feliks's sour mood.

As they wandered over to a food stall, Lazar walked a discreet couple of steps behind them – or at least as discreet as a tattooed towering bodyguard with a boxer's nose could, his bulging puffer jacket half-unzipped so he could swiftly draw his concealed MP-9 sub-machine gun at a moment's notice. The other bodyguard, Timur, had been instructed to wait with the car in case they needed to make a speedy exit.

While their pancakes were being cooked, Connor kept his eyes on the passing crowd, alert for threats. He'd noticed the FSB's black Toyota Corolla pull up to the kerb when they arrived, but hadn't seen the agent who stepped into the square. Connor had been trying to spot their tail ever since, but so far he'd had no luck.

Then a tall man in a blue beanie and black ski jacket headed their way, his hands thrust deep into his pockets. Connor tensed, wary of what his pockets might conceal. But the man walked straight past, not even looking at them.

At a nearby stall a young woman with a bob of dark hair was browsing through a display of shawls. Next to her, a smartly dressed gentleman in a fur hat was texting on his phone. He was showing no interest in the winter festival at all and Connor's sixth sense for danger buzzed. He was sure this gentleman had been loitering around the ice dragon for at least as long as they had.

Is he the agent? Another threat? A hit man for the Bratva?

Raising his alert level to Code Orange, Connor went to tell Lazar . . . when the suspect's wife and daughter arrived, greeting him with a hug, and the family disappeared happily into the crowd.

Connor eased back to Code Yellow, relaxed but still aware.

Jason handed him a warm pancake, dripping with honey. Feliks was already tucking into his own, the food seeming to have lightened his mood.

'Spot any threats?' Jason asked casually, through a mouthful of sweetened batter.

Connor shook his head. Then, just as he raised his own pancake to his lips, his attention was caught by a lean-faced man with a complexion as pale and lifeless as cigarette ash. Four stalls away, the man was inspecting an ornately painted box, but his grey eyes seemed to see straight through it; he was observing Connor and Feliks. Apart from his ashen skin, the man's features were strangely forgettable. Yet there was still something vaguely familiar about him. *Was he at the funfair?* As their eyes met, Connor felt his flesh creep.

Jason's phone beeped again. 'Ana will be here in five minutes. She's asking where to meet?'

'Tell her by the ice dragon,' Connor instructed, noting that Jason was calling her *Ana* now.

With pancakes in hand, they strolled back to the sculpture and waited. Feliks impatiently looked at his watch, every so often checking his phone, clearly hoping for a message from Anastasia too.

As Connor glanced over his shoulder to check on the grey-eyed man, the dragon suddenly exploded. Shards of lethal ice flew outward as if the beast was spitting teeth. And, alongside the shattering of the sculpture, Connor heard the telltale supersonic *crack* of a bullet.

From the moment the bullet struck, time for Connor seemed to tick by in horrifying freeze-frames. Dragon ice raining down like razor-sharp hail. Jason raising his arms as a shield. Feliks flinching forward, mouth open in a pained scream. Lazar reaching into his jacket for the MP-9. Connor discarding his pancake like a frisbee to seize Feliks. Drops of bright red blood in the trampled snow. Festival-goers whirling in wide-eyed shock as the sculpture disintegrated before them.

Then, in a rush of noise and screams, time caught up with itself and the situation accelerated like a rollercoaster. Seeing Lazar with a sub-machine gun, the crowd panicked and began to scatter. Heart pounding, Connor hustled Feliks towards the shelter of the nearest market stall, Jason in front, barging people out of the way, Lazar covering behind, his MP-9 seeking out the enemy . . .

Another bullet tore through the air.

Connor dived with Feliks into the compacted snow, coming up hard against the wooden panels of the tea stall. Hunkering down, he covered Feliks with his body, his jacket acting as a bulletproof shield for them both. Jason did the same on the other side before noticing streaks of blood running down Feliks's pale face.

'He's been shot,' said Jason.

Connor made a quick inspection and found a small gash across Feliks's scalp. 'It's just a grazing shot,' said Connor with relief.

'Where's Lazar?' asked a groggy Feliks.

Connor looked back and saw the bodyguard sprawled in the snow, blood spilling from a large hole in his throat, as if the dagger tattoo on his neck had pierced his very skin. Having taken the full impact of the second bullet, the bodyguard had likely saved Feliks's life.

In spite of his horrific injury, Lazar clawed at the snow, trying to drag himself into cover. But a second later another bullet ripped into him, targeting his heart with pinpoint accuracy. The bodyguard lay lifeless in the blood-red snow.

'We've got to get out of here. NOW!' said Jason, taking hold of Feliks's arm.

'Call Timur first,' Connor ordered. 'Emergency evac. Rendezvous Point Delta.'

Before their visit to Red Square, the Russian bodyguards had agreed planned Action-On Drills in the event of a crisis. What they'd do in a bomb attack. What they'd do if they were mugged. What they'd do if they lost Feliks. And what they'd do in the event of a shooting . . .

Rendezvous Point Delta was one of four key evacuation sites. On the north-east corner of the square, near St Basil's Cathedral, it was the closest to where they now sheltered.

Connor forced a deep breath, trying to calm himself. The worst thing was to act blindly and on instinct alone. His bodyguard training had ingrained into him the importance of A-C-E.

Assess the threat. Counter the danger. Escape the kill zone. In that order.

If they made a run for it without assessing the threat first, they could head straight into the enemy's path.

Keeping Feliks covered, Connor looked around for the shooter. The scene was utter chaos, people running everywhere, slipping and sliding on the icy snow in their attempt to flee. It was easier to spot those who *weren't* moving.

Crouched in the shadow of the market stall that sold shawls was the young woman with the bob of dark hair. In her hand she held a semi-automatic pistol . . . but she didn't have it trained on them. Or for that matter on the dead Lazar. Instead her eyes were darting round the square, apparently searching for the shooter herself, more keen on self-preservation than attacking them.

Connor realized *she* had to be the FSB agent, having stupidly assumed all this time their shadow had been male.

The grey man, however, was nowhere to be seen.

'There's a shooter in the crowd,' Connor informed Jason. 'Look for a man of average build with grey eyes and –'

'No, it's a sniper,' cut in Jason.

'I spotted a *definite* suspect,' Connor stated.

'That might be the case, but I *saw* a glint of light on the roof of that building at the same time as Lazar was shot,'

Jason insisted, pointing in the direction of the GUM department store. 'It can only be a sniper's scope.'

'Whether it's a sniper or a shooter or both, we're sitting ducks here,' said Connor. He couldn't believe they were arguing over who was trying to kill them.

'Feliks has brain fade,' said Jason, indicating the glazed look in their Principal's eyes. 'He's frozen up in shock.'

'Then we'll have to drag him to the rendezvous point.'

'Yeah, but how do we evade the sniper?' asked Jason, his eyes fixed on the store's roofline.

Or the grey man, thought Connor.

'We need a diversion,' Connor said, glancing at the tall bronze samovar on the tea stall's counter.

As he crept over towards the front of the stall, leaving Feliks exposed, Jason hissed, 'What do you think you're doing?'

'Countering the danger,' Connor replied. 'We can't see the enemy, but what if they can't see us either?'

He shoved the bronze samovar off the counter. It clattered to the ground, spilling its contents everywhere. The wave of boiling water evaporated the snow in its path, sending up great clouds of steam.

'Go! Go! Go!' Connor ordered as he grabbed Feliks's other arm and dashed with Jason into the billowing mist.

Jason took no prisoners as he shoulder-barged his way to the rendezvous point, bulldozing anyone who stepped into their path. Connor followed close on his tail, urging the dazed Feliks on and shielding his Principal as best he could. By now the mist had evaporated and the three of them were exposed to the mystery shooter. But the riot of panicking people helped cover their movements and by some miracle they reached the north-east corner of the square without getting shot.

They hunkered down behind the last stall. Timur was waiting at the kerbside and sprang the doors as soon as he spotted them. Connor scanned the area for threats. They had to sprint across fifteen or so metres of open ground to reach the safety of the armoured vehicle. That would take three to four seconds – more than enough time for a professional hit man to take aim and fire off an entire clip.

'It's now or never,' said Jason, glancing nervously at the roof of the GUM department store.

Connor couldn't see his gunman anywhere, or the supposed sniper. Still, that didn't mean the assassin wasn't watching and waiting for his target to break cover. Then Connor spotted the FSB agent pushing through the crowd, her gun held aloft as she talked rapidly into a radio. They had no choice but to risk running.

With a nod to Jason, the three of them charged over to the waiting Mercedes. Feet pounding on the tarmac, Connor braced himself for a lethal round to take him or Feliks down.

Ten metres . . . five metres . . . three metres . . .

Jason dived into the back of the car, followed by Feliks and finally Connor, who slammed the door shut behind them.

Wheels screeching, the Mercedes tore away.

'There's Ana!' cried Jason, as they whipped past a metro station.

Connor caught a glimpse of ice-blonde hair and the black oblong backpack of her violin case. Then she was gone.

'Don't worry,' said Connor, seeing the concern on Jason's face. 'She looked as if she was heading away from the danger.'

Police sirens wailed throughout the city as Red Square was put into lockdown. Timur took a hard right and the three of them were thrown around in the back seat. Riding up the kerb, weaving between vehicles and speeding down the wrong side of the road, Timur drove the Mercedes like a rally racing car.

Connor and Jason strapped Feliks into his seat belt before securing themselves.

'Where's Lazar?' grunted Timur, his brow a knot of concentration as he drove.

Connor caught the bodyguard's eye in the rear-view mirror. 'He didn't make it,' he replied.

Timur punched the steering wheel and swore heavily in Russian. 'What happened?' he demanded, his voice gruffer than ever.

'Professional hit,' Connor replied. 'Gunman in the crowd –'

'Sniper!' corrected Jason.

Connor wasn't going to argue with Jason's opinion as more furious swearing issued forth from the bodyguard. In fact, it was best to keep all options open. He was aware there could easily have been more than one gunman.

With Feliks strapped in, Connor did his best to patch up the bleeding graze to his Principal's head with the emergency first-aid kit from his Go-bag.

'Connor, I must admit that was quick thinking back there,' said Jason, passing him a bandage. 'That steam cloud was genius!'

'Thanks,' Connor replied. He half-smiled at his partner. 'And you did a good job of clearing a path through that crowd. You see, we do make a good team!'

'Don't get all mushy on me,' said Jason. But Connor could see that his partner was smiling too. Was this a breakthrough in their relationship?

'Wouldn't dream of it!' Connor replied as he tied off the bandage round Feliks's head and checked he was OK.

Feliks gave a wide-eyed nod. Then Connor took out his smartphone and dialled Buddyguard HQ to report in. The attack would soon register on their international security feed and he wanted Charley to know they were safely out of the kill zone.

'Another hailstorm!' he informed Charley. 'Assassination attempt. Little Bear secure, but Alpha BG down. Jason thinks it was a sniper, but I also saw a suspect shooter in the crowd.'

'Did you ID the shooter?' asked Charley.

'No, but I swear I've seen him somewhere before.'

'Can you describe him?'

'Yeah, he's of average build, with a greyish complexion and . . .' Connor frowned. The man's features were fading from his memory like sand through his fingers. 'Sorry, I can't remember much about him. It was crazy back there.'

'Don't worry,' said Charley. 'Amir tells me your contact lens should have recorded the last hour automatically. He's going to remotely upload the video file to our server to identify the man you're talking about.'

'But how will he know which one I mean?'

'Amir says the camera automatically focuses on where you're looking. It should be obvious. I'll report back to you as soon as we have an ID match.'

The Mercedes pulled up to the mansion's main gate, having crossed Moscow in record time. 'We're back at the cave,' Connor told her.

'Thank goodness,' said Charley, relief in her voice. 'Stay safe, Connor.' She signed off.

As the Mercedes rolled to a stop by the driveway's marble fountain, they were greeted by an unexpected sight.

'Papa!' called Feliks, suddenly breaking from his daze and jumping out of the car.

Waiting on the stone steps, Viktor Malkov clasped his son tightly in his arms. The billionaire looked drawn and haggard from his time in jail, but also hardened like a beaten nail. He glanced over at the car as Timur, Connor and Jason emerged.

'Lazar?' he questioned.

Timur simply shook his head.

A scowl like a thundercloud descended over Viktor's expression. 'The Bratva will pay dearly for this,' he declared.

Entering the cathedral, Roman Gurov made the sign of the cross and strode towards the imposing iconostasis, the gilded screen of religious icons rising up like an army to the ceiling. With his assistant close on his heels, their footsteps echoed off the tiled floor as they passed between the stone pillars of faith and approached the man who stood silent before the screen's holy doors. Hands clasped in front of his chest, head bowed in prayer, he remained as stock-still as the icons he paid tribute to. Then he crossed himself and made his way over to a golden urn bristling with candles, their flames flickering like dying souls in the gloom.

The Pakhan and his assistant joined him in selecting a long thin beeswax candle and lighting it in an offering. The delicate scent of sweet honey perfumed the chill air.

'An assassination attempt in Red Square!' hissed their comrade in a low harsh whisper. 'Are you out of your mind?'

'It wasn't our work,' said Roman stiffly.

The man's eyes narrowed, the flames of a dozen candles glinting in his dark pupils. 'You mean . . . there's another player in the game?'

Roman nodded.

'Who?'

'We've yet to find out,' Roman admitted.

'Eyes on the ground reported sniper fire,' Nika replied on her boss's behalf. 'So it could be a lone wolf, but the careful planning of the attack suggests otherwise. The assassin had to know timings, locations, vantage points, escape routes and so forth, all in advance. The mark of a professional hit.'

'But the attempt failed,' pointed out their comrade.

'That's the assumption,' replied Nika.

A frown creased the man's smooth forehead. 'Are you suggesting the boy *wasn't* the target?'

Nika gave a non-committal shrug. 'All evidence suggests the assassin was a highly skilled marksman. The shots were made over a distance of two hundred metres with a fair crosswind. Yet the bodyguard Lazar was hit straight through the neck, then in the heart. Both with pinpoint accuracy.'

Their comrade pursed his thin lips. 'Surely the bodyguard was protecting the boy. Took the bullets for him.'

'That's what I thought,' said Roman.

'And that is a distinct possibility,' agreed Nika. 'If so, the boy was extremely fortunate. Interestingly, our operative remarked on Feliks's two cousins. They could be the real reason the boy is still alive.'

The man looked sideways at the Pakhan's assistant. 'Go on.'

'It may just have been survival instinct, but the two cousins gave body-cover to the boy and extracted him in what was observed to be a *professional* manner.'

Roman and his comrade exchanged dark looks.

'This is the second time these *cousins* have intervened,' his comrade remarked, the man's tone taking on the steely edge of a honed blade. 'You need to find out who they *really* are.'

'I'm already on to it,' assured Roman. 'I've also got men hunting down this rogue sniper. I don't like loose cannons.'

'And what about the Black King? How come he's walked free?'

Roman's jaw tightened, his reply low and furious. 'He had a battalion of lawyers and an influential unknown backer. Some strings were pulled, some threatened, some even cut! The Black King isn't working alone.'

His face half in shadow, the comrade stared up at an ancient fresco of a long-dead martyr. 'You suspect the Americans?'

Roman shook his head. 'Not their style to get their hands so dirty. But it has all the signs of foreign intervention.'

The comrade's eyes burned into Roman. 'Do I need to worry? Is this situation getting out of hand?'

'No!' Roman replied firmly. 'I intend for our asset to take the Black King out of the game.'

'I still question whether that's the best move.'

A cruel smile sliced across Roman's face. 'Wasn't it Stalin who said, *Death solves all problems – no man, no problem.*'

His comrade conceded the point with the smallest of nods. 'And what about the boy?'

'The pawn is still in play,' he replied. 'But not for much longer.'

CHAPTER 43

'I've been so worried for you,' said Anastasia, hurrying over as Connor, Jason and Feliks entered the Year 11 common room.

'Aww, no need to be,' said Jason, puffing out his chest. 'I'm fine.'

Anastasia flashed him a smile in passing, then embraced Feliks. 'Are you OK?' she asked him.

Connor tried not to laugh at Jason's crestfallen look. Feliks nodded, a slight flush rising in his cheeks at her unexpected display of affection.

'Red Square was shut down when I got there,' she explained. 'The place was in total chaos. Police everywhere. They said it was a terrorist attack.'

'No, it was an assassination attempt,' Connor corrected her, keeping his voice low. 'Against Feliks.'

Anastasia put a hand to her mouth. 'Oh my –'

'It's all good,' Feliks reassured her. 'My bodyguard took the bullet for me.'

Anastasia collapsed into a chair. 'That sounds horrible. Did Lazar die?'

Feliks gave a brief nod as he sat down next to her. 'He was shot through the neck. Then the heart. Blood spewed everywhere. It was like a horror movie.'

'Oh, I'm so sorry,' said Anastasia, resting a hand on Feliks's arm. 'You must be devastated.'

Feliks shrugged indifferently. 'That was his job. He knew the risks.'

Connor exchanged a look of disbelief with Jason. Feliks's lack of grief was telling: Lazar's sacrifice was no more than expected service to him. It made Connor question why he was risking his life for someone who obviously valued it so little.

'So how did you escape?' Anastasia asked.

'Connor and Ja–'

'We were lucky, I guess,' said Connor, cutting Feliks off before he gave too much away. 'The other bodyguard, Timur, was close by in his car and we managed to reach it.'

Anastasia sighed. 'Well, I'm just glad you're all safe,' she said, her gaze lingering briefly on Jason. Turning back to Feliks, she let out a faltering laugh. 'We're not having much luck with our dates, are we? And it's such a shame they've closed off the festival in Red Square. I was looking forward to seeing the ice sculptures with you.'

Feliks fished out his phone. 'I think I got a couple of shots of the ice dragon before it was destroyed,' he said, flicking through his photo album.

Anastasia shifted closer to take a look. 'Wow! It's huge,' she exclaimed.

As she admired the dragon sculpture, Connor felt his own phone vibrate in his pocket. He glanced at the screen. 'Excuse me,' he said.

Stepping out into the corridor, Connor found a quiet corner to speak. 'Hi, Charley, everything OK?'

'Amir has isolated your suspect from the lens video,' she replied. 'I'm sending over the picture to your phone now. Is that him?'

An image downloaded of a lean-faced man with a pale complexion. While his features were otherwise unremarkable, the deadness in his bone-grey eyes was instantly and chillingly familiar.

'That's him,' said Connor. 'Who is he?'

'That's the thing,' said Charley. 'We've no idea. He doesn't register on any criminal databases – police, MI5, CIA, Interpol. In fact he doesn't show up on the grid at all.'

'How can that be?'

'Either he is completely clean,' explained Charley, 'or he has somehow globally deleted any files referencing him.'

Connor frowned. 'Is that even possible?'

'According to Amir, yes. But it would require high-end, government-level resources to achieve. So it's unlikely. Furthermore, Jason's video feed sighted a muzzle flash on the roof of the GUM department store, confirming his suspicion there was a sniper.'

Connor grimaced; Jason *had* been right. 'Then he wasn't a threat?' he said, wondering why he still didn't feel at ease.

There was a pause on the end of the line, then Charley asked, 'What does your gut instinct say?'

Connor replied without hesitation. 'He's dangerous.'

'Then if you see him again, consider him a threat,' said Charley, the slight crack in her voice betraying her concern. 'Amir has uploaded the suspect to your contact lens's facial recognition software. Let's hope it doesn't flash red.'

Signing off, Connor pocketed his phone and returned to the common room. Jason was now settled on a sofa with Anastasia, chatting away. As he approached, she rose to her feet. 'I was just going for a drink,' she said, nodding at the vending machine in the corner. 'Do you want anything?'

'No, I'm fine,' he replied vaguely, his mind on the mystery grey man. Something about him tugged at his memory. Then, looking around, he turned to Jason. 'Where's Feliks?'

Jason's gaze followed Anastasia as she headed over to the vending machine. 'Oh, he's gone to the toilet,' he said absently.

'You didn't go with him?' questioned Connor.

Jason gave Connor a weird look. 'Hey, mate, I may be his bodyguard, but I'm not going to hold it for him!'

Connor glared at his partner. 'After Red Square we shouldn't be leaving Feliks alone, even for one second.'

Jason waved off his concern. 'Chill out, Connor! We're in school. This is a secure zone.'

Connor fought back the urge to shout at him. He couldn't believe his partner was prioritizing his chat-up attempts over protecting their Principal. He needed to have serious words with Jason – maybe even report him – but now wasn't the time. Not if he wanted to ensure their Principal was safe. 'What about Stas and Vadik?'

Jason pointed out of the window. 'I saw them outside on the field just a few minutes ago. They're not anywhere near Feliks.'

The field, knee-deep in snow, was dotted with clusters of students engaged in enthusiastic snowball fights. Connor sighted a couple of Stas's gang but couldn't see Stas or Vadik. 'So where are they now?'

Jason shrugged irritably. 'I don't know. Building a snowman? Listen, Feliks will be back in a minute and you'll have worried over nothing.'

'You two OK?' asked Anastasia, handing Jason a bottle of apple juice.

'Yeah, like two roos in a pouch!' joked Jason.

Connor rolled his eyes and strode out of the common room. The toilet block was only a few metres down the corridor. As he headed towards the door, Connor just hoped Jason was right – that he was simply being too uptight. He knew there was security on the school gates and, apart from Stas and Vadik, there'd been no evidence of any threats in the school grounds. If their Principal couldn't even go to the toilet on his own, it meant they studied in a seriously dangerous school.

Entering the boys' toilets, Connor called out. 'Feliks?'

His voice echoed off the tiles. No one answered.

He checked every cubicle. All empty.

Had he missed Feliks coming out? If so, where had he gone? Connor cursed Jason for taking his eye off the Principal.

Then as he exited the toilet block, Connor spotted Feliks's phone on the floor, its screen smashed.

Feliks's attackers had taken him by surprise, coming up behind as he stood at the urinal. A bag had been thrust over his head, then his face smashed into the wall, stunning him. In moments his wrists and ankles were bound with plastic ties, and he was bundled into a jumbo-sized kitbag. He'd called for help but got a knee in the head for his efforts. His vision swam and stars had blistered in the stifling darkness. Clots of blood from his smashed nose had seeped down the back of his throat, causing him to splutter and gag. Then he'd swung like a pendulum as his attackers had hauled him out of the toilet block and down the corridor. The voices of other pupils passed by tantalizingly close. A set of doors had squeaked open and his straitjacket of a bag was hit by a blast of sub-zero air . . .

Disorientated, Feliks felt himself and the bag being dragged through the freezing snow. Panic and fury consumed him. Where were Connor and Jason when he needed them? Why weren't they doing their job? They were supposed to protect him from this sort of thing! *Die* for him!

Another door grated open. Suddenly the bag was tossed forward and he tumbled down a flight of stone steps. Unable to protect himself, his head, shoulders and back hit the edges hard and he came to rest in a bruised heap at the bottom.

Sick with pain, Feliks heard the long zip of the kitbag open. Then he was heaved out and thrown into a hard wooden chair. His ties were cut, then his hands and feet rebound to the chair's arms and legs.

Still hooded and blind, he called out, 'Wh-who are you?'

Silence. But he could hear his attackers moving round him, as well as strange *whirrs* of machinery.

'W-w-what do you want?'

Feliks felt the cool press of steel against the back of his left hand. There was a clunk and two sharp spikes penetrated his skin. He cried out in shock and pain.

'*Confess!*' hissed a voice.

'C-c-confess what?' cried Feliks.

The steel, now warm with his blood, was pressed against his other hand. His skin was skewered by two more needle-tipped prongs and he let out a shriek.

'*Confess!*'

Feliks groaned. Nausea rose in his throat from the pain. He just hoped he wouldn't throw up in the hood. A sheen of slick sweat coated his brow and he fought for breath. 'Please ... I don't know what you're talking ab–'

Another stab of pain, this time piercing his left forearm. Each spike was like the bite of a fanged snake.

'*Confess, traitor!*'

Feliks screamed in terror as he felt the stinging steel tear at his bare neck.

Connor stormed back to the common room. 'Feliks is gone!'

Jason spun round in his seat, shock and disbelief battling it out in his eyes. 'Are you serious?'

'I think someone has taken him.'

A doubtful frown crossed Jason's brow. 'You're not overreacting again, are you?'

'You call this an overreaction?' said Connor, holding up Feliks's smashed phone.

The gravity of the situation hit Jason and he leapt to his feet, swearing loudly.

'Is Feliks all right?' asked Anastasia, putting aside her can of soda.

'I honestly don't know,' Connor replied, heading for the door with Jason. 'But we need to find him fast.'

Anastasia tagged along behind. 'I'll help,' she said.

'It's all right – we've got this,' said Jason.

Connor knew his partner was trying to maintain the secrecy of their roles, but their priority was to find Feliks. 'Another pair of eyes would be useful,' he said.

Jason nodded his agreement.

'Let's start at the toilet block,' Connor instructed.

They did a quick sweep of the boys' toilets but found no other clues. The windows were too small to escape through and were also locked. The only exit was the main door.

'OK, Feliks can only have gone in one of two directions,' said Connor, looking up and down the corridor. Students milled about, and the end-of-lunchtime bell was due to go. 'Someone must have seen him.'

'I'll take the right-hand corridor,' said Jason. 'You go left.'

Jason strode off with Anastasia in tow, asking people as they went. Connor headed the other way, back towards the common room. But surely if Feliks had come this way he would have seen him? He'd been in the corridor talking on his phone at the time, but his back had been turned to the toilets. There was a slim chance that –

'Hey, Connor!'

He spun round. Anastasia was waving to him.

'You found him?' he called, running back along the corridor.

Anastasia shook her head. 'No, but look at this.'

She pointed to the fire exit, only a short distance from the toilets. The doors weren't completely shut and fresh snow was melting on the tiled floor. 'No students are supposed to use the fire exits,' she said.

'She's bloody Sherlock Holmes!' said Jason as they pushed open the doors.

'Well spotted,' said Connor, impressed. Anastasia was once again proving her potential as a buddyguard.

The snow on the other side was trampled down and a mash of footprints headed away from the building. Between them, like the trail of a huge snake, was a deep groove, evidence of something or *someone* being dragged through the snow.

'Come on,' said Connor, not even bothering with a coat as he followed the tracks.

They crossed the now-deserted playing field and Jason said in a shamed whisper, 'Sorry about this, Connor, I should've –'

'Too late for sorrys,' said Connor, his breath frosting in the chill air. 'Let's just find him.'

'But what if this trail leads nowhere?' asked Anastasia. 'What if I'm wrong?'

'Then we'll have to backtrack and search the school,' replied Connor. 'Room by room.'

The trail took them in a direct line to the school's maintenance building. Rounding the corner, they followed the footprints to a rusted metal door. That's when they heard the tortured scream.

'Shut him up,' ordered a gruff voice. 'We don't want the whole school hearing.'

The hood was ripped off. Blinking in the gloom, Feliks looked fearfully around. The room was humid and airless, with a heavy stench of burning oil. The walls sweated grease and grime and in the corner an old industrial boiler clunked and kettled. The only window was a sliver of glass at the very top near the ceiling, a weak shaft of sunlight falling upon him.

As he went to cry out for help, an oily rag was stuffed into his mouth.

'Good. That should stop the crybaby.'

Though Feliks hadn't yet seen his kidnappers, he had a clear view of the industrial-size staple gun that one of them held. And, piercing his own hands and forearms, glints of metal strips shone like exclamation marks, circled by blood that dripped in lines to the floor.

'*Confess, traitor!*' said the voice once more.

Inside the hood Feliks hadn't heard the voice clearly, but now he recognized it . . . Stas!

His tormentor stepped out of the shadows, Vadik to his right, the high-powered spring-loaded staple gun primed like a real automatic weapon. Alexei, Zak and Gleb hung round too, vampires to the brutal interrogation.

'Do it!' Stas ordered.

With a sadistic grin, Vadik pressed the staple gun to the side of Feliks's neck and pulled the trigger.

Feliks's eyes flared wide. The heavy-duty staples felt like red-hot pins being driven through his skin. He let out an almighty scream, only for it to be smothered by the rag.

'*CONFESS!*' Stas repeated. The word sounded like a hammer blow to Feliks each time.

Feliks tried to talk, but all that came out was a muffled whimper.

With an amused smirk, Stas pulled out the gag. 'Are you ready to confess?'

'W-w-what do you want me to confess to?' Feliks spluttered.

'Boris's *accident*,' said Stas. 'We know he was pushed. We know you arranged it.'

'I don't know what you're talk–'

Stas rammed the rag back in and Vadik raised the staple gun again.

'Put a staple in his eye,' ordered Stas.

Vadik looked twice at his friend. 'Are you sure –'

'Do as I order.'

Vadik shrugged and lined up the gun.

'Hold on! Aren't you going a bit far, Stas?' questioned Gleb. He and Alexei both looked uncomfortable at the direction the interrogation was taking.

Stas glared at him. 'Do I need to remind you that Boris still has his leg in a cast?' he snapped. 'This little runt Feliks has got to admit his guilt. Then justice can be served and we can *punish* him for his crime.'

As Vadik approached, gun in hand, Feliks struggled wildly in the chair, whipping his head from side to side, trying to shift out of the line of fire.

'Gleb, hold his head,' Stas ordered. When Gleb didn't move, he barked, '*Now!*'

Reluctantly, Gleb took Feliks's head in his hands. But he needed Alexei's help.

As the dark line of the staple gun's mouth drew closer and closer, Feliks clamped his eyelids shut, yelling and screaming through his gag. Hoping against hope they wouldn't really do it.

Then he felt fingers prising his eyelids open. And he knew they would.

'He's in the boiler room!' said Connor, rushing to the door and yanking on the handle.

But the door wouldn't budge.

A voice they knew only too well demanded, 'This is your last chance . . . *CONFESS!*'

Through a narrow grimy window at knee-height, Connor spotted Stas looming over the sorry figure of their Principal bound to a chair and bleeding. Vadik held a staple gun levelled at Feliks's right eye.

'They're torturing him!' cried Anastasia. 'You've got to stop them!'

Jason now leant his weight against the door. In the basement Feliks looked like he was desperately trying to speak and Stas pulled a rag from his mouth.

'OK, OK, I confess!' Feliks blabbed, tears running down his cheeks. 'I got my bodyguard Timur to rough Boris up . . . but the way he treated me at the club, he deserved it!'

Stas crossed his arms in triumph. 'And *you*, Feliks, deserve a bit more face control. Vadik, staple back his ears!'

Together Connor and Jason barged their shoulders against the door. It grated open a fraction. They charged once more and the three of them rushed inside.

'STOP!' Connor shouted as Vadik pressed the staple gun to Feliks's ear.

Vadik glanced up, sneering. 'Your guardian angels are too late, Feliks.'

The staple gun *kechunked* and planted its metal prongs into Feliks's right earlobe, pinning it to his skull. Feliks let out a wail of pain.

Jason bounded down the stairs and rugby-tackled Vadik. The two of them went flying, the staple gun skittering across the concrete floor. Connor was right behind him, charging over to protect Feliks.

But the mop-haired Alexei stepped into his path. The boy had picked up a piece of steel pipe from a toolbox and now swung it at Connor's head. Connor barely ducked in time and was forced to retreat as Alexei lashed out with the pipe.

Anastasia darted forward to rescue Feliks, but was grabbed from behind by the meat mountain Gleb. She struggled wildly in his iron grip. Meanwhile Jason and Vadik wrestled on the ground. Then Vadik managed to pin Jason down and began pounding him in the face with his fist.

'Time to break *your* nose now!' he snarled.

Stas watched the melee with ruthless glee. 'No mercy, boys. They're as guilty as this traitor.'

Stas punched the bound Feliks in the gut. Feliks doubled over in his chair. Wild-eyed and gasping for breath, he could only watch as his rescuers were beaten to a pulp.

Cornered by Alexei, Connor wished he had the XT torch with him. But it was still in his Go-bag in the common room. Connor caught a glancing blow to his left arm, the pain jolting like an electric stun gun. Then Alexei took an overhead swing at his head. Connor raised his other arm to protect himself, bracing himself for a broken bone. But the tip of the pipe smashed into an overhead duct instead, and a geyser of scorching steam gushed into the room.

With Alexei distracted by the steam, Connor dived forward, ramming his shoulder into his attacker's midriff. The boy let out a pained gasp and Connor propelled Alexei into the boiler behind. Then, as if he was back in the kickboxing ring, Connor drove his fist in a ferocious upper cut, catching Alexei under the jaw. The boy's head rocked back, his eyes rolled in their sockets and he collapsed to the floor. The pipe clattered away under the boiler.

Connor turned to help the others. Through the haze of steam he saw that Jason was still locked in a vicious brawl with Vadik. His bottom lip was split, his nose bleeding and his left eye swollen, but at least he'd wriggled out of the pin-down. Meanwhile Gleb had lifted Anastasia off the ground and was crushing the breath from her in a bear hug. But she was still fighting on. Snapping her head back, she smashed Gleb on the bridge of the nose. He staggered under the impact and Anastasia slipped free of his grip. Then she roundhouse-kicked him in the thigh.

Realizing that Anastasia could handle her own battle, Connor rushed to release Feliks, only to be confronted by Stas.

'Get out of my way,' warned Connor.

'Never mess with a Russian,' Stas replied. Out of nowhere he pulled a flick-knife. The blade swiped through the air, its tip flashing like lightning.

Connor leapt back as the steel sliced across his chest. Its razor edge cut the front of his school shirt to shreds . . . but thankfully the stab-proof fabric of his T-shirt beneath stopped the blade going any further. Stas slashed again. This time the knife hit Connor's left forearm. With nothing to protect him, the blade lacerated his bare skin. His arm still numb from the pipe attack, Connor hardly felt the cut, but blood ran freely from the wound.

Stas advanced, the blade flicking out like the stinger of a scorpion.

It's not knife defence. It's knife survival. His instructor's words of warning came back to Connor as he ducked, dived and dodged to avoid the lethal blade.

Seize, Strike and Subdue.

As Stas thrust at his stomach, Connor stepped swiftly to one side and grabbed the outstretched arm. Spinning into Stas's body, Connor put him into an armlock and wrenched hard on the elbow joint to force him to let go of the knife. But Stas clung on. In their tussle for control, they lurched round the room, banging into the boiler, then the pipes, then the wall. Stas was strong and Connor was fast losing his grip. After enduring two fights and with an injured arm, his chances of surviving this brawl were low. As they rebounded off a wall and passed beneath the damaged pipe, in a last desperate effort to disarm him, Connor shoved Stas's hand into the blistering hot steam. Stas screamed and dropped the knife. Then Connor hit him in the jaw with a spinning elbow-strike. The boy fell to his knees, dazed and clutching his scalded hand.

Seize, Strike and *Subdue*!

And Anastasia had subdued Gleb. Pinned against the wall, his face screwed up in agony, the boy was begging her to stop as she drove a knuckle into the base of his neck. Connor couldn't help smiling: she was targeting a particularly excruciating *kyusho* nerve point. The girl had some serious martial arts skills! Meanwhile, Jason had managed to put Vadik in a sleeper hold until the boy passed out in his arms.

Panting hard, Jason joined Connor in the middle of the room. The basement looked like a war zone, bodies lying everywhere.

'You OK?' asked Jason, nodding at Connor's arm.

A quick inspection confirmed the cut wasn't deep, but it still stung like hell. 'I'll live,' Connor said. 'How about you?'

Jason sucked at his split lip and tentatively touched his bleeding nose and bruised eye. 'Pretty decent war wounds, I'd say.'

'Hey, is someone going to free me?' demanded Feliks.

Retrieving Stas's flick-knife, Connor cut his bonds. 'Are you all right?' he asked.

Feliks shook him off, strode over to Stas and kicked him in the gut. Groaning, Stas curled into the foetal position as Feliks kicked him again, before picking up the staple gun. 'Hold him down,' Feliks ordered, a sadistic grin twisting his thin lips. 'Let's see how *he* likes being staple-gunned!'

Connor shook his head. 'No, Feliks! I know you're angry and hurting. But that isn't the way to solve this.'

'Perhaps not, but it will make me feel better.' Feliks held the staple gun to Stas's forehead and fired.

Stas howled in agony, blood springing from the two puncture wounds. Then Feliks grabbed him by the hair and forced the gun to his lips. 'Now his big mouth!'

As Connor moved to stop Feliks, a voice bellowed, '*What the hell is going on down here?*'

Connor turned to see the oil-stained figure of the school's caretaker at the top of the stairs, his face a thunderstorm of fury and outrage.

Stas stared down at the bearskin rug at his feet, the two staple holes in his forehead witness to the flush of bitter shame rising in his cheeks. His father sat stiff in his leather armchair in the mansion's oak-panelled study, his hands clenching the armrests so hard he looked like he might rip them off.

'I-I-I'm sorry, P–'

'Speak up!'

'I'm sorry, Papa, but it wasn't my fault. We were –'

A brutal slap across his face cut him off mid-sentence.

'I don't want excuses,' snapped his father, the man's deep-set eyes blazing with fury. 'Suspended! Maybe even expelled! That isn't what's expected of the son of the Director of the FSB.'

Stas's cheek stung like fire and his head rang. He swallowed hard, trying to hold back the hot rush of tears. He knew from bitter experience that crying would do him no good. That would just result in another beating. Much as Stas admired his father, he was a man to be feared. One who punished rather than praised. As he so often reminded

Stas, he hadn't risen to the top of the FSB security agency by being soft or weak-minded.

'I gave you a simple job to do,' said his father, his tone dangerously even. 'How come you failed me?'

Stas looked up, angry defiance in his eyes. 'I've done everything you've asked of me. I've bullied Feliks, spread rumours, isolated him at school, even *tortured* him. The boy was broken!'

'I'm not talking about that,' said his father dismissively. 'Your prime mistake was to get *caught*.'

His father shook his head in dismay. 'If you're to follow in my footsteps, you'll have to cover your tracks better than that. Now *I* have to mop up your mess! Clear our name and our connection to this debacle.'

Stas held his father's glare. 'We wouldn't have been caught if it wasn't for his stupid cousins!'

His father frowned. 'His cousins?'

Stas nodded. 'They're martial arts experts of some sort, even that new girl. We stood no chance.'

His father leant forward in his chair, suddenly interested. 'Tell me everything you know about these so-called cousins.'

Stas began listing his observations, when his mother entered the study. A short, plump woman with curly brown hair, she was the complete opposite to her husband – warm, gentle and caring.

'Stas, my boy, dinner's ready,' she said, her joyful smile wilting as she noted the red mark on her son's cheek. She turned to her husband. But years of living with the man had taught her not to intervene in such matters. 'Will you be joining us for dinner?'

His father gave a single nod.

'That makes a nice change,' said his mother, her tone light. But Stas understood the insinuation in her reply. His father had been spending one too many nights away from home.

'By the way, the office called,' his mother added as she led Stas towards the dining room. 'Your assistant says a banker has been found murdered in the Khimki Forest. An FSB agent has been assigned and is looking into it. He believes it's a Bratva hit job.'

His father swore under his breath. 'That's all I need, what with Viktor Malkov's rally happening tomorrow!'

His mother shook her head in sympathetic dismay. 'The Bratva certainly make life difficult for you, my dear.'

His father rose from his chair. 'Oh, I wouldn't say that, but I will have to check it out.'

'What, now?' his mother exclaimed. 'What about dinner?'

His father let out a weary sigh. 'You're right. The dead banker is going nowhere. I'll deal with it in the morning.'

'Look at the crowds!' said Feliks, pointing with glee to the masses gathered in Triumfalnaya Square for the *Our Russia* rally. 'They've all come to see *my* father.'

This was the first time Connor had witnessed Feliks truly smile since his assault in the boiler room the previous day. Perhaps even since the start of the operation. His humiliation and torture at the hands of Stas and Vadik had left Feliks more morose than ever and in desperate need of a boost in self-esteem. A situation made worse due to their suspension from school pending further investigation – and the possibility of expulsion hanging over them, even for Stas and Vadik.

But for now the brutal battle in the boiler room seemed a world away from the cheering chaos of the rally, and it was obvious Felix was not only proud of his father but bolstered by his father's popularity too. Yet harsh reminders of the incident could be seen on all of them. Feliks was dotted with plasters on his hands, arms, ears and neck. And though Jason had managed to escape having his nose broken, he looked like he'd been in a car crash, with a black eye, swollen lip and bruised cheek. Connor had his left arm bandaged, the knife cut superficial yet painful. Anastasia had got off the lightest with just a few bruised ribs and Connor guessed the worst for her was the threat of expulsion.

They all stood together on one side of a scaffolded stage, sheltered behind a tower of speakers. The throng of faces and waving flags stretched in all directions, filling the square and spilling over into the nearby streets. Dominating the centre of the demonstration stood the resolute and imperious statue of the famous Russian poet Vladimir Mayakovsky. And at the far end of the square, rising up like a Soviet rocket, was the sand-coloured facade of the Peking Hotel with its neo-Gothic clock tower and golden spire.

Connor scanned the crowd. He quickly spotted the FSB agent with the bob of dark hair, trying to blend in with the *Our Russia* supporters. But he was careful not to show any recognition, wanting to maintain the small advantage he now had over her. The other people around her appeared to be genuine supporters. There was a heavy police presence in the square and Malkov's security team guarded the stage. While Viktor was the prime target for an attack at the rally, Connor knew that Feliks was at risk too – no more proof was needed than the two attempts at the ice rink and Red Square, first to kidnap him, then to kill him. It would have been far safer for him to stay at the mansion, but there'd been no way Feliks was going to miss his father's rally.

Timur stood close, the big man packing a concealed MP-9. Jason was on equally high alert, having learnt his lesson the previous day. So Connor got no arguments this time when he told him to take point. In fact Jason was following all his orders without a single complaint. In their debrief to HQ over Feliks's abduction, Connor had left out his partner's failure to keep watch over their Principal, for which Jason was grateful. He knew he'd failed in his duty and clearly appreciated Connor covering for him.

'I wish my parents could see this,' said Anastasia, gazing in wonder at the vast crowd. 'So *many* people taking a stand against corruption.'

'Perhaps they'll see it on TV,' Feliks suggested.

'That's if the state media doesn't censor the coverage,' said his father with a wry grin. 'Even if they do, though, news of this rally will spread through our supporters.'

Viktor put an arm round his son, obviously enjoying the mass of people chanting his name to the wintry sky. 'This is what it's all about, Feliks,' he said. 'Planting the thought of freedom in people's minds. Watering it with words, and letting the seed grow. Until it blossoms into something great and powerful.'

Viktor looked his son in the eye. 'And when I'm in power, no one will dare touch you again. Not even the son of the FSB Director!'

Feliks gazed at his father in awe and admiration.

Dmitry approached. 'We're all set to go,' he informed Viktor. 'But I still have concerns.'

Viktor smiled. 'What do you have to be concerned about, my friend? Just look at the support we have. This is a true turning point in Russian history.'

'I too want to make history, but not at the expense of your life,' said Dmitry gravely.

Viktor frowned. 'What do you mean?'

Dmitry glanced in the direction of Timur, then lowered his voice. 'Without Lazar overseeing the team, security isn't as tight as I'd like.'

Viktor put a hand on his adviser's shoulder and whispered, 'Listen, losing Lazar was like losing a brother for me. He'd been at my side since I started my political career back in Salsk. But he of all people wouldn't want me to pull out now. Timur might not be as sharp as Lazar, but he's loyal. Besides, we have the *guarantee* of our backer.'

Dmitry sighed. 'That may be the case. But we haven't been able to check all areas.' He gave Viktor a hard look. 'The authorities have denied our security teams access to certain buildings surrounding the square. They say only the police have the jurisdiction to carry out such searches. But I suspect foul play.'

Viktor stared out across the crowd, eyeing the windows that looked blankly down on to the square. Any one of them potentially harboured a sniper. 'I know the risks. I always have. There's trusted security in place round the stage. I'm wearing my bulletproof vest as always, and just look at the police presence,' he said, pointing to the ranks of officers lining the square. 'No one would be foolish enough to attempt anything today.'

'Yes, but the police aren't here to protect you,' Dmitry reminded him. 'They're here to disperse the rally.'

'Then let's start with my speech before they do.'

From the lofty heights of the church-like spire that topped the Peking Hotel, the assassin had a bird's-eye view over Triumfalnaya Square. Below, the mass of demonstrators swelled like a rippling ocean. The cause of *Our Russia* was gaining ever-increasing momentum and thousands of supporters had flocked to see its leader and vent their fury and frustration at the current government. At the far end of the square, like a lifeboat among the waves of flags and banners, was the stage. And upon the stage stood a lone microphone, awaiting the presence of Viktor Malkov.

Sniper rifle assembled. Magazine loaded. Sights zeroed. Bullet chambered. The assassin too was awaiting the billionaire's appearance.

Keeping an eye on the wind speed, the assassin focused the rifle's scope on the microphone stand. Even at a distance of a hundred and fifty metres, it would be child's play to knock the stand over with a single shot.

Then the real target strode on to the stage.

The crowd erupted with cheers, whistles and whoops as Viktor Malkov raised his fists in a two-handed salute.

There was a squeal of feedback from the PA system, then the leader of *Our Russia* spoke, his voice booming across the square.

'For over half a century, this square has been a symbol of protest,' he declared. 'From the banned poetry readings of the sixties, to the anti-Communist rallies of the eighties, to the Strategy-31 demonstrations of the past decade. And now today we stand here to make our protest! To make a change! To make *Our Russia* ours again!'

The crowd burst into applause.

'The voice of the people *will* be heard!'

More cheers and shouts of approval echoed round the square.

'Our protests will turn into a mighty river and sweep away the pillars of lies and corruption!'

The square became a blur of banners and a roar of noise, the people's cheers rising up like a wave and breaking against the rooftop parapet that concealed the assassin.

Once the crowd had calmed, Viktor continued in a quieter, grave tone. 'The fish rots from the head,' he told them. 'And the head of Mother Russia is infested with maggots. The government is plagued with members of the Bratva, who feed and grow fat on *your* labours –'

The assassin's earpiece crackled. '*Execute the Black King now!*'

With a final check of wind speed and a measured slowness of breath, the assassin lined up the target in the rifle's sights. It would have to be a head shot. The assassin had been warned that the target would be wearing body armour.

Viktor Malkov's face appeared sharp in the scope, his eyes dead centre of the cross hairs.

The assassin's finger rested upon the trigger, a light squeeze all that was now required.

Three breaths. Then the assassin would fire in the momentary stillness following the final exhale.

Three . . . two . . .

The hard snub of a gun barrel was pressed against the back of the assassin's skull.

'What's the victim's name?' asked the FSB Director, staring down into the shallow grave. The deep snow had been cleared to reveal a muddy hole in the forest floor where a decomposing body lay at the bottom. Apparently a hiker had discovered the murder victim when her dog, hunting for rabbits, had dug up the remains.

The FSB agent, an eager young man with a slick of black hair and sharp inquisitive eyes, glanced at his notes. 'Nikolay Antonov. A financial manager for Vorstock Bank. His wife reported him missing three weeks ago.'

He knelt down beside the hole and pointed at the corpse's wrists where the skin had been rubbed raw. 'His hands were bound. And you can see here and here . . .' He indicated the burn marks on the man's chest. 'The victim was tortured, most likely electrocuted, before being –' he pointed to the dark circular hole in the man's forehead – 'executed.'

The agent stood up and, clearly wishing to impress his boss, continued with his report. 'From my initial research, the victim appears to be a high-profile banker with suspected connections to the Moscow Bratva. In fact there's a very good chance he was their primary money-launderer. With your permission, I'd like to launch a full –'

'Bury it,' said the FSB Director, cutting him off mid-flow.

The agent frowned. 'You mean . . . the body?'

'No, I mean the whole investigation.'

'B-but this could be the FSB's biggest lead into the Moscow Bratva in years,' argued the agent. 'This man may have had direct contact with the Pakhan himself. There's even a possibility that we could uncover the mafia boss's actual identity!'

The FSB Director gave the agent a hard stare. 'Are you disobeying a direct order?'

The agent stiffened. 'Of course not, sir!'

'Then bury it,' he commanded as a red-headed woman strode over, her black leather boots crunching in the thick snow. The FSB Director turned to his assistant. 'What is it?'

'Sorry to interrupt, Mr Gurov, but I've an urgent update on the Malkov rally.'

Roman Gurov nodded and headed back towards his car with his assistant at his side. He glanced back over his shoulder at the agent, who was now instructing his team to remove the body from its shallow grave. 'Reassign that agent to a Siberian outpost.'

'Of course, Mr Gurov,' replied Nika with a thin smile. She almost pitied the poor agent, who had no clue that the mighty head of the FSB, Roman Gurov, was also the merciless leader of the Bratva.

In a harsh low whisper, Roman added, 'And punish whichever *krysha* enforcer was responsible for Nikolay's death. I said to dispose of the banker *permanently*. I cannot have corpses coming back to haunt me! Not in my position.'

'Of course not,' said Nika, stiffening. As both FSB Director and Pakhan of the Moscow mafia, her boss walked a razor-thin line. In fact, the lines often blurred. On the outside, the FSB and the Bratva appeared to be two very different organizations: the former upholding law and security; the latter spawning crime and disorder. But, on the inside, much of the same blood flowed, her boss having recruited a dozen or so FSB officials to operate in the interests of the Bratva, and Nika being his first and most loyal employee.

As they approached his car, Roman asked, 'So, do you have good news for me?'

'I'm afraid not,' Nika replied, coming to a stop by the passenger door. 'After giving the order to execute the Black King, we lost communication with the asset. I sent an agent to investigate. The asset was found dead, a bullet to the back of his head.'

Roman's expression became stony. He didn't even blink. 'Are you telling me someone assassinated our assassin?'

Nika swallowed, sensing the rage building in her boss. 'It would appear so.'

'And what's happening at the rally now?'

'Malkov is still addressing the crowd.'

Roman slammed a fist on top of the car roof, denting the metalwork. 'He must be silenced! Do *whatever* it takes to stop him!'

'It is better to be slapped with the truth than kissed with a lie,' Viktor Malkov declared to the crowd. 'The government is the Bratva; the Bratva is the government. They claim your economic woes are the result of foreign intervention, but the truth is they are bleeding Mother Russia dry!'

Boos and jeers rumbled through Triumfalnaya Square at the mention of the Bratva and a shadow fell over the rally's jubilant atmosphere. Connor sensed the change in mood and his alert level shot up another notch. Feliks was by his side, the boy lapping up his father's rousing speech. But Connor was barely listening; his entire focus was on the crowd and their surroundings, watchful for the slightest hint of danger.

'But I vow to fight for you, the good people of Russia,' Viktor went on. 'To represent a new Russia. *Our* Russia.'

The boos transformed into cheers and applause, and the rally's euphoric atmosphere returned.

Viktor gripped the microphone in both hands. 'So let's take a stand. Vote for change! Vote for *Our* Russia!'

Chants of 'MALKOV! MALKOV! MALKOV!' exploded from his supporters and grew so loud that the windows in the surrounding buildings literally shook in their frames. As their leader raised his arms in his customary two-fisted salute, a cheer went up like the roaring launch of a fighter jet.

Connor was relieved the speech was almost at an end and that they could soon head back to the safety of the mansion. The crowd had swelled to an almost unimaginable size. Half the city seemed to have turned out to hear the billionaire speak. And all the time Connor had been on edge, waiting for some threat against Viktor or Feliks to materialize.

When it did, the attack came from the least expected quarter.

Without warning, as Viktor began making his closing remarks, the police suddenly moved in to disperse the crowd. Although the supporters were behaving peacefully and within the law, the police acted as if a riot was taking place. They fired tear-gas canisters, the toxic smoke spewing out like dragon's breath across the square. As people tried to escape the choking fumes, the police hemmed them in with riot shields. And when the crowd pushed back, the police beat them viciously with their batons.

Viktor appealed for calm, but the police appeared to have their own agenda. They tore into his supporters, goading them to react, then arresting any who did.

A unit of heavily armed police officers made a beeline for the stage.

'Get Viktor out of here!' Dmitry ordered Timur.

The hulking bodyguard hustled Viktor off the stage and down the scaffolded steps. Joined by three of the security team, they formed a defensive human shield round the billionaire and made for the evac point, with Dmitry close behind. Following them, Connor and Jason grabbed Feliks and bundled him down the steps, Anastasia hot on their heels.

Acting like a snowplough, Timur and his men drove a wedge through the crowd and headed for Viktor's limo and the back-up SUV. The vehicles were parked in a nearby side street that had been barricaded off so that the route remained clear on to the main Garden Ring Road. But with people and police pressing in on all sides Connor and the others started to trail behind. He noticed the FSB agent on their tail too.

'Keep up!' Connor shouted at Anastasia, not wanting to lose her in the crush. Buffeted like lifebuoys in a storm, Connor and Jason fought to hold on to Feliks. The square was so packed they were drowning in bodies, and a few times Feliks was almost torn from their grip. At the same time the police continued to tighten their net round Viktor and his men.

A tear-gas canister whizzed past, acrid smoke clouding the air.

Feliks began coughing and Connor's eyes started streaming.

'Jason!' cried Anastasia, her ice-blonde locks disappearing in the haze of smoke as she fell further and further behind. She desperately reached out to them, but the crowd swallowed her up.

'We can't leave her!' Jason gasped, the tear gas searing his throat.

As much as he hated to say it, Connor reminded him, 'Feliks is our priority.'

'That's right,' said Feliks, coughing and his dark eyes shining with terror and tears. '*I'm* your priority.'

The boy's total selfishness appalled Connor. He couldn't believe Feliks was so quickly abandoning his friend, perhaps his only friend, and one who'd recently fought to help him. Through stinging bloodshot eyes Connor looked at Jason, who was furious and distraught. They both knew their duty was to protect Feliks first. Yet, after everything they'd been through with Anastasia, Connor considered her one of them. He made up his mind. 'I've got Feliks,' he gasped. 'You get Anastasia.'

With a brief nod, Jason turned back and disappeared into the sea of bodies. Connor pressed on with Feliks. The tear gas was starting to disperse the crowd, enough for them to close the gap on his father. But it had also allowed some of the police through.

A gas-masked officer seized Dmitry from behind. As two more pounced on him, Timur and the other bodyguards were forced to leave the adviser. Clear who their priority was, they forged on with Viktor. Connor and Feliks – not recognized as targets by the police – managed to slip past while the three officers subdued Dmitry with a heavy barrage of blows from their batons.

The rest of the police unit continued to fight its way through the crowd, aiming to cut off Viktor's escape route. But his supporters, recognizing the threat to their leader, closed ranks and blocked the police advance. Batons rained down and more tear gas filled the air. In spite of the police's efforts, the crowd held firm just long enough to allow Viktor and his bodyguards to reach the side street. Connor and Feliks weren't far behind, their tail of an FSB agent lost in the carnage. Clambering over the barrier, they raced for the limo, its engine already running.

Timur almost threw Viktor into the limo's back seat. Connor shoved Feliks through the open door, then leapt in after. Timur clambered into the limo's front passenger seat as the other bodyguards piled into the escort vehicle.

Coughing and spluttering, Viktor asked, 'Where's Dmitry?'

'He was arrested,' Connor replied.

'Nothing we can do. Let's go!' Timur commanded the driver.

'Not yet!' shouted Connor, desperately looking back for Jason and Anastasia. Beyond the barrier, chaos reigned. The square looked like a battle zone, blood streaming down people's faces, women and children screaming, smoke rising like bomb blasts into the sky. But there was no sign of Jason or Anastasia.

'SHUT THE DOOR!' Timur barked.

'No, wait – I see Jason!' Connor pleaded as he spotted his partner vault the barrier and come sprinting down the road with Anastasia in tow.

The escort vehicle honked impatiently for them to depart. Timur ordered the driver to go. Even as they pulled away, Connor kept the door open, praying the two of them would catch up. By now the police had mounted the barrier and were firing warning shots. As Jason came up alongside the limo, he bundled Anastasia through the open door. Connor grabbed her arm and pulled her inside.

'My bag!' she cried.

'*Leave it*,' Connor shouted as the limo gained speed.

But, with a deft swipe, Jason managed to snatch up the black bag. Then in one last-ditch effort he sprinted after them.

'Come on, Jason!' Connor cried as more shots ricocheted down the street. But Jason was flagging, his breathing harsh from the tear gas. He wasn't going to make it.

Then, as they slowed to take the corner on to the ring road, he dived head first into the limo.

Like a sleek black tank, the armoured stretch limo cruised along the Garden Ring Road unchallenged, the escort vehicle behind, an ever-watchful guardian. Inside the air-conditioned limo, Viktor began laughing, his voice slightly hoarse from the after-effects of the tear gas. 'That was close,' he said.

'Too close,' Connor agreed, blinking the acrid tears from his eyes.

'No, not really. The wolves may be howling, but they're no longer biting.'

'But what about Dmitry?' asked Connor.

Viktor waved away his concern. 'Don't worry. I'll have my lawyers on to it straight away. If they can get me out of jail, then they can certainly free Dmitry.'

Connor just hoped Dmitry *was* in jail. By the looks of the beating he'd had from the police officers, he could just as easily end up in hospital.

'But why did the police attack in the first place?' demanded Feliks angrily, wheezing from the tear gas. 'I couldn't see any reason for it.'

'They didn't need a reason, my son,' said Viktor with another hoarse laugh. '*Our Russia* has become a force to be reckoned with and that scares the establishment. It was inevitable they'd try to break up the rally at some point. I'm just surprised they let me talk for so long. But the police can't have anticipated such huge numbers attending. That's why they hesitated.'

'I wouldn't call tear gas and riot police exactly hesitating,' said Jason.

'No, but they failed to stop the rally. And that's what counts,' replied Viktor, his tone triumphant. 'In the forthcoming elections I'll sweep away the old guard. It's time for a new Russia.'

'Will it really be a *new* Russia?' asked Anastasia.

Viktor nodded. 'I promise to root out all the corruption and make those responsible pay for their crimes. The Russia you'll grow up in, my dear, will be a far cry from the Russia of today.'

Anastasia responded with a brief smile. 'I'm glad to hear it,' she said, before breaking into a hacking cough.

'Are you OK?' Jason asked, putting an arm round her.

Anastasia nodded. 'Just . . . the tear gas.'

'It's horrible, isn't it?' said Feliks, wiping at his bloodshot eyes. 'If I had my way, I'd gas the whole police force.' He noticed Jason's arm round Anastasia and put his hand on her knee. 'I was worried for you. I really was. That's why I sent Jason back.'

Jason's mouth dropped open as he exchanged an incredulous look with Connor. But before he could protest

Anastasia clasped Feliks's hand, saying, 'Thank you, Feliks. I appreciate that. Jason was a true lifesaver.'

The limo entered the mansion grounds, wound its way along the gravel drive and pulled up beside the marble fountain in the centre of the forecourt. Frosted in fresh snow, the mansion looked like an enchanted castle in the late-afternoon sun. Ski-jacketed security guards patrolled the gardens and two armed men were stationed either side of the main entrance. Timur clambered out of the front passenger seat and opened the door for his boss as the escort vehicle behind disgorged the security team.

'Well, I'd better start phoning my lawyers,' said Viktor, stepping out into the chill air.

Timur and the security team escorted Viktor towards the mansion. Feliks followed his father across the forecourt, Connor flanking him, and Jason at Anastasia's side.

'You've forgotten your bag,' the driver called after them. He reached into the vehicle and pulled out a black bag and waved it at Anastasia.

Anastasia frowned. 'That's not mine,' she replied, holding up her own and walking on.

At the exact same moment Connor spotted a ghost-like face peering through an upper window of the mansion. The heads-up-display on his contact lens flashed red three times, confirming the sighting.

Connor's sixth sense went haywire. The grey man. The unidentified bag. It couldn't be coincidence. Connor dived at Feliks and shouted, 'GET DO–'

Then the world turned into a roar of noise, fire and death.

'When I said do whatever it takes, you certainly took me by my word, Nika.'

Roman Gurov strode over to his drinks cabinet, selected a pair of shot glasses and poured out two measures of finest Russian vodka. On the far wall of his office a television screen displayed a news report of the smoking devastation at the Malkov mansion.

Handing Nika a brimming glass, he raised his own in a toast. 'To *My Russia*,' he said with a smirk.

When his assistant didn't join him in the toast, the FSB Director paused, the glass hovering at his lips. 'Why don't you drink? Is the Black King not dead?'

Nika set aside her glass. 'Preliminary reports confirm multiple deaths and casualties. But Viktor Malkov isn't one of them.'

With a furious snort, Roman knocked back his vodka, then hurled the empty glass into the fireplace, where it exploded in a shower of flaming sparks. 'That man has more lives than a cat!'

The FSB Director paced the room. 'Tell me exactly what happened. Why have *you* failed yet again?'

Nika stiffened, realizing that not only her job but possibly her life could be on the line. Those out of favour with the irascible director had a habit of disappearing ... rumour had it, to a Siberian prison camp. 'As per *your* orders,' she emphasized, 'our strategy was to stop the rally and silence Malkov. The police were instructed to move in, disperse the crowds and discredit *Our Russia* supporters. They made numerous arrests. Unfortunately Malkov escaped. The bomb, however, *wasn't* part of the plan.'

Roman stopped pacing and stared at his assistant in astonishment. 'We didn't plant it! Then who did?'

Nika shrugged. 'Agents are searching the site for evidence, as we speak. There's a chance our asset planted it before he was killed, as a back-up in case the shooting failed. But my gut instinct tells me it's another attack by the Red Square lone wolf.'

Roman walked over to the window and stared out at the wintry sky. 'I only wish we had this lone wolf on our team,' he muttered, glancing over at his assistant, and added icily, 'Then we might have more success.'

Nika smarted at her boss's tone. She wasn't to blame for this fiasco. But, as ever, she'd have to clean it up.

'So what have you found out about this lone wolf?' Roman asked.

'Very little, I'm afraid,' said Nika, placing a slim folder on the director's desk. 'He left few traces at the GUM store. All tracks in the snow were cleared. Gun shell casings collected. No fingerprints found anywhere. And CCTV revealed no likely suspects. All we can determine is that the lone wolf is highly trained, a meticulous planner and fires a sniper rifle with 7.62 mm calibre bullets. It's as if this lone wolf is a ghost.'

'Sounds like the perfect assassin to me.'

'I'm hoping the bomb site will provide us with more clues,' said Nika. She placed another folder, slightly thicker, on the desk. 'However, we have had more success with the two supposed cousins. They're definitely not family. While Viktor's son does have distant relatives on his late mother's side, they're still living in the Ukraine.'

'Then who are they?'

'According to their personal records online, just ordinary kids,' said Nika. 'But digging a little deeper, we discovered the records had been doctored. Connor Reeves and Jason King are actually connected to an organization called Buddyguard, a covert training programme for young bodyguards.'

'Young bodyguards!' snorted Roman. 'Don't make me laugh!'

'It's no joke. And you can't deny their effectiveness,' said Nika. 'They took out one of our teams and extracted a Principal under sniper fire. Viktor Malkov has evidently hired them to protect his son. And, by all accounts, they're doing an excellent job.'

Roman grunted. 'No wonder Stas had such trouble with them.' He looked Nika in the eye. 'If this is the case, the two boys are now legitimate targets. *Expendable.* Understood?'

Nika nodded as the FSB Director strode back to the drinks cabinet and poured himself another shot of vodka. 'So tell me, where is Viktor Malkov now?'

'He's pulling back to his dacha in the country. After the attack on the mansion, it's the most secure position f–'

Roman held up a hand, cutting her off. 'I don't care if the dacha's as secure as the Kremlin, I want the Black King *dead.*'

Nika now picked up her own shot glass and took a confident sip. Always in possession of a back-up plan, she informed her boss with a sly smile, 'We do have one piece left in play. A Trojan horse.'

The explosion spread out in a wave of fire and heat. Instantly vaporized, the surrounding snow – and the driver – might never have existed. But the limo stood firm, its armoured panels forcing the blast wave outwards. And in a hail of white marble the fountain of Neptune exploded, one of its lethal shards spearing Timur in the back. The bodyguard fell across Viktor, shielding his boss, while all the other bodyguards were cut to shreds.

The hailstorm of marble struck Jason and Anastasia too. Jason tried to use his jacket to shield them, but they were thrown to the ground, their bodies battered, bleeding and lifeless.

Caught out in the open, only Connor's fast reactions saved his Principal. As he wrapped himself round Feliks, the blast wave knocked them off their feet and marble shrapnel rained down. But Connor's bulletproof jacket absorbed the impacts. Flung forward by the shock wave, Connor's head struck the mansion's stone steps with an explosion of stars and ringing in his ears. Then a curtain

of darkness covered him as the ringing grew louder ...
and louder ... and LOUDER ...

Connor opened his eyes, waking from the nightmare. On the bedside table his smartphone was ringing. He picked it up and mumbled, 'Hello?'

'Connor, it's Charley. How are you doing?'

Connor sat up in bed. Shafts of golden sunlight pushed through the curtains, picking out dust motes and spotlighting the old wooden floorboards. 'OK . . . but I think I've overslept,' he replied, rubbing his eyes, then pinching the bridge of his nose as a dull headache gripped him.

'You're in recovery,' said Charley. 'You're bound to feel a bit groggy.'

Connor glanced round the room. He lay on an iron bedstead. There were no solid gold lampstands and the furniture was simple rustic rather than priceless antique. The velvet burgundy curtains were now plain white cotton and the en-suite bathroom housed a large free-standing bathtub but no chandelier. He was no longer in the mansion, that was for sure. 'Where am I?' he asked.

'Viktor Malkov's dacha. For safety reasons you've been moved to his country estate outside Moscow.'

'How come I don't remember?' he asked, his thoughts foggy and disjointed.

'You've suffered a concussion,' explained Charley. 'Short-term memory loss is to be expected, but let me know if it persists.'

'Sorry . . . *who* are you again?'

'Connor, it's Charley!' she said, suddenly sounding alarmed. 'Please tell me you remember me –'

'Only joking,' said Connor with a laugh. 'You'd have to chop off my head before I'd forget you!'

He slid out of bed, a little wobbly on his feet but otherwise fine as he made his way to the bedroom window. Parting the curtains, he gazed out across the snow-covered grounds of the estate. The dacha, a large, two-storey, wooden country house, was surrounded by tall trees on all sides, their branches frosted white. A long garden dotted with sculptures stretched down to a frozen lake and a thick pine forest.

'That wasn't funny! You seriously had me worried for a moment,' Charley told him sharply. 'In fact the whole bomb attack has us all concerned.'

An image of Jason and Anastasia lying lifeless in the wreckage flashed before Connor's eyes. 'How are the others?' he asked urgently.

'Apart from a few cuts, Jason's fine. So is Anastasia. Like you and Feliks, they were saved by his bulletproof jacket and graphene-fibre trousers. And the statue's pedestal shielded them from the worst of the blast. But Timur was killed, along with the driver, and there were several casualties among the security team. Considering the force of the explosion, it's a miracle you survived at all.'

Connor spotted Jason, Anastasia and Feliks walking round the lake, confirming Charley's words. Relieved, he turned his attention back to Charley. 'Has the bomber been caught?' he asked.

'No,' Charley replied. 'The police have questioned the usual suspects, but no one has claimed responsibility – not even the Bratva. The authorities don't have a clue who it might be.'

Connor narrowed his eyes. Despite his concussion, he hadn't forgotten the face he'd seen in the window. 'I know who it is,' he said.

'Who?'

He told Charley his suspicions.

'You'd better warn Mr Malkov then. By the way, Anastasia's background check has come back clear … apart from one anomaly.'

'Go on,' said Connor.

'I'm pretty sure it's a clerical error, but can you confirm her surname is spelt K-O-M-O-L-O-V-A?'

'Yes, I think so. Why?'

'Well, the only girl the Moscow registry office could find with that name died two years ago.'

Connor watched as Jason followed Anastasia over to a boathouse on the edge of the lake. 'Well, I can assure you she's definitely alive.'

'I know,' said Charley. 'I've seen her picture. She's very attractive.'

'Can't say I've noticed,' Connor replied a little too quickly.

'Nice try, Romeo.' Charley laughed. 'But I'd be worried *you* were dead if you hadn't noticed her looks.'

Connor felt his cheeks flush and was glad this wasn't a video call. 'No comment,' he said. 'But should this be ringing alarm bells?'

'No, as I mentioned before, Russian bureaucracy is a nightmare. I think the registry office has made a mistake and muddled her with someone else. Their records seem a total mess. I just wanted to check the spelling before trying again with Bugsy's help. However, if *I'm* having this much trouble finding out about her past, it'll be a huge advantage to her becoming a buddyguard.'

'So,' said Connor, 'I can recommend her to the colonel for recruitment?'

'I already have,' Charley replied, much to Connor's surprise. 'He's preparing the entry tests for her right now. Once Operation Snowstorm is over, they'll make an approach.'

'That's great news,' said Connor, confident that Anastasia would pass the tests and be an asset to their team.

On the other end of the line Connor heard Charley clear her throat, then say, 'Before we sign off, do you want to hear some more good news?'

Connor plopped himself down on the bed. 'Absolutely. It makes a change from all the bad news here.'

'Well, I don't want to get my hopes up,' Charley said, suddenly sounding unsure. 'But I've been contacted by a Chinese medical research group about a new breakthrough development for spinal injuries. They're seeking a volunteer to try out a pioneering therapy.'

Connor sat up. 'That's wonderful! What sort of therapy?'

'It involves a combination of advanced cell transplantation and microchip implantation.'

'Wow, sounds like they want to turn you into the Bionic Woman. How did they find out about you?'

'That's the strange thing – I don't know. Perhaps the hospital. But I suspect Ash might have something to do with it.'

Connor suppressed a twinge of jealousy at the mention of the name. Ash Wild was a world-famous teen rock star who Charley had once been assigned to protect, and during the course of her assignment they'd fallen for each other. But then she'd suffered her tragic accident. In the aftermath they'd split up, but Ash had donated all the royalties from a song he'd written for her into a recovery fund.

'Sounds like his doing,' said Connor, keeping his tone casual.

'I realize it's a long shot,' Charley admitted. 'I might not even get selected. But if I did, then maybe I could . . . well, who knows. They're not promising anything.'

Connor smiled encouragingly. 'Well, if anyone can make it happen, you can.'

CHAPTER 56

Washed and dressed, Connor felt a whole lot better and after a couple of tablets his headache was gone. Hurrying to join the others by the lake, he grabbed his jacket – the one that had saved his life – and made his way downstairs. Recalling the layout of Malkov's dacha from the operation briefing notes, he passed along the upper landing and down the wide wooden staircase to the main entrance hall, where the antlered head of a stag was mounted proudly over the door.

Dachas were the traditional country retreats for Muscovites. Most were modest affairs with just a small cottage and a plot for growing fruit and vegetables. But Viktor's – like many of Russia's elite – was the equivalent of a rural mansion. While not as grand as his main residence in the city, the dacha still boasted six bedrooms, an indoor swimming pool, a games room, separate staff quarters, the lake for fishing and a thirty-acre forest for hunting.

As he headed for the front door, Connor heard voices in the drawing room.

'I *can't* be seen to be hiding.'

'I appreciate that, Viktor, but it's best you remain here until we secure operations in the city.'

'I won't be intimidated out of Moscow! And *Our Russia*'s rise certainly won't be undermined by one bomb!'

'Need I remind you, the bomb hasn't been the only threat . . .'

At first Connor thought Viktor was speaking with his adviser. But then he remembered Dmitry had been arrested at the rally. And the voice didn't have the same nasal tone as Dmitry's. This one was low, almost breathless, the sort of voice Connor imagined a snake or lizard might have.

'That's why I've extra men patrolling the perimeter of the estate, as well as guarding the house. This is the best location for the time being.'

With both Lazar and Timur dead, Connor guessed the man was the new head of security. Whoever it was, though, Connor had to interrupt the meeting. He had important information. He knew who the bomber was.

'But what about Equilibrium?' Viktor went on. 'Won't they see this as a weakness?'

'Don't worry, Viktor. Your sponsor – and my employer – doesn't question your unwavering commitment to the cause –'

Connor knocked on the door. The voices stopped.

'Come in!' said Viktor.

Connor entered the drawing room. Warm and welcoming, the wood-panelled room was carpeted with a dark-red woven rug over polished floorboards. An antique gold-framed mirror hung above a mahogany drinks cabinet and a cream-coloured Chesterfield sofa with matching armchairs was cosily arranged round a crackling fire in the hearth. Above the mantelpiece a stuffed wolf's head stared ravenously down at him, its teeth set in a snarl.

Viktor sat in one of the armchairs, a cut healing on his cheek and a bandage on his right hand.

Then, as Connor looked round, all the warmth seemed to drain from the room.

Standing by the fire was the bomber.

'Connor, glad to see you up and about,' said Viktor with a grin. 'I've yet to personally thank you for saving my son's life. Without your lightning-fast reactions, he'd have gone the same way as Timur.'

Connor didn't respond, his eyes locked on the threat in the room. Although a fire blazed in the grate, none of its warmth or colour seemed to touch the man, as if he stood in a permanent cold spot in the room – or in fact he *was* the cold spot. The bomber's ice-grey eyes returned his gaze with disturbing indifference. No acknowledgement that they'd seen each other before. No concern that Connor might recognize him. And, what was worse, no indication of any humanity behind those eyes. He was like the wolf mounted above the mantelpiece.

A shiver ran down Connor's spine. Again there was that nagging tug in his mind that he *knew* this man.

Connor finally found his tongue. 'Mr Malkov, call security!'

Viktor stiffened in his chair. 'Why? What's happened now?'

261

Connor moved across to protect the billionaire. 'I suspect this man's behind the bombing and other attacks on you and your son.'

Viktor blinked. 'What did you just say?'

'This man was in your mansion as the bomb went off,' Connor explained. 'I also spotted him just before Feliks was shot at in Red Square. I suspect he followed us in Gorky Park and at the ice rink before the attempted kidnapping. That's one time too many to be a coincidence.'

Viktor looked from Connor to the accused and back again, then laughed. The billionaire stood and joined the bomber by the fire.

'Mr Grey is an associate of mine,' said Viktor, resting a hand briefly on the man's shoulder. 'Our dealings go way back. In fact, he's the one that's been *protecting* me.'

Connor's jaw went slack, his accusation coming back at him like a punch to the gut.

'Mr Grey prevented an assassination attempt at the rally,' explained the billionaire. 'He's also responsible for getting me released from jail so quickly. And he's been watching over Feliks.'

'*Watching over Feliks?*' exclaimed Connor.

'In case other security measures failed,' said Mr Grey pointedly.

'Which they didn't, thanks to Connor and Jason,' acknowledged Viktor. 'I've been telling Mr Grey all about your Buddyguard organization. He's very interested in how you work.'

Connor was shocked. 'B-but, Mr Malkov, you're not

meant to disclose our organization to anyone who hasn't been approved!'

'Don't worry. Mr Grey is very circumspect,' replied the billionaire. 'Besides, now Lazar and Timur are no longer with us, Mr Grey is taking responsibility for security and will be my personal bodyguard.'

Connor felt deceived by Viktor. 'If he knew about me and Jason, then why didn't you tell us about *him*?' he demanded, pointing a finger at Mr Grey.

Viktor's expression hardened. 'Just as my adviser Dmitry doesn't know about your role here, certain facts are kept from you too,' he said sharply.

'Like the fact that Feliks's previous bodyguard was shot in a carjacking?' Connor snapped, annoyed that another crucial piece of security information had been withheld.

Viktor frowned. 'What are you talking about? Colonel Black is well aware of that incident. I told him about it in our first meeting.'

Now Connor *was* confused. Which one of them – Viktor or the colonel – was telling the truth?

'It appears our friend is suffering from concussion,' said Mr Grey. 'Perhaps he should go and lie down.'

His icy tone more an order than a suggestion, Mr Grey guided Connor over to the door. Bewildered, Connor allowed himself to be shown out. But, as he glanced up into the man's pale face, he experienced another shiver of recognition. 'I'm *sure* we've met before.'

'I doubt it,' said Mr Grey curtly, firmly closing the door on him.

Tugging on his boots, Connor stepped out into the brittle cold. He clapped his gloved hands together and rubbed them for warmth. Frozen crystal-white, the garden and surrounding forest were utterly still and silent, the sounds of the world muffled beneath a thick blanket of snow.

A waft of cigarette smoke alerted Connor to the two security guards stationed either side of the front door. One stomped his feet in an effort to keep warm, while the other drew hard on the stub of a cigarette, a scattering of blackened butts in the snow evidence of his chain-smoking.

Connor gave them both a brief nod as he passed through, but they ignored him – either too cold, too bored or too rude to respond.

As he trudged down to the lake, his feet crunching in the thick snow and his breath fogging out before him, the fresh air helped clear his mind. Connor didn't trust the new head of security – even if Viktor Malkov did. There was something dangerous about the man. Besides the persistent yet infuriatingly vague recollection of him, Mr Grey's manner gave the impression that he *harmed* people more than he protected them.

Connor resolved to keep a close eye on the so-called Mr Grey.

Coming across a wooden summer-house tucked behind a clump of trees, Connor spotted Feliks alone on a bench. Shoulders hunched over his phone, and head bent, he appeared to be playing a zombie horror game.

'Hey, Feliks, you OK?' Connor asked, heading over.

Barely bothering to look up, Feliks shrugged.

'Glad to see you're in one piece,' said Connor. 'I honestly thought that bomb would be the end of us.'

Feliks grunted, monosyllabic as ever. While Connor hadn't expected a lively conversation, he'd hoped for a simple thank-you for saving the boy's life. Operation Snowstorm had become a lethal thunderstorm. Kidnap attempts, snipers, assassinations, riots, car bombs . . . there seemed no limit to the lengths Viktor's enemies would go to, to destroy him and his family. Charley's fears about the mission were proving well founded. Connor wondered how long they'd be staying at the dacha. While it was arguably more secure than Moscow, the Bratva would no doubt know its location. Meaning nowhere was safe.

Connor glanced around. 'Where are Jason and Anastasia?'

Feliks raised his chin in the direction of the boathouse.

'Why aren't you with them?'

'I got the impression they wanted to be alone,' he muttered.

Now Connor understood the boy's mood. He couldn't help feeling annoyed that Jason had left their Principal unprotected yet again. 'Well, let's join the party,' he suggested.

Feliks put aside his phone and slouched against the bench. 'You go. I can't be bothered.'

'Come on, don't be such a sulk. Anastasia's with us because she wants to spend time with you.'

'*Really?*' snorted Feliks. 'You could have fooled me. Besides, I thought she was here for her own safety.'

Connor sat down next to Feliks. 'She is. But she's interested in *you*, not Jason.'

Feliks shot him an incredulous look. 'Jason's her *lifesaver*,' he said acidly. 'She's totally in love with him now he's rescued her twice!'

'Anastasia may be thankful to him, but I've seen the way she looks at you. She likes you.'

Feliks spun on him. '*No one* likes me! You know that from being at school. I've got no friends. I mean, you and Jason are the closest and you're *paid* to be my friends. So I don't even know why Anastasia hangs around with me.'

Connor seriously didn't know why either. It would help if he wasn't so sullen and unsociable, but Connor didn't want to completely crush the boy's spirit. 'Listen, you stay here,' he said. 'I'll get the others, then we'll have a game of pool together back at the dacha.'

'Whatever,' Feliks replied, picking up his phone and resuming his game.

Leaving Feliks to slash and kill his way through hordes of zombies, Connor set off towards the boathouse. It wasn't far and he had a clear line of sight back to the summer-house, so he could still keep watch over his Principal.

As he approached the boathouse, he heard Jason talking. 'It was my father's idea. Thought the training would give me discipline and direction. Ex-army, he was a bit of a hard man. I thought by joining I'd gain his respect.'

Connor stopped just outside the boathouse doors. He'd never known Jason to open up about his past or his family. To Connor this was a revelation.

'And did you?' asked Anastasia.

'Maybe. Who knows? The old man died from lung cancer halfway through my training. He was a drinker and a smoker. Since he didn't have any life insurance, we were hard up for cash. And that's when I was approached by Colonel Black –'

Suddenly realizing Jason was about to expose the organization and their role as buddyguards, Connor strode into the boathouse. He found the two lovebirds nestled in a wooden rowing boat.

'Oh! Connor, you're up,' said Jason, casually unwrapping his arm from Anastasia's shoulders.

'Alive and kicking,' he replied, giving his partner a hard stare.

Unflustered by Connor's surprise entrance, Anastasia graced him with one of her dazzling smiles. 'Jason was just telling me about his army cadet training. If it wasn't for that, I guess we'd both be dead from the bomb.'

'I guess you would,' said Connor, as Jason clambered out of the boat with Anastasia.

'Feliks decided to head back to the dacha,' said Jason in answer to Connor's stare.

Connor nodded. 'I bumped into him at the summer-house.'

Lowering his voice, Jason said, 'I thought he'd be fine, given the security around the place.'

'Like at the mansion?' challenged Connor. He knew he was being hard on Jason, but the bomb had shown nowhere was safe.

'Come on, you two,' said Anastasia, heading out of the door. 'I can see Feliks waiting for us and I'm getting cold.'

'I thought Russians never got cold!' Jason called after her.

'Only in winter!' she replied.

Picking up Feliks on their way past the summer-house, Anastasia walked ahead with him, giving Connor a chance to speak with Jason. 'You were just about to tell her about Buddyguard!' he accused, not wanting Jason to steal his thunder.

Jason gave a defensive shrug. 'She was asking loads of questions about how I knew what to do in a bomb situation. So I told her the truth about my army cadet training. I wasn't intending to expose our role . . . but she's so easy to talk to. Anyway, I don't see what your problem is. No harm's done – I only mentioned the colonel's name.'

Connor shook his head in dismay. 'By the end of this mission, the whole world's going to know about us!'

Jason frowned. 'What do you mean?'

'Forget it,' said Connor, deciding to keep his concerns about Mr Grey to himself. 'Anyway, Anastasia will know about Buddyguard soon enough. I've suggested to the colonel that we recruit her.'

Jason looked at Connor in surprise. 'Recruit Ana?'

'Why not? She's got all the skills.'

Jason suddenly looked flustered. 'Yeah, but . . . I don't think that's a good idea . . . Ling wouldn't . . . I mean, shouldn't the colonel –'

'What do you care what Ling thinks?' cut in Connor. 'I thought you said you two had broken up. Unless you're thinking of getting back together? Whatever – your flirting with Anastasia is upsetting the Principal. And it's a line that shouldn't be crossed. You have to stop.'

Jason halted in his tracks. 'Just who the hell do you think you are, telling me what to do?' he snarled. 'I mean, you're a fine one to talk. On your first mission you snogged the President's daughter, for heaven's sake! *That's* crossing a line.' With a final angry glare at Connor, he stomped off.

Connor let out a heavy sigh. Perhaps Jason had a point. Who was he to lecture his partner? His personal record wasn't exactly blemish-free.

As they approached the dacha, the two security guards opened the front doors and let them in. Kicking the snow from their boots, they stepped inside the entrance hall just as Viktor came out of the drawing room.

'Ah! There you all are,' he said. 'Just to let you know, we've got an early start tomorrow morning. We're going on a hunt!'

'Cool,' said Feliks, the glimmer of a grin breaking through his sullen mood.

'I thought you'd like that,' said his father, ruffling his son's hair. He turned to Anastasia. 'My security guard informs me you've brought your violin. Is that right?'

Anastasia nodded. 'I hope you don't mind. I need to practise, even if we are suspended from school.'

'Of course not,' said Viktor, looking kindly upon her. 'In fact, I'd love to hear you play. My late wife was a concert violinist. Ever since she . . . well, you know . . . I've missed the sound of it in our household.'

Connor noticed Anastasia shifting a little uncomfortably on her feet.

'I can't promise to live up to your wife,' she said, looking down as if checking for snow on her boots. 'I'm honestly not that good.'

'Don't be so modest,' chided the billionaire. 'I'm sure your performance will knock me dead.'

Anastasia offered him a hesitant smile. 'I hope so.'

Viktor clapped his hands together. 'Then it's agreed. You'll play for us tomorrow after the hunt.' He headed off towards his study, then paused at the threshold. 'Oh, by the way, Anastasia, I've tried to get in contact with your parents, but haven't had any luck. The number you gave me keeps going to answerphone.'

Anastasia sighed. 'Yep, sounds like my parents. They're probably somewhere in the Arctic with no signal. As ever!'

Viktor gave her a sympathetic smile. 'Well, I'm sure they'll be in touch as soon as they get my message.'

The face loomed out of the darkness. A skull with skin stretched tight over the bone. Ice-grey eyes that promised death. Wreathed in black smoke and flames from a blazing tanker, the figure hissed poisonous words: 'You crop up in all the wrong places and at all the wrong times –'

Connor woke in a cold sweat, the nightmare clinging to him like a monstrous spiderweb . . . with Mr Grey at its centre.

Connor tried to shake away the horrific images in his head. He sat up, switched on the bedside light and rubbed his eyes. But still the unsettling vision of Mr Grey remained.

The nightmare had felt *real*, and Connor realized he'd been reliving his traumatic mission in the Indian Ocean against Somali pirates. But what was Mr Grey doing there? Connor knew that hadn't really happened. *Or had it?* His mind must still be feeling the effects of his concussion after the car bomb.

Connor dry-swallowed. His throat was sore and his mouth tasted like sawdust. Sliding out of bed, he pulled on jeans and a T-shirt and headed downstairs for the kitchen. A glass of milk would sort him out. As he passed through the dacha's darkened entrance hall, Connor noticed a wedge of light escaping from the drawing room, the door partly ajar. Low voices could be heard, one of them Viktor's.

'Dmitry, it warms my heart to see you. I can't believe you've been released so quickly.'

'Nor can I,' replied his adviser's familiar voice. Connor smiled with relief to hear that Dmitry had survived his ordeal.

'Our new lawyer is certainly worth his weight in gold,' Viktor went on. 'Did the police torture you at all? Threaten you?'

'You know how it goes, Viktor.'

'Yes, I do. I'm sorry, my friend, that you had to suffer . . .'

Connor couldn't help but listen in. He wanted to know more about Dmitry's release. Praying none of the floorboards would creak, he crept over to the drawing-room door and concealed himself in the shadows. Through the gap between the door and its frame, he spied Viktor sitting in his armchair next to the fire. Opposite him was Dmitry, his face pale and drawn, dark circles under his eyes, and his beard tinged a little greyer than before.

'The rally was a major success,' Dmitry remarked with a bittersweet smile. 'As you said, Viktor, a true turning point in Russian history. So I suppose any amount of suffering is worth the result.'

Viktor grinned. 'That's the spirit, Dmitry!'

'Talking of spirits, Viktor, I think we should celebrate my release with a drink, don't you?'

'Dmitry, that's your best advice ever!' Viktor laughed, rising from his chair.

Dmitry waved Viktor back down and got up himself. He headed over to the mahogany drinks cabinet and selected a bottle of finest vodka. That's when Connor spotted the third man in the room.

Mr Grey.

He'd been standing so still he could have been a mannequin. His ashen face shared the same lifeless waxwork-like quality. Connor shuddered, recalling his earlier nightmare.

'Mr Grey, won't you join us for a toast?' asked Dmitry, offering up a glass. There was a slight tremble to his hand.

Mr Grey didn't even glance at the vodka. 'I don't drink.'

'Of course not,' said Dmitry with a nervous smile. 'I forget you're a true professional.'

'You've never drunk in all the time I've known you,' Viktor remarked with a wry smile. 'Aren't you even the slightest bit curious as to its taste?'

'Curiosity killed the cat,' Mr Grey replied.

Connor suddenly experienced the strongest sense of déjà vu. The drawing room almost seemed to sway, as if he had motion sickness.

Curiosity killed the cat. He'd heard Mr Grey say that exact phrase before.

Connor squeezed his eyes shut, pierced by a crippling headache. Mr Grey's voice echoed in his ears: *Forget my face . . . I never existed . . . You never heard my name . . . Equilibrium means nothing . . . I am just a ghost to you . . .*

As if floodgates had been opened in his mind, memories came surging out.

Mr Grey *had* been involved in the pirate attack on the Sterlings' yacht. He'd been with him on that blazing tanker.

Now the vision of a ferocious jungle battle flashed before Connor's eyes, with Mr Grey pointing a pistol at him from across a raging river. *I never miss . . . I shot exactly who I meant to . . .*

His head spinning, Connor grabbed for the door frame to stop himself falling. He realized he'd encountered Mr Grey during his African assignment too. In fact, the man had been the architect of the coup and diamond smuggling in Burundi. And during that last encounter Mr Grey had hypnotized Connor to make him forget . . .

But now Connor remembered. He remembered everything.

Mr Grey was an assassin. A cold, calculating killer.

That meant Viktor Malkov was in grave danger and Connor had to warn him.

Now Connor's eye caught sight of Mr Grey's reflection in the gold-framed mirror above the drinks cabinet. The assassin's hands were behind his back, a gun concealed in his palm.

Connor's heart began to race. Should he call Jason for back-up? But if he did the two of them might return to the drawing room too late – the assassin having already killed his target.

There was no time. Connor readied himself to Seize, Strike and Subdue. Disarming a trained assassin would be almost suicidal, but he still had the element of surprise on his side.

Dmitry passed Viktor his drink and Connor heard the *clink* of glasses.

'To *Our Russia*!' Dmitry said, raising his shot of vodka in a toast.

The billionaire raised his own glass at the same time as Mr Grey flicked off the safety catch on his hidden gun.

Connor burst into the room. 'GET DOWN!' he shouted.

The three men spun towards Connor as he charged at Mr Grey. The assassin neatly side-stepped Connor's attack, tripped him up and sent him crashing to the floor. Connor instinctively rolled back to his feet and turned to confront the assassin, but Mr Grey already had his gun trained on him.

'Connor, what is the meaning of this?' Viktor demanded, putting down his drink and glaring at him.

Mr Grey had his finger on the trigger but had yet to fire. Connor raised his hands in surrender. If he could just get close enough, he still had a chance of disarming him. 'Mr Malkov, I realize you *think* you know this man, but you don't.'

Viktor narrowed his eyes. 'Explain yourself.'

'I've met Mr Grey on previous operations in Somalia and in Burundi. He's no bodyguard. He's an assassin!'

Mr Grey's trigger finger twitched, but his glacial eyes still gave nothing away.

'He's been sent to kill you,' Connor went on, readying himself to lunge at the assassin.

Mr Grey's thin lips curled into a vampire's smile – soulless and sinister. 'I'm not the assassin here, Connor,' he said. 'Dmitry Smirnov is.'

He turned his weapon on Viktor's adviser. Confronted by the barrel of a gun, Dmitry's already pale face went ashen. 'W-w-what are you talking about?'

'Let's not play games, Dmitry,' said Mr Grey. 'The FSB released you on one condition: that you kill Viktor.'

The billionaire stared at his friend in shock. 'Is this true?'

Connor was equally stunned by the revelation, but Dmitry shook his head vehemently. 'No, of course not.'

With his gun still aimed at the adviser, Mr Grey took Viktor's shot glass from the table and presented it to Dmitry. 'Then you won't mind drinking his vodka.'

Dmitry held up a hand in polite refusal. 'I have my own, thank you,' he said.

'Drink *this* one.'

When the adviser refused to take the glass, Mr Grey pressed the hard snub of his gun against Dmitry's temple. 'Drink!'

Dmitry began to tremble. His eyes glassy and wide, he looked to the billionaire. 'Viktor, listen to the boy! This Mr Grey is a mad man. He's feeding you lies. He's trying to –'

Mr Grey now forced the glass to Dmitry's lips. '*Drink!*'

With Mr Grey distracted, Connor lunged for his gun. But Viktor grabbed him by the shoulder and dragged him back. 'Keep out of it! This is none of your business, Connor.'

Mr Grey began to pour the vodka into Dmitry's mouth.

'No! No! Stop!' spluttered Dmitry, turning his head away. Then he began to weep. 'Viktor . . . I'm sorry. It's true . . . the FSB gave me the poison . . .' He turned to the billionaire with pleading eyes. 'You must understand. They were going to torture Natasha . . . and . . . *my little Tanya.*'

Viktor stared back, pitiless and unmoved. 'You back-stabbing snake in the grass!'

Dmitry dropped to his knees, sobbing. 'No, no. Please understand . . . I had no choice!'

Viktor sighed. 'And neither do I.'

He gave Mr Grey a nod. Connor watched in horror as Mr Grey yanked back Dmitry's head and poured in the remainder of the vodka. Clamping his hand over the man's mouth, he waited until Dmitry had swallowed it all. Then he let the adviser go and Dmitry collapsed on the carpet beside the fire. For several long seconds, he just lay there, looking up at Viktor like a loyal but scolded dog.

Then Dmitry gasped and began clawing at his throat. As he fought for breath, his face turned purple and the veins in his neck became distended. He writhed on the carpet, eyes bulging, breathing ragged. All of a sudden he stiffened, then fell still.

'Is there *no one* I can trust?' said Viktor, spitting on Dmitry's dead body.

'Viktor *ordered* Mr Grey to kill his friend,' Connor whispered, his gaze flicking towards the bedroom door, half-expecting the assassin to burst in at any moment. 'They murdered him right in front of me.'

Connor perched on the end of Jason's bed, his face as ghostly pale as the silver moonlight seeping through the curtains. Bleary-eyed and his hair in knots, Jason propped himself up against his pillows. He frowned, looking as if he didn't quite believe Connor.

'You said Dmitry tried to poison Viktor first. So isn't it sort of justified?'

'How can you even think that, Jason? His family had been threatened!' exclaimed Connor, struggling to keep his voice low. 'Dmitry was pleading for his life. It wasn't as if there was even a trial!'

Jason ran a hand through his tangled hair. 'Remember what Charley said, it's Russia – normal rules don't apply.'

Connor gave a derisive snort. 'Yeah, Viktor explained that it was *Russian justice*. That Dmitry had been caught in the act and admitted his guilt. That the appropriate punishment had been served. And that I should simply forget about it. But how can I?'

He got up and paced the room. The image of Dmitry clawing at his throat while the poison ate away at his insides was seared into Connor's memory. 'Malkov claims he's fighting for democracy and freedom, but what I just witnessed surely goes against all that? Then there's his connection to Mr Grey.'

'What about him?' said Jason, rubbing his eyes.

Connor stopped pacing. 'He's an assassin, for heaven's sake! A trained killer. What's he doing protecting Viktor Malkov?'

Jason shrugged. 'Are you sure you're not confusing this Mr Grey with someone else? I mean, it sounds a bit far-fetched to me that this supposed assassin *hypnotized* you. Perhaps the knock to your head scrambled your mind? Jumbled up your memories?'

'No! If anything, the knock straightened them out.' Connor sat down on the bed again. 'Remember my assignment protecting the Sterling sisters? The doctor said Emily had been brainwashed and that subliminal suggestions had been planted in her mind, hypnotism being the most likely method. I *know* it was Mr Grey I saw on that tanker. And I believe he was responsible for Emily's brainwashing. I think that he wiped my mind to protect his identity. He promised that if we ever met again, it wouldn't end well for me. Now he knows that I remember him, I'll be next on his hit list.'

'OK, if you're that worried, contact the colonel,' Jason suggested, stifling a yawn.

'I intend to,' said Connor. 'Charley was right – there's something very wrong about this assignment. The colonel needs to withdraw us immediately.'

'Seriously?' said Jason, giving Connor a dubious look. 'Aren't you overreacting? Colonel Black would have vetted Mr Malkov before agreeing to take him on as a client. And Mr Malkov obviously trusts Mr Grey – he's put him in charge of security.'

'True, but should *we* be trusting Viktor?'

'Come on, Connor – he's a billionaire and politician, not some mass murderer –'

There was a creak outside on the landing and Connor's eyes shot to the door. Putting a finger to his lips to warn Jason to be quiet, he slipped off the bed and silently crossed the room. Hearing another faint creak of floorboards, he eased the XT torch from his pocket and extended the baton. Last time Mr Grey had got the better of him. This time he intended to strike first and fast.

Grasping the handle, he yanked the door open –

Anastasia almost fell into the room and Connor had to stop himself mid-strike.

'What are you doing out there?' he exclaimed, his baton still raised.

Her eyes wide with alarm, she responded with a nervous smile. 'I . . . couldn't sleep. Then I heard you talking and wondered if everything was all right?'

Jason shot her a reassuring grin and jumped out of bed. 'Yeah, everything's fine, Ana.' He pushed past Connor. 'Put the baton down, Connor.'

Jason guided a rather startled Anastasia over to a wicker chair by the window. As she settled on the cushion, she asked, 'Why's he got a baton?'

Connor sheepishly pocketed the weapon.

Pulling over another chair, Jason sat down opposite Anastasia. 'I think it's time we let you into a little secret,' he said.

Connor stepped forward and interrupted him. 'Before that, I've got a couple of questions for her.'

Now that he'd revealed his hand and Jason had decided to broach the subject of Buddyguard, Connor thought they might as well go the whole distance and try to recruit her. But first there were a few blanks that needed to be filled in.

Anastasia shifted in her chair, a sudden anxious look on her face. 'Am I in trouble?'

'No,' said Connor. 'But I am interested in why you're so skilled at martial arts? The way you took down Feliks's kidnappers at the ice rink and dealt with Gleb in the boiler room suggests you've had formal training – and we're not talking school judo sessions either.'

Anastasia held his interrogating gaze. 'In Russia, sadly, girls are often harassed and attacked by Bratva gangs. My parents wanted me to be able to handle myself, especially as they're away so much. So I learnt the Russian martial art of Systema.'

Connor nodded, pleased at her answer. 'Talking of your parents, Viktor's had trouble contacting them. We've also had difficulty getting in touch. Why is that?'

Anastasia stiffened. 'Why are you trying to contact my parents? As I said before, they're in the Arctic with no signal. Their oil job demands secrecy.'

'Fine, but we haven't been able to verify other things about you. For instance, we couldn't find your birth certificate at the Moscow registry office. The only one under your name is for a girl who died two years ago.'

Now Anastasia looked very alarmed. 'That's because I wasn't born in Moscow!' She stood up, a thunderous expression on her pale face. 'Why have you been looking into my life? You've no right –'

Jason took her hand and tried to calm her. 'Please, just hear us out.'

He gestured to the chair. She reluctantly sat back down.

'We're not Feliks's cousins,' Jason explained. 'We're his bodyguards.'

Anastasia's eyes flicked between Jason and Connor, waiting to see if they were playing a joke on her, then she smiled. 'I suspected as much.' She turned to Jason. 'No wonder you're so good at saving my life! But why are you telling me this?'

Connor replied, 'Because we think you'd make an excellent buddyguard.'

Anastasia laughed. '*Buddy*guard?'

'Yes, we work for a covert protection agency that specializes in young bodyguards,' explained Jason. 'And we're always on the lookout for good recruits. That's why we've been investigating your background.'

Anastasia fell silent, her expression unreadable.

'So what do you say?' asked Connor.

She chewed on her lower lip, seeming to consider their offer seriously.

'It's very flattering that you think I could be a bodyguard,' she eventually replied. 'But that's not where I see my life heading.'

Connor's shoulders slumped a little, unable to hide his disappointment. Then again, he'd taken some convincing before he'd agreed to such a life-changing decision. 'That's perfectly understandable. But think about it. If you change your mind, let us know. And obviously keep all this to yourself.'

'Of course,' Anastasia replied, rising from the chair. 'Well then . . . I'll leave you boys to your bodyguarding. See you in a few hours for Viktor's hunt.'

Withdrawing from Jason's bedroom, she headed across the landing for the staircase. On her way she picked up her violin case that she'd left outside Jason's door.

'You had your violin with you?' asked Connor, curious since it was the middle of the night.

Anastasia shrugged as if this was normal. 'As I said, I couldn't sleep. I was going to find a quiet room to practise for tomorrow.'

'Well, I wouldn't go downstairs if I were you,' said Connor.

'Why not?' she asked, her brow wrinkling in puzzlement.

'The new security guards are a little on edge,' he explained, thinking of Dmitry's dead body in the study. 'I wouldn't want them mistaking you for an assassin or anything!'

Anastasia laughed and pointed to her pink pyjamas. 'Little chance of that!'

Roman Gurov balled his hands into fists. He wanted to drive his knuckles through the wall. Smash the mahogany coffee table to pieces. Snap the marble chessboard in half. But it wouldn't do to wreck the stateroom of Moscow's most exclusive private members' club or to display his rage in front of his chess opponent. Instead he channelled all his fury into the grainy surveillance photo of a middle-aged yet trim man with short hair, a pale complexion and plain looks that were disturbing in their very ordinariness.

Nika stood at a prudent arm's length from her boss. 'According to our source, this man neutralized our Trojan horse,' she informed him.

Through clenched teeth, Roman asked, 'Who is he?'

Nika laid a single sheet of paper on the coffee table – a pro forma, most of the boxes blank.

Roman cast his eye over it. 'Is this *all* the intelligence you've gathered on him?'

Nika nodded. 'He exists off-grid. Doesn't register on any databases. All online records of him have been erased. Our agents went back over two decades and only gleaned a few facts. What we do know is that the man is an assassin for hire. A top-level one, likely government-trained. We may even have hired him ourselves in the past!'

Roman exchanged a thunderstruck look with his chess opponent.

'He's known on the circuit only as Mr Grey and is presumed to travel under various pseudonyms – none of which we know. But we did find evidence of links to several major criminal organizations, including the Sinaloa cartel, the Yamaguchi yakuza and the Camorra mafia. And our source reports he has ties with something called Equilibrium. We also suspect he's –'

'*Equilibrium?*' interrupted Roman's chess opponent.

Nika nodded. The man's face darkened. Roman swallowed as if something sharp was stuck in his throat, then cursed viciously under his breath.

'*That* changes everything,' said his opponent.

'How so?' asked Nika.

'If Equilibrium is involved, then the Malkov problem goes beyond these borders.'

Roman stared at the fire blazing in the stateroom's hearth, his dark eyes reflecting the flames. 'This explains why the Black King has been virtually untouchable,' he snarled.

Nika looked in confusion at the two men. 'But . . . what is Equilibrium?'

In an almost reverential tone, Roman's opponent explained, 'Equilibrium is a shadow organization. Maybe even a myth. But definitely a threat.'

'An American threat?' asked Nika.

'Not as far as we know. Equilibrium is rumoured to have its base in China, although its core council may well be international.'

Roman turned to his comrade. 'But why is Equilibrium backing the Black King?'

'Isn't it obvious?' said his opponent. 'To overthrow this government and take power through him.'

He picked up the namesake's chesspiece from the board and studied it in the flickering firelight. 'Their involvement with the Black King is tantamount to war. The game is over, Roman. You need to end this and end it *now*. Not only for your sake but for Russia's.'

Roman Gurov stood and buttoned his jacket. 'I'll personally assemble an elite force of FSB agents.'

'No, keep the government out of it. This'll be a dirty job and I want our hands clean. Wear your *other* hat, Roman. As the Bratva, send in your *krysha* enforcers.' His opponent tossed the wooden king into the fire and watched as the chesspiece was consumed by the flames. 'Burn the Black King and his castle to the ground!'

Connor crouched behind the trunk of a tree, his breath misting in the frigid air. Rays from the dawn sun penetrated the forest like splinters of ice, but the ground remained in semi-darkness. Jason and Anastasia lay silhouetted against the crisp white snow, neither daring to move. Feliks was stretched out beside them, perfectly still, his eye to the scope of his rifle.

They'd left the dacha two hours before sunrise, riding on snowmobiles, their headlights cutting a path through the blackness. Viktor, Mr Grey and a four-man unit of security guards had led the way, with Feliks and Connor following on one snowmobile and Jason and Anastasia on another.

Once deep in the forest, they'd all dismounted and spread out in a line to begin a slow advance in their hunt for prey. At first the forest appeared like a frozen wasteland and it was difficult to spot any animal tracks or signs of life. But, as dawn approached, evidence of fresh droppings and the imprints of small hooves became visible.

Following the tracks, they'd been about to enter a small clearing when an unsuspecting grouse crossed Feliks's path. The bird pecked at the frozen ground, rooting out any food it could find.

With a final adjustment to his line of fire, Feliks steadied his breathing, then squeezed the trigger. The gunshot shattered the silence of the forest, echoing off the trees until it faded into the distance.

'Got it!' Feliks cried, leaping to his feet and hurrying over to the kill. He picked up the dead grouse by its feathered legs. The bird hung limp from his hand, blood dripping in red beads on to the snow.

'Good shooting, Feliks,' praised his father, raising a gloved fist in the air. 'First kill of the morning.'

Not true, thought Connor, unable to suppress the image of Dmitry writhing on the carpet in Viktor's drawing room.

'I shot it straight through the heart!' Feliks exclaimed as he closely examined the bloody hole in the bird's chest. His skill with the rifle was testament to the time spent hunting with his father, but Connor was deeply unsettled at his Principal's macabre delight in killing the creature.

Connor had no love of hunting. He could understand it in the context of survival or as a source of food. *But for sport?* It seemed barbaric and cruelly unfair. Surely the opponent should be given an equal chance? Yet he didn't see the grouse wielding a Remington bolt-action rifle!

From the sickened look on Anastasia's face, he could tell she didn't approve either. Jason, however, clearly had more of the hunter spirit in him, patting Feliks on the back in congratulations. Clasped under his arm was the rifle Viktor had loaned him and, judging from the way he was checking the sights and confirming a bullet was chambered, Jason was itching to notch up a grouse of his own.

Returning to the snowmobile, Feliks tied his 'trophy' on the back and Connor took the opportunity to look at his phone. It had been the middle of the night in the UK when he'd called Buddyguard HQ and left an urgent message for the colonel to contact him. He'd also emailed a mission update, detailing the killing of Dmitry and his fears about Mr Grey. Even if the colonel had responded, though, Connor wouldn't receive his message. There was no signal at all in the remote forest.

'Let's bag some bigger game,' said Viktor, as Feliks returned and reloaded his rifle. 'Like a deer or a boar!'

They spread out again, this time Viktor heading in a southerly direction and Feliks going north. Mr Grey and three security guards stayed with the billionaire, while the fourth guard joined their party – Feliks, Jason and the guard out front, Anastasia trailing behind with Connor.

Aware of each other's reluctance to join in the hunt, Connor shared a disconsolate smile with Anastasia. While tinged with sadness, her smile was still radiant and Connor was struck again by how beautiful she was. Yet he was conscious of a deep well of grief in her ice-blue eyes. He recalled her scarred back and wished he could somehow get her to talk about it. But this wasn't the time or the place. Maybe if she did decide to join Buddyguard, they'd have a moment to talk and he could help ease her hidden sorrow. So Connor just walked in silence by her side, hoping that was comfort enough.

The forest was magical at this time in the morning – branches frosted like icing, crisp snow as white as cotton, the light pure and clear. A crystalline winter paradise . . . into which they, as hunters, were intruding.

Connor prayed any deer or other animal would steer clear. But they hadn't gone far when he spied movement among the trees. A fleeting glimpse of white.

He didn't alert Feliks or Jason, hoping they had missed a second kill.

Then Connor caught sight of a branch twitching on a young sapling, the snow dislodged from its pine needles – a sure sign an animal had recently passed by.

Anastasia noticed it too. Feliks and Jason were still scouting up ahead with the guard, oblivious to this potential prey. Anastasia quickened her pace and caught up with Jason. They'd been warned of wolves and even bears in the forest, and Connor didn't blame her for wanting to be with the main group.

Connor spotted more movement, this time on a low rocky outcrop. Then he froze in his tracks. To his left the dark barrel of a gun poked out from behind a nearby tree, its sights targeted on his chest.

Peering through the scope was none other than Mr Grey.

How convenient for the assassin, thought Connor, his pulse quickening. *A hunting accident.*

He could run, dive behind a tree, even rush the assassin. But he was caught in the open and all Mr Grey had to do was pull the trigger. Connor braced himself for the inevitable shot –

Mr Grey lowered his gun. 'Luckily for you, we're on the same side.'

His eyes flicked round the forest, appearing to search for new prey.

Connor breathed again. His heart still thudding in his chest, he stared defiantly back at the assassin. 'Are we?' he challenged.

Mr Grey slung his rifle and strode over, the air seeming to drop several degrees at his approach. He leant in close to Connor's ear. 'At the moment we are.'

A soft whistle like birdsong caused them both to turn round. At the top of a small rise, Viktor was waving them over, signing for them to keep low. Joined by the others, they crept up the slope and hunkered down behind a large fallen log. Without saying a word, Viktor pointed into a clearing on the other side. A lone grey wolf was feeding on the carcass of a baby deer.

'*My* prize,' Viktor whispered, shouldering his rifle. Flicking off the safety catch, the billionaire lined up the animal in his sights.

The wolf's ears pricked up. His head turned, all his senses attuned to danger. But the wolf wasn't looking in their direction.

As Viktor went to take his shot, the forest erupted with gunfire.

Mr Grey was already in motion, diving on top of Viktor as a bullet ricocheted off the log. Splinters flew like arrows and Connor shoved Feliks to the ground, shielding him with his body. Jason tried to cover Feliks *and* Anastasia, but his bulletproof jacket wasn't large enough to protect them both. A splinter of wood struck Anastasia in the face, gouging a bloody line across her cheek.

The four security guards drew their compact MP7 sub-machine guns and began firing back.

But who are they firing at? wondered Connor, his eyes darting round the forest. Evidently what he thought had been a deer moving through the undergrowth earlier had in fact been their attackers. How ironic! Feliks and his father had believed they were the hunters, when in truth they were the ones being hunted.

The wolf long gone, the forest thundered to the roar of automatic gunfire and the *zing* of steel-jacketed rounds. Despite the shelter offered by the fallen tree trunk, Connor and the others were still dangerously exposed on top of the rise. One of the guards jerked forward, crying out as he was shot in the back. He slumped across the log, blood spurting out and staining the snow scarlet.

'We're surrounded!' yelled one of the surviving guards, firing with wild abandon at the trees behind.

Mr Grey was the only one among them seeming not to panic. With one hand planted firmly on Viktor's shoulder to keep him down and the other gripping his gun, the assassin's cold gaze swept the forest.

'Not completely. Rolan, focus your fire on that outcrop over there,' he ordered, his tone calm but firm. 'Koldan, the trees behind to your left. Ivan, you come with me.'

As bullets peppered the ground millimetres from them, Feliks yelped and curled up into a tight ball. Anastasia flinched. Mr Grey, unfazed by the close attack, turned to Connor and Jason, his eyes like shards of steel. 'Let's see what you two are really made of. Get Feliks to the dacha. Viktor, time to go!'

Leaving two guards to lay down suppressing fire, Mr Grey and Ivan rushed Viktor down the slope to the snowmobiles. Connor glanced at Jason, who shrugged. They both knew it was a suicidal run, but what choice did they have? Connor yanked Feliks to his feet and sprinted after them, with Jason and Anastasia hot on their heels.

Bullets chased them all the way, rounds searing overhead, ripping into tree trunks and tearing apart the bark. Keeping low, Connor zigzagged between the trees, hoping to make himself and Feliks less of a target. As the snowmobiles came into sight, Feliks stumbled over a root. He sprawled face first in the snow, dropping his rifle. In that moment the forest seemed to rain bullets and Connor dived on top of him.

'Don't move!' he ordered, tensing his whole body for the brutal impacts to come.

'*Feliks!*' cried his father in despair as gunfire stitched the snow around them.

Out of the corner of his eye, Connor spied Jason and Anastasia pressed flat against the trunk of a tree in a desperate attempt to shelter from the barrage –

Then Connor was hit. Hard in the lower back.

Pain flared outwards with such explosive force that he could no longer breathe. His vision contracted until the snow-filled forest was just a pinprick of light in the blackness. As he lost consciousness, the sounds of battle faded, the gunfire clattering like a distant train at the far end of a long tunnel . . .

Then out of that tunnel the headlight of the train came hurtling back towards him, its light becoming painfully bright and the chaotic noise of its wheels on the track growing more and more ferocious . . . until he heard his name being called above the thunder of gunfire: 'CONNOR!'

Dazed and confused, Connor raised his head and opened his eyes. He still lay on top of Feliks. Jason was at his side, shaking his arm. The hail of enemy bullets had ceased momentarily as Ivan retaliated with his MP7 sub-machine gun.

'GET MOVING!' shouted Mr Grey.

Numbly aware that his bulletproof jacket had absorbed the lethal round and he was still alive, Connor got unsteadily to his feet with Jason's help. Then together they pulled Feliks to standing.

'You OK?' asked Jason.

'Yeah,' said Feliks, dusting off the snow.

'I was talking to Connor!' said Jason sharply.

Connor nodded. 'I'll live,' he groaned. But it felt like he'd been run over by a ten-ton truck.

In a lolloping run he staggered the last twenty metres to the snowmobiles. Mr Grey and Viktor, their engines revving to the max, were already speeding out of the danger zone. Jason and Anastasia clambered on to their snowmobile.

'But my rifle!' cried Feliks, turning back for the weapon.

'Leave it!' gasped Connor, mounting the snowmobile and gunning the ignition. His back ached like hell but the adrenalin was masking much of the pain. 'Get on!' he yelled at Feliks just as Ivan's gun clicked empty.

There was a moment of stunned silence – as if the forest had taken a breath – then a blast of retaliating fire cut the guard down. With Feliks clinging to him, Connor thumbed the throttle hard and their snowmobile shot away through the trees.

CHAPTER 65

Pursued by gunfire, Connor rode as fast as he dared, branches whipping at their faces. A volley of bullets strafed across the back of their snowmobile, pulverizing the dead grouse that hung off the end, feathers and blood flying. Feliks shrieked in his ear as they weaved hard right to avoid hitting a tree head-on. Connor was trying to follow in Viktor and Mr Grey's tracks and catch them up. But he'd only ever ridden jet skis before this morning and he was pushing the snowmobile and his skills to the limit. Behind he could hear Jason and Anastasia's snowmobile right on their tail. And in the distance the battle still raged as the two remaining guards fought for their lives.

Ahead he spotted the tail lights of Viktor's snowmobile. But as soon as he caught them up they rode straight into another ambush. In white ski jackets and carrying assault rifles, four gunmen began firing. Mr Grey and Viktor veered hard left. On instinct Connor turned right. He didn't have time to see what happened to Jason and Anastasia. Bullets shredded the trees and undergrowth as he and

Feliks slunk low on their snowmobile, only their speed saving them from being blasted out of their seats.

Through a blur of vegetation and snow, Connor spotted one of the enemy blocking Mr Grey and Viktor's escape route. Taking the offensive, Mr Grey drew his handgun and, steering one-handed, shot the man straight through the head.

But the other three gunmen were still a threat.

One leapt directly into Connor's path. There was no way to avoid the man or his bullets.

As the gunman took aim with his rifle, Connor recalled his instructor Jody's advice for surviving an ambush: *if there's an armed attacker in front of your vehicle, you either drive into, around or over that attacker.* So Connor accelerated hard and steered the snowmobile up and off a sharp rise in the track. The snowmobile cleared the air and flew like a guided missile towards their attacker. As the man instinctively ducked, he was struck by the tail end of the machine. His rifle was smashed from his grasp and he was knocked off his feet. Then the snowmobile hit the ground with a bone-shuddering *thump*. Wrestling with the handlebars to keep it on the track, Connor glanced back to see the gunman out cold in the snow. Connor allowed himself a brief triumphant grin – he'd pulled off the stunt of the century! Driving the throttle all the way, he tore a path through the trees, leaving the deadly ambush behind.

The next time he looked over his shoulder, he and Feliks were on their own.

'Who were those men?' Feliks shouted above the growl of the snowmobile's engine.

'Bratva! FSB! The Russian Army! Who knows, Feliks?' replied Connor, gritting his teeth as he concentrated on keeping the snowmobile upright while they traversed a slope. 'Your father has many enemies.'

He leant into a sharp turn, the rear end sliding out and clipping a tree.

'Slow down!' Feliks pleaded, gripping Connor even more tightly round the waist.

Even though the sound of gunfire had receded into the distance, Connor had no intention of slowing down. They zoomed past a pair of dead bodies in the snow – a dacha security patrol, judging by their uniforms. Now Connor feared that the whole estate had been overrun.

'Do you know where you're going?' Feliks demanded.

Connor realized he didn't. He'd just been intent on escaping the immediate threat. He took his thumb off the throttle, the snowmobile ground to a halt and he looked around. They were still deep in the forest, every direction looked the same and, with fresh snow falling and covering the ground, there were no obvious tracks. Connor knew the dacha lay east of where they'd been hunting and he tried to get his bearings from the weak sun peeking through the tree canopy.

'Do you even have an escape plan?' complained Feliks.

Connor turned in his seat, wincing at the pain in his back, and glared at his Principal. He'd had enough of the ungrateful brat. 'I've just saved your life. *Again*. So at least show some gratitude.'

'Thanks,' said Feliks sarcastically. 'But I could *still* die out here.'

'Not if I can help it,' replied Connor. 'We need to get back to the dacha, regroup with the others, then extract you and your father to a safer location. *That's* the plan.'

Feliks raised an incredulous eyebrow. 'Well, the dacha's that way,' he said, pointing in a completely different direction from the way they'd been headed.

'Thanks,' said Connor with equal sarcasm. Thumbing the throttle, he turned the snowmobile round.

They rode on in silence. Connor seriously questioned why he was bothering to protect this boy who had no respect for him or his efforts to keep them both alive. Bodyguarding was hard enough when you liked the Principal; it was virtually impossible when you didn't. But Connor, bound by a sense of duty, had no intention of abandoning his role. Besides, if they were to survive this ordeal, they would have to stick together.

With no tracks to follow, Connor found the going tough and his arms started to ache from wrestling with the steering column. Every so often they'd hear an ominous exchange of gunfire. He hoped that Jason and Anastasia had managed to escape the second ambush. They'd been right behind them when they'd split. But there'd still been two gunmen and the chances of Jason and Anastasia evading being shot were slim.

Then, just as they were emerging from the forest, Connor heard the growl of another snowmobile. He slowed down to wait for them to catch up. As the noise drew closer, the one engine became two and Feliks turned to Connor with a hopeful grin. 'Must be my father and Mr Grey!'

But Feliks's relieved smile fell from his face when the snowmobiles crested the rise. Sat astride the machines – stolen from the security guards left behind at the first ambush – were two ski-jacketed gunmen.

'Over there!' shouted one, pointing his assault rifle in their direction.

As they started firing, Connor revved the engine and raced off towards the sanctuary of the dacha. The two men gave chase. Connor drove the throttle fully home. But in his rush to escape he hadn't checked the route ahead. They were speeding at over forty miles an hour when the snowmobile struck the half-buried tree stump.

Connor flipped head first through the air. In the brief seconds that followed the crash, he registered the crumpled shell of the snowmobile; the dark underbelly of the clouds; the icy whip of the wind on his cheeks; Feliks somersaulting, his arms flailing like a broken-winged bird; and then . . . the impact of the frozen snow. Hard and punishing as concrete. He tumbled over and over, finally coming to rest in a crumpled heap.

Feliks lay a little way off, writhing and moaning . . . but alive.

The guttural sound of two snowmobiles grew louder. Then the engines cut out and a strange unsettling silence descended. Stunned to his core, Connor could only lie in the compacted snow, his body failing to respond as he listened to the approaching crunch of footsteps.

A shadow fell over him.

'They're just *kids*!' said a voice so gruff the man had to be a thirty-a-day smoker.

'Yeah,' replied the other, his tone lazy and slurred as if he drank too much. 'But this one here is Malkov's son.'

303

'Does that mean we get a bonus payment?'

'Absolutely.'

'So what about this one? Is he worth anything?'

A boot was applied to Connor's side and he was rolled painfully on to his back, allowing Connor to get his first close-up look at their attackers. The man who'd turned him over was bull-necked with a heavy brow and flared nostrils. His knuckles were calloused and his ears cauliflowered like he spent every weekend cage-fighting. The other man – the apparent leader of the two – was taller with a shaven head and a brick-like jaw disfigured by a long white scar. On the back of his right hand was a crude tattoo of a black skull.

He walked over and bent close to Connor. 'I reckon he's one of them young bodyguards the Pakhan warned us about.'

The cage-fighter snorted. 'Some bodyguard! He looks half-dead.'

'Well, let's finish the job for him,' replied Skull-man, drawing a handgun from his holster. 'After all, the Pakhan did say he was *expendable*.'

At the prospect of imminent death his body finally responded. With lightning speed, Connor seized the gun's muzzle.

'What the –?' cried Skull-man as Connor's seemingly dead body came to life and fought to disarm him.

Exactly as he'd been taught in training, Connor twisted the weapon away from himself. The gun discharged and a bullet blasted the ground, sending up a plume of snow. Yet again Jody's words of wisdom sounded loud in his head: *once you get hold, you must never let go. Your life literally depends upon it.*

Connor was in no doubt about that. He kicked hard at Skull-man's right knee. The man buckled and Connor rotated the gun sharply towards his attacker. There was a sickening *crack* as the man's finger snapped in the trigger guard. Skull-man shrieked in agony. But as Connor wrestled to take full control of the weapon the other man lumbered in with a punch like a rockfall. He caught Connor across the jaw so hard that stars burst before his eyes. All his strength sapped by the hammer blow, Connor went limp, dropped the gun and crumpled to the ground.

Still howling with pain and fury, Skull-man hobbled to standing and kicked Connor in the thigh. 'On your knees!' he ordered.

His head ringing and his jaw aching, Connor struggled into a kneeling position as he was booted again.

'So there *was* a little more fight left in him.' The cage-fighter laughed. 'He broke your finger!'

Skull-man didn't laugh. Scowling at his partner, he picked up the gun in his left hand and planted the cold metal of its muzzle against Connor's forehead.

'This is an SPS handgun,' he told Connor with vindictive glee. 'My personal favourite when executing scum like you. When loaded with armour-piercing SP10 bullets, like it is, this weapon is able to penetrate thirty layers of Kevlar body armour backed by a titanium plate. Why am I telling you this?'

He paused for effect, a grin revealing uneven coffee-stained teeth.

'So you know what's going to happen to you when I pull the trigger,' he said, answering his own question. 'The bullet will literally blow your brains out and leave a hole so large in the back of your head, I'll be able to reach inside your skull and scoop out what little's left.'

'You might have trouble with your broken finger!' Connor spat, his joke a last stab at his attacker. By the murderous look in the man's eyes, Connor knew it was over. He'd had his chance to disarm him . . . and failed.

In the brief few seconds he had left to live, his thoughts turned to his mum and gran. *You shouldn't have to risk your life for ours*, his gran had pleaded. *You're in the line of fire. Risking everything. And for what?*

For you and Mum had been his answer. And it remained so. But how he wished he could be safe with his mum and gran at that very moment.

His final thoughts were of Charley. He would never again hear her voice, hold her hand or kiss her soft lips. She'd warned him not to take this mission. Why hadn't he listened to her? Now he would die in this frozen wasteland.

Skull-man put his finger to the trigger. 'Say your prayers, little bodyguard!'

When the shot came, Connor didn't expect it. Nor did Skull-man.

The bullet went straight through the man's upper chest. A second bullet drilled a hole three inches to the left of the first. As he staggered backwards, a third clipped him in the head.

Mozambique drill, Connor thought, as Skull-man keeled over in the snow.

His partner made a dash for the snowmobile, where his assault rifle hung from the handlebars. But two well-aimed shots downed him before he could reach his gun.

Connor blinked in shock. Barely a few seconds ago he'd been facing certain death. Now both his attackers lay dead. Connor glanced over his shoulder, half-expecting to see Mr Grey. But it was Jason and Anastasia who emerged from the forest, Jason with the hunting rifle still pressed to his shoulder, its muzzle targeted on the prone body of Skull-man.

Anastasia hurried over to help Feliks while Jason continued to head his way. As he passed the fallen gunman, now lying in a slush of red snow, Jason tapped him with his foot. There was no response.

'He's . . . dead,' said Jason, sounding as if he didn't quite believe it. He lowered his gun and helped Connor to his feet.

'You had no choice,' said Connor, noticing the tremble in Jason's hands. 'It was either them or me.'

'I know, a tricky decision!' said Jason with a forced laugh, its hollowness betraying his deep shock. 'Bet you're glad now I'm a better shot than you.'

'Too right. If it had been the other way round, I might have hit you!'

Jason suddenly embraced him. 'I'm just glad you're OK, bro.'

'Likewise,' said Connor, taken aback by this unexpected show of friendship.

Jason released him and for a moment an awkward silence hung between them, neither knowing what to say next.

'So . . . what happened to you?' Connor eventually asked. 'And where's your snowmobile?'

A distant report of gunfire caused Jason to glance anxiously in the direction of the forest, then he turned back to Connor. 'We lost you during that second ambush. It was chaos, but we managed to ride through. Two of the gunmen chased us on foot, then gave up. Just as we got clear, we ran into *another* unit. There must be a small army in there! We barely escaped with our lives. Then we hit a ditch a little way back and broke one of the snowmobile's skis. Had to go on foot after that.'

'Did you see if Viktor or Mr Grey made it?'

Jason shook his head. 'No, but I heard a couple of snowmobiles in the distance.'

'Could have been these two,' said Connor, nodding at the dead gunmen.

'We need to go!' Anastasia urged, as she half-carried a limping Feliks to one of the snowmobiles.

'She's right,' said Jason. 'The other gunmen aren't far behind us. You OK to walk?'

'I'll run if I have to,' Connor replied, not admitting that every bone in his body felt like it had been beaten with a hammer.

As they headed to the snowmobiles, Anastasia's eyes opened wide and she yelled, 'Watch out! *Behind you!*'

Connor and Jason spun to see Skull-man sitting up in a pool of blood-red snow, his scarred face a pale death mask. Although the first two bullets had hit home, the third had glanced off Skull-man's forehead, temporarily stunning him rather than finishing him off. His outstretched arm shook as he tried to steady his aim with the gun.

'Too late for prayers now!' spluttered Skull-man, blood spilling from his lips as he pulled the trigger.

Connor never felt the bullet's impact . . . because Jason took it for him.

In the second prior to Skull-man firing, Jason had wrapped his body round Connor's and shielded him. As the round struck him in the back, Jason stiffened and grunted with pain. Behind them, Skull-man collapsed, his final act of violence done.

'Jason!' cried Connor, holding his friend in his arms as they both sank to the ground.

'Man, that hurts!' he groaned, his face screwed up in agony. 'Real bad.'

'Don't worry, you're wearing your bulletproof jacket. You'll be fine. It's just the impact that kicks like a mule,' Connor explained, his own back still throbbing from where he'd been hit during the first ambush. Still, concerned about the risk of blunt trauma, he unzipped Jason's jacket to check for any unusual bruising . . . and discovered blood soaking through Jason's sweater.

That wasn't right.

Then Connor remembered . . . SP10 armour-piercing bullets! *This weapon is able to penetrate thirty layers of Kevlar body armour backed by a titanium plate.*

As Anastasia rushed over and snatched the gun from the dying Skull-man, Connor peeled away the bloodsoaked layers of clothing to expose an alarmingly large hole in Jason's stomach. The armour-piercing round had gone straight through him, finally being stopped by the bulletproof panel at the front of his jacket.

'Tell me the worst, doc!' Jason gasped, a sweat breaking out on his brow.

'You'll be OK,' Connor replied, applying pressure to the wound and causing Jason to cry out. But blood continued to pour through his fingers.

Connor couldn't bear the thought of losing his friend and partner. Not after all they'd been through together on this mission. He frantically reached for his Go-bag, but it had been ripped open during the snowmobile crash and the contents had scattered across the ground. But he soon spotted what he needed.

'Anastasia, grab that dressing and that packet of QuikClot over there,' he ordered, pointing to the two potentially life-saving items.

She gathered them up – and anything else she could grab – and ran across to her friends. Connor tore open the packet and poured the QuikClot agent over Jason's entry and exit wounds. The powder instantly set to work, speeding up the clotting process and arresting Jason's blood loss.

'You'll be OK,' said Connor again. But he knew this was just a temporary fix – and so did Jason. They needed to get him to the dacha fast, where there was a full trauma kit.

Jason smiled weakly. 'You keep saying that. Doesn't feel OK . . .'

Connor turned to Anastasia, who stood staring numbly at Jason's wound. 'Get one of the snowmobiles. We need to move him.'

Snapping out of her trance, she hurried off and started the engine, while Connor began to wrap the dressing around Jason's stomach.

'Hey, do me a favour,' wheezed Jason. 'Tell Ling . . . I'm sorry . . . for being such an idiot . . .'

'Tell her yourself,' replied Connor, continuing to bandage the wound.

Jason shook his head weakly. 'I don't feel right. I'm cold . . . *so* cold . . .'

'That's cos I've got your jacket open.'

'No, it's more than that. The cold's *inside* me . . .' He clasped Connor's arm. 'Promise . . . to keep Ana safe . . . promise?'

Connor nodded. 'Sure, I promise, but –'

All of a sudden Jason's body went limp and his expression slackened. 'Hey, I don't feel the pain any more. Perhaps I am OK . . .'

He gave Connor a winning smile. Then his eyes lost focus and the smile slipped from his face.

The falling snow slowly shrouded Jason in a white blanket. Connor knelt next to his dead partner, lost in a storm of grief, anger and regret.

His sorrow at the cruel death of his friend was mixed with rage at the gunman whose armour-piercing bullet had made that final killing shot. But most of all he regretted the petty squabbles with Jason, the stupid insults they'd exchanged and the trivial one-upmanship. And in all that time he hadn't taken one opportunity to show the admiration and respect he had for his partner. Now it was too late.

Too late to make amends. Too late to say sorry. Too late to be *true* friends.

The two of them had been like bickering brothers. But, despite always arguing, their training and mission had united them. And Jason had clearly felt the same way. His last words kept replaying in Connor's mind. *I'm just glad you're OK, bro.*

Connor began to choke up. When the time had come, Jason hadn't hesitated to save him. He'd leapt into the line of fire and made the ultimate sacrifice.

Anastasia rode the short distance over to Connor with the snowmobile and cut the engine. When she saw Connor's grief and the unnatural stillness of Jason's body, her ice-blue eyes melted with tears.

'No . . .' she said softly. '*Not Jason . . .*'

She slid from her seat and fell to her knees beside Jason. With a tenderness that betrayed her true feelings for him, she caressed his unruly hair and wept. Connor fought back his own tears, clenching his fists in frustrated fury, barely aware of the gunfire drawing closer.

Feliks limped over. 'Jason's dead. OK, it's tragic. But you need to get *me* out of here. Now!'

Connor didn't move, or even look up. He no longer cared. For himself, for Feliks, for anyone.

Anastasia reached over and squeezed his shoulder. 'Feliks is right. There's no point Jason sacrificing himself for you if you let yourself be killed now.'

Connor stared at her, her face appearing angelic in his blurred vision. He remembered the promise he'd made to keep Anastasia safe, and got to his feet. He hated abandoning Jason in the snow. But he vowed he'd return for his friend when this was all over.

Suddenly the forest edge erupted with gunfire. Two security guards sprinted from the treeline, only for one to be cut down a few paces later in a storm of bullets. A unit of gunmen in white ski jackets emerged and continued firing at the other guard – and at them. Connor pushed Anastasia and Feliks into the cover of the snowmobile. A percussion of bullets raked along its side, the sound like hail hitting a car roof.

'We're sitting ducks!' cried Feliks, covering his head with his hands.

More steel-jacketed rounds whizzed past. But this time the harsh *clack* of automatic weapons came from behind. Connor glanced over his shoulder and spotted three more of Mr Grey's security guards hunkered down inside the boathouse on the other side of the lake. They were laying down a wave of suppressing fire to help their comrade to escape and forcing the enemy back to the treeline.

'This is our chance,' said Connor. He reached up and twisted the snowmobile's ignition. Nothing happened. He tried again. The engine didn't even turn over. Then Connor noticed the dribble of black oil in the snow and the multiple holes in the cylinder block. The engine was dead. The other snowmobile was equally damaged, gasoline spurting from its fuel tank.

'We'll have to make a run for it,' said Connor.

Feliks looked all the way up the slope to the dacha in the distance. 'We'll never make it.'

'It's our only hope,' said Connor. 'Now let's go –'

'Wait!' said Anastasia, grabbing his arm. 'We need a distraction first.'

'Like what?' asked Connor.

She held up a small round plastic container. 'I picked these up when I was getting the dressing and QuikClot,' she explained, prising the lid off.

On the container's side, the label declared *All-Weather Survival Matches*. Connor smiled. Another life-saving item from his Go-bag. Bugsy, their surveillance tutor, had once demonstrated their effectiveness. They were more like small flares than matches. They burnt intensely for almost twelve seconds, couldn't be blown out and even continued to work in water. But they weren't any sort of grenade or smoke bomb.

'How are *those* going to help us?' said Feliks dismissively.

Anastasia flicked the match against its striker and it burst into flame. She threw the match over to the other snowmobile where it landed in a patch of petrol-soaked snow. The fuel instantly caught light and a moment later the entire snowmobile exploded in a mighty fireball, billowing black smoke into the air.

'Like that!' she said, as a wave of heat hit them. She struck another match and planted it in the ground. 'I'd advise you both to run.'

Connor glanced down and saw the dribble of black oil advancing on the match. He leapt to his feet with Feliks and they sprinted for their lives. A moment later the snowmobile detonated like a firebomb, the blast almost knocking them off their feet.

'You're crazy!' Feliks shouted at Anastasia, as parts of flaming snowmobile rained down on them.

'Crazy but clever!' said Connor, once again admiring Anastasia's natural instincts as a buddyguard.

Concealed by the smoke, they ran up the slope towards the dacha. It was tough going, the thick snow like glue around their feet. Thanks to his fitness training, Connor had the stamina and so too did Anastasia. But Feliks was flagging, his breath ragged and laboured.

'Keep going!' Connor urged as his Principal's limping pace slowed even more.

Anastasia's quick thinking had given them a head start, but now the smoke-screen was dispersing and the gunmen renewed their attack, splitting their firepower between the boathouse, the surviving security guard and the fleeing group.

Feliks collapsed in the snow, his chest heaving.

'Come on!' said Connor as deadly rounds *zinged* overhead.

'I can't . . . go . . . any further . . .' he gasped.

The security guard caught them up but didn't stop to help. Instead he ran past, more concerned for his own life than saving his boss's son. Connor had every mind to leave Feliks behind too, after his self-centred remark following Jason's death. But he'd sworn to protect Feliks and wouldn't fail in that duty. Taking him by the arm, Connor hauled him to his feet. Anastasia took his other arm and they half-dragged him up the slope.

The gunfire increased in intensity. Connor glanced back. The boathouse had been overrun and the gunmen were now in pursuit. Supporting Feliks as much as he could, Connor dug deep and ran for all he was worth. But the dacha still seemed a mile off, the garden somehow growing in length with every step they took. Suddenly the snow around them erupted and the security guard ahead screamed as one of the bullets took him down.

Connor threw himself on top of Feliks and Anastasia, shielding them as best he could with his jacket.

Pressed against the snow, her face flushed and her breathing rapid, Anastasia stared at Connor with true fear in her eyes for the first time. 'We're not going to make it, are we?'

Connor realized the chances of them *all* safely reaching the dacha were virtually zero. Exhausted and half-lame, Feliks was a dead weight and a liability. Connor had little left in the tank himself, having supported his Principal most of the way. Anastasia had the greatest chance of survival. Quick and nimble in the snow, she might just outrun the gunmen. But with every passing second their pursuers drew closer and their aim improved.

'You go ahead!' Connor told her. 'I've got Feliks.'

Anastasia hesitated.

'Just GO!' he ordered.

With the gunmen bearing down on them, Anastasia ran off towards the dacha and Connor made one last-ditch effort to save his Principal.

'You've had your rest,' he said, sliding himself off Feliks's back. 'Now get to your feet.'

'But my leg hurts,' Feliks complained, grimacing with pain as he tried to stand.

'I promise you, a bullet hurts a helluva lot more.'

Holding his Principal in front so that he acted as a shield from behind, Connor propelled Feliks up the slope. A volley of gunfire chased them and a bullet clipped Connor's arm, winging him. He wheeled round but kept his feet, the jacket doing its job and absorbing the impact. But, as he staggered on, Connor knew with dead certainty that the next direct hit would drop him.

Then, when all hope seemed lost, Mr Grey appeared like an avenging devil at the top of the slope. Crouched behind one of the garden statues, an assault rifle in his grip, he began to pick off the gunmen one by one. His precision shooting made short work of their pursuers, and soon Connor and Feliks were the only two left running up the slope.

The irony wasn't lost on Connor. Once again the assassin had saved his life!

Anastasia was waiting for them at the top of the garden. She took Feliks's arm and helped to support him as he recovered his breath.

'I see three of you made it,' remarked Mr Grey, slamming a fresh magazine into his rifle. 'But you took your time.'

Connor looked daggers at the assassin. Before Connor could reply, Mr Grey strode off towards the dacha. They hurried after him and discovered Viktor crouched inside the main entrance protected by two armed security guards. When Feliks limped into sight, Viktor ran out and embraced his son.

'I thought I'd lost you,' he said, displaying more affection for the boy than Connor had ever seen before.

'No time for happy reunions,' Mr Grey interrupted. He looked to one of the guards, the chain-smoker who'd ignored Connor the previous day. 'Where's Yuri?'

'Getting the vehicle prepped, as ordered,' replied the guard.

Mr Grey glanced round. 'Well, he should've been here by now.'

With a curt wave of his hand, Mr Grey instructed them all to follow him. Rifles primed, the two security guards kept a sharp eye on their surroundings as they skirted round the dacha and made their way towards the garage block. Feliks stayed with his father, so Connor stuck close to Anastasia.

Turning to Connor, Viktor asked in a hushed tone, 'No Jason?'

Unable to find words, Connor just shook his head.

'I'm so sor–'

Mr Grey silenced Viktor with a glare. They had to cross twenty metres of open ground to reach the garage block. Mr Grey signalled the chain-smoking guard to go ahead. The guard sprinted the short distance and entered the garage through a side door. A few seconds later, the main garage door automatically opened, revealing the grille of a white four-wheel drive Toyota Land Cruiser.

The guard appeared. 'No Yuri, but all clear!' he said, beckoning them over.

Mr Grey led the way. However, as the garage door fully opened, it completed an electrical circuit and triggered a hidden bomb. The fireball incinerated the guard and obliterated the Land Cruiser. The blast that followed vaporized the snow and knocked everyone off their feet.

Connor lay sprawled on the ground as debris rained down. A buzzing filled his ears like the static of an old TV and he coughed and wheezed as the bomb-blasted air filled his lungs. Through the haze of smoke and flames, he spotted at least ten men in white ski jackets marching towards them.

Mr Grey was on his knees, dragging Viktor back to the cover of the dacha. The other guard was dead, a jagged piece of the Toyota's metal bodywork protruding from his chest.

On willpower alone, Connor crawled over to Anastasia. Her face was smeared with ash and a thin stream of blood ran from her nose, but she was breathing. Connor shook her and shouted her name, his own voice sounding dull and distant in his head. She responded with a few blinks, then raised her head weakly. Between them, they managed to stand and stagger the short distance back to the dacha.

Mr Grey was now half-carrying Viktor towards the front door. The billionaire was calling for his son. But either the assassin didn't hear or didn't care about the boy's fate. He simply kept going.

Connor turned and saw the boy laid out on the ground. To all appearances, dead. Then he noticed a twitch of the fingers and a slight rise of the chest.

'I'm OK!' said Anastasia, her shout sounding more like a whisper. 'Get Feliks.'

Making sure Anastasia reached the front door first, Connor then went back for his Principal. A quick inspection of Feliks revealed no major injuries; the boy was just in deep shock.

He glanced up. The gunmen were closing in, but seemed in no rush to finish off their quarry.

Calling upon all his remaining strength, Connor hauled Feliks on to his shoulders and lurched towards the dacha's main entrance. No shots were fired at them and Connor was amazed to make it alive. As soon as they were inside, Mr Grey slammed the door and bolted it shut.

'What the hell's going on?' said Connor, after depositing Feliks into the arms of his father. His ears still rang, but his hearing was gradually returning. 'Bombs, ambushes, assault teams . . . It's a flipping war zone!'

'When things go bad in Russia, they usually go bad in a big way,' said Mr Grey, dragging over a heavy wooden cabinet to block the front door.

Connor lent his muscle to the task. 'But who are the men attacking us?'

'*Krysha*,' Mr Grey replied. When he caught the bemused look on Connor's face, he added, 'Bratva enforcers, recruited from the most violent ex-convicts and murderers in Russia.'

'Sounds like your sort of friends,' said Connor dryly.

Mr Grey stared at him, the joke falling flat. 'I don't have friends.'

Connor glanced over at Viktor Malkov, the billionaire clasping his son to his chest, his bloodied face a mix of thunder and fear. 'Isn't Viktor a friend?'

'He's an associate,' Mr Grey replied, his tone cool and business-like, 'and a highly valuable asset to Equilibrium.'

'What's this *Equilibrium*?' demanded Connor, recalling the name from his African assignment.

The assassin drew his Ruger SR 9c semi-automatic pistol from its holster and Connor flinched away, immediately regretting the question.

Mr Grey smirked at Connor's knee-jerk reaction. 'If we survive this, Connor Reeves, maybe I'll introduce you to them.'

The assassin checked the pistol's cartridge, half-empty, and turned to the billionaire. 'Do you have any more guns or ammo?'

Viktor gave an absent nod. 'In my study.'

As Mr Grey headed across the entrance hall, Viktor reached out and seized the assassin's arm. 'So, what's the plan *now*?' he demanded, sounding both desperate and angry. 'The grounds are overrun. The guards all dead. And our only escape vehicle has just been destroyed!'

Mr Grey looked down at Viktor's hand with something approaching distaste and the billionaire quickly released his grip. 'I've already called for back-up,' he replied.

'And how long will that take?'

Mr Grey shrugged. 'Two hours, maybe a little more. We just need to hold out until then.'

The assassin's blasé attitude to their predicament only enraged the billionaire more. 'We've barely survived the last half-hour!' he cried. 'What makes you think we can last out another *two* hours?'

Mr Grey replied in a matter-of-fact tone as stone-cold as his stare. 'Because we must.'

The assassin opened the door to the study, and Viktor snapped, 'I thought Equilibrium promised to protect me from all this!'

Mr Grey glanced back over his shoulder. 'Well, you're not dead yet, are you?' he said acidly, before disappearing into the study.

Connor felt the entrance hall breathe again. At times he didn't know who was more dangerous – the *krysha* outside or the assassin Mr Grey. Connor went over to Anastasia, who was leaning against the wall for support.

'You all right?' he asked.

She responded with a faint smile. 'I'm all in one piece, if that's what you're asking.'

Connor was amazed at her resilience. Most people would have been an emotional wreck or in total shock after being shot at, pursued by gunmen and almost blown up. In fact Feliks was a perfect example of just that as he rested his head numbly against his father, his eyes glazed over in the thousand-yard stare of a battle-weary soldier.

'Do you *really* think we'll survive long enough for back-up to arrive?' asked Anastasia, dabbing at the blood dripping from her nose with the back of her hand.

Connor found her a box of tissues from the hall's restroom, at the same time catching a glimpse of himself in the mirror. He barely recognized himself. His hair was matted and grey with dust, his face streaked with dirt and blood, his lower lip split and his cheek bruised and swollen like a prizefighter's. Judging by his appearance alone, he didn't much rate their chances of survival. But he replied, 'If Mr Grey says so. He's experienced in these sorts of situation. And I'll do everything in my power to protect you.'

Anastasia replied with a bittersweet smile, 'That's what Jason promised me too.' Then her eyes narrowed. 'What do you mean by *experienced*?'

Before Connor could reply, Mr Grey returned with a hunting rifle, a second pistol in a paddle holster and a box of bullets. He threw Viktor the hunting rifle. 'Locked and loaded, but don't waste any rounds. We're short on ammo.'

Discounting Feliks due to his state of deep shock, Mr Grey presented Connor with the handgun – a SIG Sauer P226. 'I presume you know how to use one of these?' he asked.

Connor nodded. Gunner had made sure that he and Jason were familiar with the most common semi-automatic pistols. Sliding the SIG from its holster, he checked the magazine, chamber and safety before weighing the weapon in his hand. The SIG P226 was a lot heavier than a Glock 17 due to its stainless-steel frame and Connor knew he'd have to account for this when aiming.

Mr Grey eyed Connor. 'You ever shoot someone?'

Connor shook his head, clipping the holster to his belt.

He smiled coldly. 'The first time's the hardest. After that, it's child's play.'

Connor felt an iron knot tighten in the pit of his stomach. He'd trained to protect people. Not kill them. This was a line he hadn't wanted to cross. But he understood the situation now might demand it. If faced with a choice between a *krysha* and saving Anastasia, Feliks or himself, he couldn't afford to hesitate in pulling the trigger.

'We need to make this dacha as secure as a castle,' Mr Grey instructed, heading for the kitchen. 'Lock and block all the doors. Close the windows. Pile the furniture into barricades. And do it quickly!' He snapped his fingers in front of Feliks's face, bringing the boy out of his daze. 'Did you hear me?' Feliks gave a vague nod. 'Then move!'

As they set to work battening down the hatches, Anastasia called out from the front living room, 'Why aren't they attacking?'

Having checked the rear patio doors were locked, Connor joined her in the living room and peered through the window. It seemed the ten *krysha* had fanned out round the dacha. They now stood like sentinels, watching the house.

'There's your answer,' said Mr Grey, coming up behind and pointing to the bottles in their hands.

Each of the *krysha* carried a Molotov cocktail. Upon a command they lit the rags and a gunman began shooting out the dacha's windows ... then the firebombs rained down.

The living-room window imploded in a cascade of glittering glass. Connor shielded Anastasia from the lethal shards as a Molotov cocktail was hurled through. The bottle smashed on to the wooden floor, splattering blazing liquid everywhere. As the furniture went up like a bundle of dry sticks, a roar of flame filled their ears and the air turned toxic with the stink of acrid fumes.

Battling against the wall of heat, his skin searing, Connor bundled Anastasia out of the room. Already out in the hallway, Mr Grey slammed the door shut behind them in an attempt to stop the fire spreading. But his jacket sleeve was dripping with flaming petrol and his arm was ablaze. Tearing off his jacket, he stamped on it until the fire was extinguished, wisps of smoke rising from the scorched fabric.

Viktor, his rifle over his shoulder, sprinted down the hall towards them. Right behind him was Feliks, panic etched on his pale face.

'The games room and drawing room are on fire!' said Viktor.

'The bedrooms too,' gasped Feliks, coughing from the smoke seeping round the door frames.

The wooden dacha was fast turning into a deadly bonfire. And they were in the middle of it.

'We've got to get out!' Anastasia cried, dashing to the front door and clawing at the cabinet. But she couldn't move it on her own. 'Help me!' she pleaded. 'Connor!'

Mr Grey put a hand on Connor's shoulder, holding him back, his bony fingers like talons. 'No, that's exactly what they want,' he said. 'If we run out, they'll shoot us down like dogs.'

'What other choice do we have?' said Connor, shaking off his grip.

'He's right. We'll be burnt alive if we stay here!' Viktor argued as the crackle of flames grew more intense. 'We have to surrender.'

'There is no surrender,' said Mr Grey. Anastasia was now kicking at the cabinet in her desperation to escape. Connor went over and tried to calm her. 'But there's another way,' said the assassin. 'Follow me.'

Heading into the kitchen – the one room currently spared an arson attack – he opened a drawer, pulled out several tea towels and soaked them in the sink.

'Wrap these round your faces to stop the smoke,' he instructed, handing out the sodden cloths.

Connor tied his tightly across his nose and mouth, then helped Anastasia with hers.

Mr Grey opened a small door in the kitchen wall. 'In here,' he ordered.

'But that only leads to the wine cellar,' said Viktor, his voice muffled by the cloth.

'Exactly. Now move!'

'But we'll suffocate down there,' protested Viktor.

Mr Grey stared at him, unmoved by the billionaire's argument. 'You'll burn here and die out there. Best take your chances below.'

Viktor shook his head in dismay but did as ordered, taking his son with him. Connor urged Anastasia towards the small dark opening.

'No! No! No!' she cried, shaking her head, her face a mask of terror.

The kitchen window imploded and another Molotov cocktail was flung in. Connor grabbed Anastasia and bundled her down the stairs. Viktor and Feliks were already at the bottom, Connor and Anastasia halfway down, when Mr Grey shut the door on them.

'He's locked us in!' Connor yelled, rushing back up the stairs and banging on the cellar door. 'The double-crossing snake has locked us in!'

'I'm sure it's part of his plan,' said Viktor, although he didn't look too convinced.

Connor turned on him. 'You're putting your trust in an *assassin*?'

'I've known Mr Grey for over ten years,' he replied. 'He's never let me down yet.'

'There's always a first time,' said Connor, furiously yanking on the handle. But the door wouldn't budge.

'Mr Grey's an assassin?' queried Anastasia, her voice small as she cowered in the corner, her knees hugged to her chest.

Connor could feel the handle growing hot in his grasp. He backed away from the door and descended the stairs. 'Mr Grey's a cold-blooded ruthless killer. He doesn't care about us. He doesn't care about anyone. He's locked us down here so he can make a clean escape!'

'Assassin? Bodyguard? It depends upon which end of the bullet you're on,' Viktor muttered. 'You can believe what you like about Mr Grey, but he's been employed to keep me alive.'

Connor glared at the billionaire. 'Then why's he left you to burn to death in this cellar?'

Viktor answered with a baffled shrug. 'I don't know. But he'll have his reasons.'

Connor began looking round for another exit. The bare bulbs in the ceiling cast a stark white light on the brick walls, wooden casks and rows upon rows of wine bottles. Dust lay thick on the concrete floor and mice scuttled through the shadows, desperate to escape the fire too.

'He said there was another way,' Feliks said, panicked. 'Isn't there another door or a tunnel?'

'There's *no* other way,' replied his father. 'The cellar's a dead end.'

The hope drained from Feliks's face. 'You mean ... we're trapped here?'

Viktor wrapped an arm round his son and pulled him close.

'What about an access hatch or window?' asked Connor, peering into the shadows at the far reaches of the cellar.

The billionaire shook his head. 'The cellar's a closed system. It's been designed to keep a constant temperature and level of humidity to preserve the wine.'

'Well, the temperature's only going up in here!' said Connor, now searching for anything he could prise open the door with – a crowbar, a hammer, even a screwdriver. But there were only more brick walls, bottles of wine and plastic crates.

'Papa, I'm feeling a bit dizzy,' said Feliks, swaying on his feet.

'Sit down,' said Viktor, guiding him over to a crate. 'You're just light-headed because the fire's sucking up the oxygen.'

Connor felt it too. His heart rate had increased and his breathing was laboured. The wet tea towels would absorb the worst of the smoke, but couldn't prevent them from inhaling carbon monoxide and other poisonous gases.

He went over to check on Anastasia. She was still curled up in the corner, her gaze fixed on the cellar door, eyes wide as moons, and her face just as pale. 'You OK?' he asked.

She didn't respond.

Delayed shock, Connor thought . . . or so he hoped. He sat down and put an arm round her shoulders to comfort her. As his sleeve brushed past her hair, it exposed her neck and the fine tapestry of white scars at its nape. 'Don't worry, we'll be fine –' he began.

Then the lights went out.

In the darkness, Connor could feel Anastasia trembling all over. On the other side of the cellar Feliks was moaning softly, his father trying to console him. Above them, the noise of the fire sounded like some wild beast rampaging from room to room. Connor thought he heard the stutter of gunfire, but it could equally have been the *snap-crack* of blazing wood.

A headache was starting to take hold and Connor realized that time was fast running out for them. The best they could hope for now was to fall unconscious before the flames consumed them.

As they huddled in the dark, almost suffocated by the cloying heat, Connor felt his phone vibrate in his pocket. He pulled it out and saw a text message from Colonel Black.

Call at once. Immediate withdrawal.

Too late for that, thought Connor. Regardless, he video-called headquarters.

Charley's worried face appeared on the screen. 'Connor! Where are you? What's going on? We can't make contact with *anyone*!'

Connor smiled beneath the wet cloth. 'It's good to see you, Charley.'

Her brow furrowed. 'Connor, why are you wearing that rag? Are you all right?'

He was beginning to feel sleepy and his limbs heavy. It was hard to think straight. 'We've . . . been attacked by Bratva enforcers,' he explained. 'Jason's dead.'

'No . . . not Jason!' cried Charley, shaking her head. She ran her hands through her hair, struggling to compose herself. 'Back-up is already headed for Malkov's dacha. So tell me *exactly* where you are, Connor.'

Connor felt Anastasia slump against him. 'We're trapped in the cellar beneath the dacha . . . the Bratva have set fire to the house.'

'Hold on, I'll arrange for emergency services to respond immediately,' said Charley. She picked up a phone and began dialling.

'They'll get here ... too late,' Connor slurred, his head drooping.

Tears began to run down Charley's face and she pressed a finger tenderly to the screen. 'Stay with me, Connor.'

He smiled weakly. 'I'll always ... be with you.'

'Connor, *I love you*.'

He looked at her, taking in the gentle curve of her chin, the bright blueness of her eyes and the soft sheen of her blonde hair. 'I love you too, Charley.'

Then the phone slipped from his fingers.

Connor could hear Charley's voice, distant and frantic, sounding from the phone at his feet. The glow from the screen did little to illuminate the cellar, but he could just make out Viktor and Feliks's forms slumped against one another in the darkness. By now the heat had risen so much that it felt like a furnace rather than a wine cellar. Several bottles near the ceiling exploded, spilling their contents across the walls.

Connor's head throbbed and nausea swept over him. He tried to pick up the phone, but his arm felt like lead. A lick of flame caressed the ceiling. Then another. Sparks rained down like falling stars as the blaze took hold and started to eat its way into the cellar.

Connor was fighting to keep his eyes open when the door to the kitchen burst open and Mr Grey appeared at the top of the stairs, flames rising behind him like he was the devil incarnate.

'OUT!' he yelled.

Viktor wearily rose, carrying his son with him. Helped by Mr Grey, they climbed the stairs and disappeared through the doorway. Connor knew with grim certainty that the assassin wouldn't come back for them. So, in one last superhuman effort, he willed himself to his feet and dragged the barely conscious Anastasia up after them. Each step was like climbing Everest, with his head spinning and legs that seemed made of lead. At one point he almost toppled backwards down the steps, but managed to grab hold of the rail and steady himself.

When Connor finally reached the top, he discovered the kitchen ablaze. The flames were so fierce and the heat so intense that his skin was instantly scorched and his hair singed. But Mr Grey had set up a garden hose to spray water at full blast into the room. While it couldn't stop the fire, the fountain of water was enough to reduce the flames and create a narrow pathway through to the back door.

Connor staggered out, stumbled another few paces until they were a safe distance from the dacha, then collapsed in a heap. The ice-cold air and freezing snow felt heavenly after the hellish heat of the fire. He lay there a moment, allowing his cheeks to cool against the snow and inhaling lungfuls of sweet oxygen. Once his headache had faded and his senses returned, he put Anastasia into the recovery position and got unsteadily to his feet.

The dacha was a raging inferno, its charred skeleton wreathed in yellow and red flames, thick black smoke swirling into the bleak sky like a tornado.

Mr Grey stood guard beside Viktor, who was checking on Feliks, his son weak and listless but alive. Blood ran down the assassin's right-hand sleeve where a bullet had clipped his arm. And there was a cut on his left cheek. Otherwise he appeared relatively unscathed.

The same couldn't be said for the Bratva enforcers. Their bodies were dotted round the dacha like discarded bags of rubbish. Mr Grey had laid waste to them. The *krysha* closest to Connor exhibited a classic double tap to the chest and one to the head. *Mozambique drill*, Connor thought absently and then remembered with sadness Jason entombed in the snow at the bottom of the garden. He had to go back and retrieve his fallen friend. The thought of it filled him with grief. Jason had paid the heaviest price to save him and Connor dreaded telling the other members of Alpha team about his tragic death.

'It's over,' Mr Grey declared, having completed his sweep of the grounds.

Viktor smiled with relief and went to shake his protector's hand when –

'Not quite,' said Anastasia, now standing with an SPS handgun aimed at Viktor's chest. 'You're a very hard man to kill, Mr Malkov.'

CHAPTER 74

Everyone stood perfectly still, as ash and snow fell around them, mottling the garden a funeral grey. Viktor had his hands raised in a gesture of surrender. Feliks knelt beside his father, his eyes wide and uncomprehending. Mr Grey had automatically reached for his Ruger pistol, but Connor noticed the slide was locked out, indicating the magazine was spent. Connor simply stared at Anastasia, unable to believe what she was doing. For a brief moment he wondered where she'd found the gun, then remembered her snatching it from the *krysha* who'd shot Jason.

Connor took a careful step towards her . . . then stopped as her eyes flicked in his direction, their icy glare warning him to stay back. 'Anastasia, put the gun down,' he urged. 'You're delirious from the fumes.'

'My name's not Anastasia,' she replied curtly, the pistol not wavering. 'It's Nadia.'

Connor blinked in bemused shock. *Nadia?* She *was* delirious.

Ignoring him, she addressed the billionaire. 'My father was Anton Surkov. My mother was Talya Surkov. My little brother was –' her voice cracked – 'Piotr Surkov.'

Viktor looked at her blankly. 'Am I supposed to know these people?'

'You should do,' she spat. 'You're responsible for their deaths.'

'Me?' he exclaimed, genuinely surprised. 'I don't know what you're talking about.'

Nadia sneered. 'Of course you don't. Why would you? We were just farmers. You were the mayor of Salsk.'

Viktor screwed up his face. 'That was some ten years ago.' He frowned more deeply. '*Surkov?* Now I come to think of it, I do recall that name. Wasn't there some fire at their farmhouse? Very sad. Everyone died, from what I remember.'

'Not quite everyone,' said Nadia, her finger tightening on the trigger.

Viktor held out a hand to ward off the attack. 'B-b-but what have I got to do with the fire?' he stuttered, a panicked sweat breaking out on his brow. 'It was a tragic accident. I didn't kill your parents.'

'You may not have pulled the trigger, but you're the one who loaded the weapon.' Her eyes blazed, all her rage focused on her bewildered target. But Connor saw Mr Grey's left hand sliding surreptitiously into his back pocket, clearly preparing to make a move. Not liking where the situation was headed, Connor subtly reached for the SIG on his hip.

'The fire was no accident,' continued Nadia. 'It was to cover up the attack by the Boykov Bratva. An attack *you* sanctioned as mayor, because my father was planning to resist and expose the corruption in your administration.'

'Ana – Nadia, are you sure you've got the right person here?' Connor interrupted. 'Mr Malkov is the one fighting corruption in Russia.'

Nadia let out a hollow laugh. 'He'd like everyone to believe that. As Lenin once said, a lie told often enough becomes the truth. And, Viktor, you've told yourself the lie so many times even you believe it! But *you're* the corruption that needs to be rooted out. The cancer that needs eliminating.'

Viktor raised his hands higher. 'Believe me, I had nothing to do with that attack. You're clearly confused and in shock. Your mind's been twisted by today's events. Now be a good girl and put the gun down, then we can forget all about this.'

'I can *never* forget about it,' snapped Nadia, a slight tremble in her hands as she tried to hold the gun steady. 'Every time I close my eyes. Every time I go to sleep. I see my father burning. My mother bleeding on the kitchen floor. And I hear my baby brother screaming, *screaming* . . . until his cries are silenced by a gunshot.'

'I'm truly aggrieved to hear that. It must be a living nightmare,' said Viktor, his voice soothing and calm. 'But, if you'll let me, I can help you hunt down these criminals and bring them to justice.'

'I already have,' said Nadia coolly. 'You're the last on my kill list.'

Viktor's eyes widened in disbelieving horror.

Nadia took a step closer to him. 'I *know* you were involved because I heard the Bratva scum who murdered my father say, "You can let the mayor know the weeds were rooted out before they got a chance to grow." And he was telling *that* man.' She turned the gun on Mr Grey.

The assassin froze, his hand still behind his back. '*You* were the one in the cellar,' said Mr Grey, more a confirmation than a question.

Connor was stunned. She was apparently telling the truth.

Nadia gave a single nod. 'I didn't recognize you, Mr Grey. Not until today at least. You're strangely *forgettable*. But I remembered the one with the dagger tattoo on his neck. The one who ordered my brother to be shot. The one who locked me in the cellar and set my house on fire. I didn't know his name or how to find him – as I did with Viktor – but his face and dagger tattoo were *burnt* into my memory, just like the scars on my back!'

Like a bolt of lightning Connor suddenly knew who she was talking about – Lazar! Viktor's personal bodyguard – he'd had a dagger tattoo on his neck. And it was Anastasia – or rather Nadia – who'd suggested the meeting in Red Square straight after she'd learnt that the bodyguard had been assigned to protect Feliks. It now struck Connor that Feliks had never been the target. 'So *you* were the sniper who shot Lazar?'

Nadia smiled, not with her usual warmth but with the hard edge of revenge. 'Yes, Connor. It was luck, or maybe fate, that I crossed paths with Lazar again. Whatever, I'm thankful for the chance I had to take revenge on my father's killer. And that's when all the pieces of the puzzle fell into place. Seeing Lazar, I had a flashback and recalled the lowlife who shot my brother. That's why Timur met his end with the bomb. It was meant to take out Viktor as well. But, as I said, he's a very hard man to kill.'

'But that bomb hurt so many more than just Timur,' said Connor, horrified. 'Innocent people died.'

'None of Viktor's men are innocent,' she snapped. 'They're all ex-Bratva. Every one of them has blood on their hands – if not my family's, then countless other innocent people's. Besides, the assassination was planned to be so much *cleaner.*'

She swung the gun back to Viktor. 'You were always my main target. I've spent my life preparing to kill you. Ten years in hiding, training with Chechen rebels, learning how to shoot, fight, flirt, assume another's identity . . . every conceivable skill I might need to assassinate you. I first tried to poison you at the restaurant but we were interrupted when you were arrested by FSB agents. Then it became a waiting game until I could get close enough to you again. When you invited me to stay at your dacha, I knew this would be my golden opportunity. I'd planned to shoot you last night, but Connor put a stop to that.'

'I did?' queried Connor.

Nadia gave him a pitying look. 'For a trained bodyguard, you sometimes overlook the obvious. Who'd practise the violin in the middle of the night? My case contained my gun. It was the only way I could smuggle a weapon through Malkov's security.'

Connor couldn't believe he'd been deceived so easily. He now recalled Nadia fleeing the scene at Red Square. She'd had her violin case with her there too. It must have concealed her sniper rifle! 'Can you even play the violin?' he asked.

Nadia gave him a wry smile in answer, then turned back to Viktor. Behind them the dacha groaned, then roared like a dying beast as the building collapsed in a fury of flaming timbers, flying sparks and billowing smoke.

'You burned my house to the ground. Now yours burns to the ground,' said Nadia with grim satisfaction. She aimed the gun directly at Viktor's heart. 'You took away my family, my home and my life. Now I will take yours.'

'Please, NO!' Viktor begged, his face a picture of true remorse. 'You have to understand that was the only way to exert authority back then. The nail that stuck out *had* to be hammered down. The Bratva had a stranglehold over me. But everything I have done since is to repent for those sins.'

Nadia snorted with disdain. 'What difference does that make to me and my murdered family?'

'*Our Russia* could be a new start for this country,' Viktor went on, wearing the oily smile of a politician. 'We're on the cusp of a big change. No more Bratva. No more corruption. You kill me . . . you kill the hope that your father died for.'

Nadia appeared to waver a moment. Then she gave a slow shake of the head. She clearly didn't believe him. Nor did Connor. Viktor had not only admitted his guilt; his supposed redemption was a lie. In ten years the billionaire hadn't changed at all. Connor had seen the man's true nature when he'd ordered Mr Grey to murder Dmitry in cold blood. And, although Viktor might no longer be associated with the Bratva and had every intention of bringing them and the government down, Connor knew the billionaire was connected to an organization seemingly far more sinister and dangerous – Equilibrium.

Connor found himself in a quandary. He was employed by Viktor. His duty lay with protecting Feliks. And Nadia had deceived him about her identity and her motives. Yet he and Jason had deceived her too about their roles. He'd also promised to protect her. On top of that, Viktor, believing his own lies, was the biggest deceiver of them all.

Out of the corner of his eye Connor noticed Mr Grey creeping forward. He drew his SIG Sauer pistol and took aim on the assassin. 'Stay back!' he warned.

Mr Grey stopped in his tracks, eyeing him with snake-like suspicion. 'Careful, Connor, which side you choose.'

'I think it's pretty clear which side I've chosen.'

Mr Grey shook his head in what looked like disappointment. 'I'm warning you, *don't* get in the way of Equilibrium's interests.'

Connor kept his gun trained on the assassin. 'And I'm warning you to leave Nadia alone.'

A cold sliver of a smile slid across the assassin's lips. 'I admire your courage, Connor, but I don't believe you've the guts to pull that trigger.'

'Well, do you have the guts to find out?' countered Connor.

Mr Grey didn't respond. But neither did he move.

'Surely we can settle this without further bloodshed,' said Connor, his muzzle not wavering from the assassin.

But his resolve to pull the trigger was wavering. He didn't want to shoot anyone, not even Mr Grey. 'Nadia, think about what you're doing. Didn't someone once say, an eye for an eye only makes the whole world blind? Killing Mr Malkov won't bring back your family. Report his crime to the authorities instead. Have him arrested. Tried in court. He'll be jailed for life and justice would be served.'

'Connor, you're so naive,' said Nadia. 'That might work in your country. But this is Russia. Money and power rule here. Even if the police believed me and arrested him, he'd just bribe his way to freedom. But *this* –' she held up the gun – 'is true Russian justice!'

The moment she took her aim off the billionaire, Mr Grey rushed at her, a glint of steel betraying the knife in his hand. At the same time Viktor went for the rifle slung over his shoulder. Caught between the two deadly threats, Nadia faltered for a fraction of a second before zeroing in on the billionaire. But Mr Grey was quick, covering the distance in a few paces. Seeing the assassin's blade slicing for her throat, Connor instinctively pulled the SIG's trigger. The pistol kicked, a *crack* like thunder splitting the air, and Mr Grey was blown off his feet. A second later another gunshot rang out. Viktor was hit square in the chest, but miraculously managed to keep on his feet.

He laughed at Nadia.

'Stupid girl!' he spat, chambering his rifle to return fire. 'Have you forgotten that I wear a bulletproof vest?'

'No,' she replied, her eyes like ice. 'Armour-piercing bullets.'

Viktor glanced down in shock and saw the blood seeping through a hole in his jacket. Only now did his brain register that he'd actually been shot.

'*Our Russia* votes you out,' declared Nadia as he slumped to the ground.

Even though Malkov was dead, Nadia kept her gun held out, a faint vapour trail of smoke rising from the SPS's muzzle. She appeared to be in a daze, as spent as the shell casing that had fallen at her feet. Then her arm fell limp at her side, the weapon dropping to the snow with a soft *thunk*.

Connor cautiously approached, one eye on Nadia and the other on Mr Grey, who lay sprawled on the ground, his body lifeless. The assassin had been wrong about the first time being the hardest. In the heat of the moment Connor had found the trigger all too easy to pull. It was the aftermath that was hard to cope with. He'd taken a man's life and the weight of it hung heavy on his conscience. He knew he'd had no choice, that Mr Grey would have killed Nadia with a vicious slice of his blade if Connor hadn't pulled the trigger. But that fact didn't dull the deep shock he was feeling.

It appeared that Nadia was also stunned by her actions. She stared blankly at the man responsible for her family's brutal murder. 'I thought I'd feel happier, my grief lessened,' she murmured. 'But I just feel . . . *empty*.'

'You're in shock,' said Connor, gently resting a hand on her shoulder.

Nadia flinched. She looked at him as if from a faraway distance. 'You . . . protected *me*.'

Connor nodded. 'I'd made a promise to Jason that I would.'

Nadia responded with a faint smile.

'So what are you going to do now?' he asked.

She looked up at the sky, snowflakes and ash drifting down from the grey clouds. 'My whole life has been spent preparing for this moment. Revenge was my only motivation – the only thing that stopped me going mad with grief. Now I've avenged my family's deaths and delivered justice, I've no idea . . . I'm a bit lost . . .'

Connor felt for her. Nadia's family had been murdered in the most brutal way. Somehow she'd survived ten years alone with only the thought of revenge for company. So, despite having just shot Viktor in cold blood, *she* was the true victim, the one who deserved sympathy and help. Connor could see that Nadia needed a new purpose. A way to keep her life on track. And with her skills in martial arts, firearms and surveillance it was obvious she'd make a formidable bodyguard. Yet her recent actions really made her . . . *an assassin*.

Still, there was always the chance of redemption.

'Nadia, I can talk to Colonel Black about you becoming a buddyguard. There's a possibility that, in light of everything, he'll *still* consider you for recruitment.'

Nadia gave a hollow laugh. 'You really think someone would trust me with their life? After what I've done? I'm sorry, Connor, but –'

'You weren't interested in me at all, were you?' said a forlorn voice from behind.

Connor spun round to see Feliks standing beside his father's bloodsoaked body, his eyes still glazed over with the shell-shocked look of a traumatized soldier.

Nadia gave him a pitying smile and shook her head. 'Sorry, Feliks, but no.'

His shoulders sagged. 'You used me to get to my father.'

He bent down as if only now realizing that his father had been killed. Then he picked up the rifle, rested the butt against his shoulder and took aim.

'NO!' shouted Connor, leaping in between the gun and Nadia. He realized Feliks had cracked. The combined strain of the attacks, the fire and his father's death had snapped his already fragile state of mind. Connor held up a hand, begging him to stop. 'Hasn't there been enough killing today?'

Feliks gave a little shrug. 'Perhaps . . . so what difference does taking one more life make?'

Connor stood his ground, shielding Nadia behind him. He had his SIG in his other hand, but didn't raise it in case he prompted Feliks to shoot. 'Don't do it, Feliks. This won't solve anything. You're in shock. You don't know what you're doing.'

Feliks cocked his head to one side, his eyebrows wrinkling in bemusement. 'You're supposed to be *my* bodyguard. Well, if you won't move, Connor, I'll just have to fire you.'

The rifle boomed and Connor was knocked backwards. He slumped to the ground at Nadia's feet, his chest throbbing as if a locomotive had ploughed into it. But the bulletproof jacket had saved his life once more. Fighting for breath and consciousness, he looked up at Nadia and managed to gasp, '*Run!*'

Nadia retreated a few steps, then stopped. She knew – like Connor did – it was pointless to flee. Feliks was a crack-shot with the rifle. If he'd been wielding a handgun, then she might have had a chance. But with a hunting rifle he would just shoot her down like a deer in the forest.

She spotted her SPS handgun in the snow and dived for it. Snatching up the weapon, Nadia pulled the trigger. The gun clicked dry.

'Oh dear, no more bullets,' said Feliks, rechambering his rifle. 'Would you like one of mine?'

With a faint shake of her head, Nadia dropped her gun in defeat.

'Go on, run,' said Feliks with a sneer on his lips. 'I'll give you until the count of ten.'

Nadia didn't move.

Feliks shouldered the rifle. 'Ten . . . nine . . . eight . . .'

She bolted. Connor watched her race down the garden, heading for the treeline.

'. . . seven . . . six . . . five . . .'

She wasn't going to make it. Connor caught a glimpse of his SIG Sauer pistol half-buried in the snow. His fingers scrabbled for it, but the grip was just out of reach.

'Four . . . three . . .'

Feliks closed one eye and took careful aim. 'Two . . .'

Connor lunged and snatched up the gun and –

'ONE!'

A double blast echoed round the garden. Feliks let out an agonized scream and collapsed to the ground. Nadia whirled round like a winged bird, then crumpled.

'NO!' cried Connor.

Ignoring the wounded Feliks and the pain in his own chest, Connor staggered down the garden to Nadia. She lay in the white snow, blood fanning out like red wings beneath her.

Despite her injuries, she smiled up at him. 'I told you, Connor . . .' she wheezed, 'that Russian girls are full of surprises.'

'I'm sorry, I'm so sorry,' he said, dropping to his knees beside her, his apology both for her and for the broken promise he'd made to Jason. 'I tried my best to protect you.'

'I know you did,' she rasped. 'I know Jason did too.'

Connor stared at Nadia. 'He *knew* about your past?'

Nadia weakly shook her head. 'No, but he was my lifesaver. Always will be. If it wasn't for him, I wouldn't have –' She winced as a shudder of pain ran through her.

Connor began to unzip her jacket, looking for the entry wound, hoping to stem the bleeding.

'No, Connor, don't,' she said, grasping his hand with surprising strength.

He looked at her in confusion. In the distance he could hear the plaintive wail of sirens. 'But help is on its way.'

'I don't need help,' she replied, squeezing his hand. 'I'm ready to die . . . *happy* to die. Mama and Papa are waiting for me. And I'll see my baby brother . . . very soon . . .'

Connor felt her grip slacken and a final breath misted in the frigid air, hanging briefly over her . . . then it was gone. He continued to hold her hand, tears clouding his vision until Nadia was just a blur. Snowflakes fell, glistening against her pale skin as they settled on her face. Her ice-blue eyes gazed unseeing at the sky. And a serene smile graced her lips.

Nadia was finally at peace.

'The Black King is dead,' announced Nika, pocketing her phone and approaching the two men who sat at the polished walnut desk in the centre of the Kremlin office. A chess game was in play, lit from above by a huge crystal chandelier.

Roman Gurov pounded a fist into his palm, a grin of deep satisfaction cracking his stony face. 'At last!'

His opponent glanced up from the chessboard. 'Any survivors?'

Nika nodded. 'Feliks Malkov and one of the young bodyguards, Connor Reeves.'

'What about the assassin?' asked Roman's opponent. 'The one connected to Equilibrium.'

'Reeves reports Mr Grey was fatally shot –'

'Good –'

'But the body's missing.'

'*What?*' exclaimed Roman, sitting up straight in his chair.

'The boy showed our agent where the assassin supposedly fell. But there was no body, not even any tracks, just a patch of blood,' Nika explained. 'Either the boy is lying or the assassin survived and escaped.'

Roman scowled. 'Whatever the truth is, this assassin is alive and on the run. You need to find and eliminate him. We can have no loose ends.'

'A full clean-up is in progress,' Nika informed them with confidence. 'But what about the Reeves boy? He's currently being held by the police. You stated he was *expendable*.'

The FSB Director rubbed a hand across his dimpled chin. 'That I did. And after giving my son a black eye, expendable he is.'

Roman's opponent leant back in his chair and steepled his long fingers. 'It might be good to have a survivor or two, someone who can corroborate your story of a Bratva attack. If the boy dies in custody – especially a foreign boy with security connections – questions will be asked.'

The FSB Director hissed through clenched teeth, then waved a hand at Nika. 'Draft up a pre-prepared statement *in Russian*. Get the Reeves boy to sign it . . . whatever it takes. Then deport him.'

'And what about Feliks Malkov?' asked Nika. 'He's on his way to hospital but . . . we could let him bleed out before he got there?'

'Death does solve all problems,' agreed Roman, twisting the gold ring on his forefinger and nodding sagely.

His chess opponent shook his head. 'The boy's death *after* the event might appear a little too convenient. Besides, the problem's been solved with Malkov's demise.

Without their leader, the *Our Russia* movement is dead in the water. And the snake that is Equilibrium has had its figurehead cut off in Russia. It'll be some time before they try to infiltrate us again –'

There was a knock at the door and an elegant blonde woman in a smart black dress entered.

'Sorry to interrupt, President Blatov, but it's time for your cabinet meeting.'

President Blatov held up a finger. 'One moment, Anya, I've some important business to finish.'

As his PA left the room, President Blatov contemplated the chessboard for a moment, then picked up his queen and moved her three spaces, opposite the black king. He smiled in triumph at Roman Gurov.

'Checkmate.'

Alpha team stood in a small huddle round the open grave. A drizzle of rain thrummed upon the black domes of their umbrellas and dripped on to the sodden ground. The little tree-bound cemetery was nestled behind the school chapel, a solitary flintstone building with a single stained-glass window, and was home to a dozen or so lichen-covered tombstones. Among them, a polished white marble headstone glistened in the rain. In the distance the rugged peaks of the Brecon Beacons were shrouded in mist, and there was a chill in the air so deep that it worked its way to the bone. But Connor and the others ignored the cold as they listened in respectful silence to the priest.

'We have entrusted the soul of our dear departed to God's mercy, and we now commit this body to the ground,' intoned the priest, reading from the red leather-bound book clasped in his pudgy hands. 'Earth to earth, ashes to ashes, dust to dust; in sure and certain hope of the Resurrection to eternal life, through our Lord Jesus Christ, Amen.'

At the priest's beckoning, Connor tossed a handful of earth into the grave, the dirt clattering sad and hollow upon the wooden coffin below. As he fought back his tears, he felt Charley's hand take his and offer a consoling squeeze. The other members of Alpha team now cast their scatterings of soil and duly paid their respects.

'It could have so easily been your funeral too,' said Ling, resting her hand tenderly on Jason's broad shoulders.

Jason glanced up, his eyes rimmed red. 'Yeah, I know,' he croaked. 'You've got Connor to thank for delaying that little celebration!'

'And Mother Nature for turning you into an ice cube,' said Connor, patting his friend on the back. Jason winced slightly, his wounds still raw. His face was pale and gaunt, dark shadows ringing his eyes, and he sat hunched and unusually small in the wheelchair. But he was alive – a miracle considering he had been clinically dead for almost two hours.

The Russian doctors put his incredible survival down to two things: QuikClot and snow. First, Connor's application of the clotting agent had stopped Jason bleeding out. Then the tomb of ice-cold snow that had slowly encased him had super-cooled his body, dramatically slowing cellular activity and leaving him in a state of suspended animation. This had given the medics the crucial time window to transport Jason to the hospital, complete surgery on his gunshot wounds and carry out a blood transfusion before his brain cells began to die. For several hours it had been touch-and-go. The groundbreaking procedure known as EPR – 'Emergency Preservation and Resuscitation' – was still in its trial stages. Yet, as

Jason was resuscitated and oxygen reintroduced to his bloodstream, there was a huge risk of cell destruction, organ failure and even brain damage. But Connor knew Jason would be just fine when he heard his partner wisecracking to the doctor, 'I'd need a brain for there to be any damage!'

The funeral was not for Jason. It was for Nadia.

With no living relatives or any money besides her school scholarship, she'd been destined for a pauper's grave. And there'd been no way Connor was going to leave Nadia to be buried alone and forgotten in Russia. So he'd asked the FSB agent assigned to him if her body could be flown to Wales for burial instead. To his surprise, the agent – a tough yet striking redhead who'd introduced herself as Nika – had been extremely helpful. She'd just required him to sign some official documents first, each one in Russian and in triplicate. Then he'd been put on a private medical plane, with Jason on life support and Nadia's body in the hold, and sent home.

It was almost as if Russia couldn't wait to get rid of them.

'I know I never met her,' said Charley, after scattering earth on her grave, 'but from what I discovered during my research – once I had her real name – Nadia was a truly remarkable girl.'

Connor and Jason nodded in agreement.

'I've seen photos of her family's farmhouse after the fire,' Charley went on. 'It was burned to the ground. I've no idea how Nadia escaped from that cellar alive. But she did. Then, despite horrific burns to her back and being only five years old, she managed to walk over ten miles through freezing snow to her grandmother's house in the next village. *Ten miles!*'

Charley shook her head in disbelief at the ordeal. 'Then the poor girl couldn't go to hospital or the police, because she was the only living witness to her family's massacre. Which meant that she was a threat to the local Bratva gang and would be killed on sight. With corrupt officials offering her no protection, her grandmother somehow managed to keep Nadia's existence a secret for almost five years.'

The rain pattered loudly on their umbrellas as the funeral party listened in astonished silence to Nadia's life story.

'But Nadia's troubles weren't over,' said Charley with a sigh. 'She'd barely turned ten when her grandmother died. Imagine being ten, orphaned and a target for the mafia! No wonder she was desperate enough to join Chechen rebels. I couldn't find out much about her time with them. Only that it would have been a tough life. But her skills in firearms, unarmed combat and surveillance proved her determination to seek justice for her family's murder. The fact that she managed to assume a completely new identity as Anastasia Komolova and secure a music scholarship at the International Europa School proves Nadia was not only cunning but talented and bright.'

'You mean she could actually play the violin?' asked Connor, thinking of the deadly weapons the violin case had concealed.

Charley nodded. 'Nadia was a gifted violinist, according to her music teacher at the school.' She swept her gaze round the congregation. 'Nadia overcame every hardship thrown at her and never gave up. It's a shame she didn't live to become one of us.'

Connor hugged Charley, as much to stop his own tears as to thank her for giving them Nadia's life story. Everyone now knew who Nadia really was.

Jason threw in his handful of dirt and, eyes red with tears, gazed silently at Nadia's headstone. A small angel was carved on top, its wings spread in flight, and a few words had been engraved into the marble face:

Earth has no sorrow that heaven cannot heal.

The simple yet touching service over, Alpha team slowly made its way back to Buddyguard HQ. Connor and Jason were among the last to leave. When the rain turned from a drizzle to a downpour, Ling unlocked the brake on Jason's wheelchair, eased him round and rolled him along the path.

'This is . . . only temporary,' said Jason, grimacing with each bump and jolt. 'Until I recover.'

'Well, you'd better recover fast,' said Ling, fumbling with the umbrella at the same time as trying to steer. 'I'm not pushing you around for the rest of your life.' She glanced guiltily across at Charley. 'I'm so sorry . . . that was insensitive.'

'Don't worry,' Charley replied, and gave her own chair a pat. 'If I have my way, this will only be temporary too.'

Connor stopped in his tracks, raindrops splashing in the puddles at his feet. 'You mean to say, you've been selected by that spinal research group?'

Charley nodded, barely able to suppress her grin.

'Why didn't you tell me?' he said, a smile breaking through his grief. 'This is wonderful news.'

'Well, you've had a few other things on your mind,' she explained. 'And I thought it best to wait until the funeral was over.'

'So, when are you off?' he asked.

Charley shifted awkwardly in her chair, seeming reluctant to tell him. 'I fly to Shanghai next week.'

'I still can't believe you *shot* your Principal!' Amir laughed, shaking his head in disbelief.

'Only in the leg,' Connor replied defensively. He'd had no intention of killing Feliks when he pulled the gun's trigger. He'd just been aiming to wound and stop his Principal shooting Nadia. But he'd been a second too late to save her.

Connor plonked himself down in one of the armchairs in Alpha team's common room. He felt flat and cheerless. He'd just come off the phone from his gran; his mum was stable but no better. She needed round-the-clock care more than ever. He'd also seen Charley off at the airport and already he was missing her.

'Feliks more than deserved it,' said Jason bitterly. 'Just a shame you didn't go for a head shot!'

'That's a bit harsh,' said Richie, sprawled on the sofa, looking up from his manga comic.

'Harsh but fair,' Jason muttered. 'He killed Ana.'

'Nadia,' Connor corrected.

Jason waved him off. 'Whatever. She'll always be Ana to me.'

'And what will I be?' said Ling, striding into the room with Marc. 'Second best?'

Jason spun round in his chair, flashing her his broadest grin. 'You'll always be my first and true love.'

Ling stuck her fingers down her throat and pretended to be sick.

Marc laughed. 'You'll have to sweet-talk her better than that!'

'Too right,' said Ling. 'You've got a lot of making up to do before I'll fall for your Aussie charms again.' She brought over a tray of Jason's medicines. 'Now, as your nurse, you'd better be extra nice to me or I might swap your painkillers for laxatives.'

Jason gave her a look that verged on panic. 'You wouldn't, would you?'

'Who says I haven't already?' Ling replied, a smirk on her lips. 'Now be a good boy and take your medicine.' She offered him a suspiciously large brown pill.

Jason held it in the palm of his hand. 'Can I have a glass of water, please?'

Ling grinned even more. 'You don't swallow it, you stick it up your –'

'Connor! The colonel wants to see you,' interrupted Jody, their instructor, appearing in the doorway as Alpha team fell into fits of laughter at Jason's wide-eyed look of horror.

Dragging himself out of the armchair, Connor headed along the corridor to the colonel's office and knocked on the solid oak door.

'Enter!' responded a gruff voice.

Colonel Black sat behind his fortress of a desk, the debrief report on Operation Snowstorm open on its polished mahogany surface.

'Glad to see you're fighting fit after Russia,' he remarked. 'That was some ordeal.'

Connor nodded. Still suffering from a bruised chest, burns to his hands and a black eye, he didn't consider himself fighting fit. But there was nothing to be gained in arguing the point with a hardened military man like the colonel.

But he did want to raise another issue. 'The mission would have gone a lot smoother if we'd had *all* the facts,' he said.

Colonel Black held up a hand in acknowledgement. 'Such omissions were unfortunate. Viktor Malkov proved to be a habitual liar. I can assure you future clients will be more rigorously vetted and operational information fully completed. Talking of which –' he tapped a page in the report – 'this Mr Grey and the Equilibrium organization. Are you certain you've encountered them before?'

'Absolutely,' said Connor.

'And you say you shot the assassin?'

'Point-blank. But I guess he must have been wearing a bulletproof vest.'

Ever since returning from Russia Connor hadn't been sleeping easy. He knew Mr Grey was ruthless and relentless, and half-expected the assassin to slit his throat in the middle of the night. Was it likely the assassin could track him down? Connor had no doubt that he could. But, with the entire Russian Secret Service hunting the man, would such a cold-hearted killer be interested in personal vengeance? Given their previous encounters, quite possibly. Only time would tell.

The colonel closed the file and set it aside. 'I'll have Bugsy investigate further. If Equilibrium is even half as dangerous and pervasive as your report implies, then it'll have serious implications for future operations. Now, on to your next mission.'

Connor's jaw dropped. '*What?* I thought we'd agreed I could have a break from active duty.'

'Yes, we did,' the colonel replied, his rugged face expressionless. 'With Charley away and Jason out of action, though, you're back in.'

Thrown by this railroading of his request for leave, Connor stared out of the window. In the darkening dusk the cemetery and its tombstones were just shadows. Only the white marble of Nadia's gravestone stood out, a reminder of the perils on every assignment. And, after four straight operations in a row, the risk of mission fatigue and a fatal mistake only grew.

'Can't another team take up the slack?' he asked.

'They're already committed,' the colonel replied firmly.

'What about Ling or Richie or Marc? I can head up the operations from HQ.'

Colonel Black shook his head. 'That'll be Jason's role while he's in recovery. Listen, Connor, I wouldn't ask this of you if I had an alternative. But you're the most qualified and capable recruit among Alpha team. Your father's blood runs through you like the steel in a samurai sword. Besides, you fit this mission's profile.'

He took out an operation folder and dropped it on the desk. The location was designated as Mexico.

'Cover this one, then we'll discuss extended leave,' he said. 'It's only a short assignment. You'll be back in time for Charley's return.'

Connor glanced at the folder. The colonel clearly wasn't taking no for an answer. And, if he was honest with himself, he was tempted. With Charley away and his mum no better, he needed an assignment to occupy himself. Besides, he knew from past experience that after a week or two he'd be longing for the challenge of an operation and craving the adrenalin rush that came with protecting a Principal. His gran had been right when she'd said he was just like his father.

One more mission. *What harm could that do?*

Perched on the roof of a skyscraper, the golf range overlooked the sprawling urban mass of Shanghai. A patch of perfect green grass, it was an oasis against the glaring neon of the city. Far below, the constant flow of traffic washed by like a distant river, the honk of horns and drone of cars drifting up on the polluted haze. The day's humidity had begun to ease with the approach of evening and a light breeze cooled Mr Grey's brow as the Director carefully lined up the golf ball.

With a precise stroke of the putter, the Director struck the dimpled ball and watched it roll smoothly across the grass and into the hole. An impressive shot at twenty-five yards. Still without acknowledging the assassin's presence, the Director took a sip from a tall glass of iced tea before bending down to set up another putt.

'So Malkov is dead,' said the Director, without taking an eye off the ball. 'You were assigned to protect him. Why didn't you step into the line of fire to save our investment?'

'I'm an assassin, not a bodyguard,' Mr Grey replied curtly. His arm was bandaged and his cracked ribs were healing, but the pain of his failed mission remained raw and festering.

The Director now focused on the flagstick at the far end of the rooftop green. 'And you say Connor Reeves, from that Buddyguard organization, was to blame?'

'Yes. He protected the girl . . . by shooting *me*.'

The Director raised a slim eyebrow. 'Perhaps we should think of recruiting him instead?'

Mr Grey scowled darkly.

The Director took a practice swing. 'Yet this isn't the first time that boy has thwarted our plans.'

'No,' Mr Grey replied. 'He's become somewhat of a thorn in our side.'

The Director stopped mid-swing. 'What does he know about Equilibrium?'

'Very little. Our name, but not our purpose.'

The Director paused a moment longer in thought. 'Yet an ant may well destroy a whole dam.' With a sideways glance at the assassin, the Director said pointedly, 'It's prudent never to underestimate such threats, Mr Grey.'

'What would you have me do?' asked the assassin.

'Eliminate the ant,' the Director ordered, resuming the swing and striking the ball. Mr Grey followed the path of the shot – the golf ball sank into the hole without a trace. 'In fact, destroy the whole nest.'

With each Bodyguard book, the missions become harder, more challenging and ever more daring – not just for my hero Connor but for me as a writer too. In order to satisfy my own, as well as my fans', high expectations, I have to ensure each story is better than the last – tonally different yet still familiar; fresh in plot yet containing the same core ingredients that will guarantee my readers devour each chapter in the series. And so I hope you've enjoyed the thrill of *Assassin* and are eager for the next instalment . . . *Fugitive!*

However, while a story is written by a single author, the finished book is the sum of many people's hard work and efforts. And I'd like to thank those who have played a crucial role in producing *Assassin*:

First and always first, my family – Sarah and our two little assassins, Zach and Leo; Mum and Dad; Simon, Steve and Sam; and my best friend, Karen.

Next, my agent and dear friend, Charlie Viney. Your loyalty and honesty is always appreciated, as much as your killer instincts!

My Bodyguard squad at Puffin: Tig Wallace, the ultimate assassin (sorry – I mean, editor!); Wendy Shakespeare, my longest-serving bodyguard; Helen Gray, a copy-editor extraordinaire (who must have an editing eye sharper than an assassin's knife!); my PR and marketing 'Assault Unit' – Hannah Sidorjak and Rebecca Booth; Matt Jones, the mystery hitman behind the covers; and all the other Puffins who work tirelessly to produce and promote my books.

All the hard-working and dedicated librarians and teachers assassinating illiteracy in schools around the world with only a Bodyguard or Young Samurai book as their weapon.

Finally, a huge thanks to my readers – without you reading and recommending my books, I'm simply writing in an empty room.

Stay safe,
Chris

Any fans can keep in touch with me and the progress of the Bodyguard series on my Facebook page, or via the website at *www.bodyguard-books.co.uk*